THE WAR WITHIN

Sharlene Leker

Sharlene Leker

ISBN 978-1-63814-796-1 (Paperback)
ISBN 978-1-63814-798-5 (Hardcover)
ISBN 978-1-63814-797-8 (Digital)

Copyright © 2021 Sharlene Leker
All rights reserved
First Edition

All rights reserved. No part of this publication may be reproduced, distributed, or transmitted in any form or by any means, including photocopying, recording, or other electronic or mechanical methods without the prior written permission of the publisher. For permission requests, solicit the publisher via the address below.

Covenant Books, Inc.
11661 Hwy 707
Murrells Inlet, SC 29576
www.covenantbooks.com

For Gary, my big brother.

PROLOGUE

The altar was abandoned, except for him. He was oblivious to his surroundings and had not noticed that one by one, others who had knelt there had returned to their pews and eventually left the church, hurrying off to their Sunday meals. His back was toward me. I just kept staring at him. He wore an angora sweater, large stripes of white and pale blue.

Kneeling, his head lowered as if in deep conversation with God, I wondered what had caused him to linger. Was it a thankful heart? Or a burden too heavy to bear? He was seventeen. I was nine, and I loved him with all my heart.

My brother: a prankster, joker, and a tease. I know because he practiced his antics on me. We didn't have a lot in common in those early years. I was just the little sister who wanted to tag along with my big brother, my mentor, my rock. But despite our age difference and the endless teasing, I knew he loved me.

Years have passed, and the age gap between us seems to have diminished. I don't know exactly when it happened, but somehow, we had traded places. Now I am the one giving emotional support. I have become his rock.

CHAPTER 1

Today was hot! Like most summer days in the Valley, the temperature would rise above one hundred degrees. Now the mercury had already edged its way up to a record-breaking mark for June. The hottest day of the year so far and not even a hint of a breeze. I could feel the sting of sweat as it ran down my forehead and into my eyes. I had forgotten my hat, and the sun was turning my neck into leather. I would pay for this later.

All I could think about was standing in front of the cooler with the air blowing over my parched skin. We didn't have air-conditioning, just a swamp cooler. Situated in the window at the end of our shotgun house, it kept us reasonably cool. Putting vinegar on the sunburn to soothe the pain would have to wait. I couldn't take time to go back home now.

I grew up in the San Joaquin Valley, smack-dab in the middle of California. The small town, considered a farming community, was regarded as quiet and peaceful among the residents. It must have always been that way because it's called Tranquillity. Mama, Daddy, my little sister, Katie, and I lived in a small house in the country, nearly five miles from town. We had a few close neighbors but were mostly surrounded by wide open spaces and agricultural fields.

Daddy was a farmer. He didn't own the farm—he just worked the land. He drove a D-8 Caterpillar six days a week for a paycheck that barely kept our small family clothed and fed. Once, when I was quite a bit younger, I asked Daddy what he did when he went to work. He answered, "I ride that big cat 'round and 'round all day long." That created quite the visual for a kid until I understood that the "cat" was actually a tractor.

Instead of wheels, each side of this tractor had long continuous tracks that clawed at the earth as it slowly crawled along the fields, obliterating anything in its path. A disc, attached to the rear of the tractor trailed behind, ripping the ground, turning up any remnants of old crops in preparation for planting new ones. It's easy to spot Daddy at work. I would look for a cloud of dust and puffs of black smoke the tractor's exhaust pipe had coughed into the air. Even from far away, I could hear the faint sound of the powerful engine chugging along, escorted by loud squeaks from the rotating tracks.

Daddy's tractor didn't have an air-conditioned cab, air-ride seats, or state-of-the-art stereo system. There was just him with his farmer's tan and hat, out in the open air, soaking up the sun, churning up dust, and breathing it in. It was his job, and he never complained.

Throughout the year, he planted rice, alfalfa, barley, and cotton. He tended to each crop the same way a mother tends to her children—caring and attentive to every detail. My favorite is the alfalfa. When in bloom, little yellow butterflies seemed to appear out of nowhere, and the fresh, fragrant aroma filled the air during harvest.

Then there was cotton—lots of cotton. From start to finish, our entire family had a hand in the cotton, Daddy on the tractor, and me and Mama walking the rows, chopping out weeds that threatened the tender plants. To avoid hiring someone to stay at home with Katie, Mama brought her with us. Katie often carried her books and drawing pad to occupy the time until she was old enough to wield her own hoe. This is how I spent my summers.

During cotton season, Mama taught me everything I know about fieldwork. She always made sure our hoes were sharp and reminded me to wear a hat, a long-sleeve white shirt, and to bring plenty of cold water.

Daddy always had cold water with him on the tractor. He would fill a clean plastic jug halfway the night before and let it freeze solid. Before the sun came up, he topped off the jug with tap water, wrapped it in a burlap bag—we called it a tow sack—then he saturated the bag with water, and set it by his feet on the tractor.

As the cotton grew, so did the weeds. When weeding cotton, you take on the role of a hunter, walking row after row "hunting" for weeds.

THE WAR WITHIN

Morning glory is a beautiful plant. It is a green vine with purple or white blossoms. Some would call it a flower, but to the field-worker, it's a weed. A noxious weed. A vining weed that will violate the space of healthy plants and choke the life right out of them. If cotton had morning glory, you understood why someone coined the phrase, "That's a tough row to hoe." Thanks to morning glory, we got to work the same fields a couple of times over the summer. This is how we made our money.

Helen is a longtime friend of Mama's and visited often. She had impeccable timing and, more times than not, would drop by to visit right before mealtime, knowing she would be invited to eat. Helen is short, and as she called it, "Big Boned." Her double chin served as a cover for her thick neck. She kept her jet-black hair short and greasy. She always wore a dirty dress that was loose and frumpy. The faded floral print disguised leftover stains from previous meals. Bathing was not on her priority list. I nicknamed her Smellin' Helen although I never called her that to her face. Mama wondered what had changed Helen. She used to wear makeup and nylons, curl her hair, and dress to the nines. All that just to go shopping.

On this particular day, we all came in from the fields to have lunch and cool off. Mama made us bologna sandwiches and sweet tea with lots of ice. Daddy was sitting at the kitchen table right in line with the cool breeze from the swamp cooler, and sure enough, here comes Helen. Feeling no need to knock, she barges in and positions herself right in front of the cooler, raises her arms, and announces, "It's so stinking hot." She was right about the heat and the stink. Daddy began to silently gag, so Mama quickly invited Helen to come on in to the kitchen and have lunch just to get her away from the airflow. Helen, as always, replied, "I didn't come to eat." But we all knew she did. Mama said she didn't mind that Helen came over at mealtime—our kitchen was always open for family and friends.

Working the fields during the hot, dry summer is hard labor. Not the way a teenager wants to spend summer vacation: clothes drenched with sweat, aching feet, and hands sporting blisters. Yet this is my only source of income. Little did I know that this need for money would be a pivotal point for me. It would take me down a dark, perilous road that lasted a lifetime.

CHAPTER 2

My life as a teenager was uneventful. School, homework, and church three times a week left little time for fun. Graduation was quickly approaching, and the school counselors were hounding the seniors about our future plans. I always had a desire to be a dentist, but deep down, in the depth of my soul, I feel a calling. An inner compulsion I can't ignore—a burning desire to share God's Word. Now that I'm facing that decision, I want to be a preacher. I not only want to be a preacher, but I also need to be a preacher—a collaborator with Christ.

I'm not a seasoned speaker, and when I stand in front of a crowd, my nerves usually get the best of me. I often meet with our pastor and discuss my plans of becoming a preacher. He encourages me and is delighted that one of his flock is willing to carry the torch.

This Sunday, after church, he approaches me and asks if I would be willing to preach the following Sunday.

"Me?" was my nervous reply. "But…I don't know how to preach. That's why I'm going to college!"

His face showed no sign that I had convinced him, so I continued with my argument.

"I enjoy teaching Sunday school, but that's not preaching."

"I spoke at youth group once, in front of a small group of my friends, but that's not preaching."

"I read Bible verses to the folks at the nursing home, but that's not preaching."

Then in desperation, I said, "I'm not going to get up in front of a big crowd and try to preach a hellfire and brimstone sermon!"

There, I said it.

THE WAR WITHIN

Pastor simply replied, "You don't have to. Taking the first step is always the hardest. Just speak from your heart."

Each day, I studied, and prayed, and jotted down my thoughts. By the end of the week, the trash can was overflowing with crumpled, discarded sermon notes. By Saturday evening, I had prepared three viable sermons and was feeling somewhat comfortable about preaching on Sunday. I would decide which sermon to use in the morning.

I donned my only suit and sat on the front pew, waiting for my turn to speak. My knee kept bouncing, shaking the entire bench. Pastor let me know I had thirty minutes to deliver my sermon, but then whispered, "Take all the time you need." Sunday school was over, and the main service began. My knee was still bouncing, and my palms clammy from sweat. The last hymn was sung, and the pastor informed the congregation that they were in for a real treat and introduced me as "Today's special speaker." I stepped up onto the platform and stood behind the pulpit. As I looked out at the congregation, I spotted Mama and Daddy grinning from ear to ear, their faces beaming with pride and anticipation. Katie, my little sister, was waving at me as if she hadn't seen me in months. I took in a deep breath and exhaled, trying to calm my nerves. With trembling hands, I spread my notes on the pulpit and began to speak. I was keenly aware that the hands of the clock on the back wall had stalled, or so it seemed.

The next time I peered at the clock, fifteen minutes had ticked by, and I had preached all three of my sermons. I stepped off the platform and returned to my seat in the front row. We all stood and sang the doxology, then the pastor guided me to the back door. I shook hands with everyone as they left. Some offered words of encouragement, and some even said they looked forward to hearing me speak again. Others just enjoyed getting out of church early that day. Pastor was right. The first step was the hardest.

CHAPTER 3

It's a strange feeling. I'm excited and at the same time afraid of what lies ahead. My entire twelve years of school were right here in this tiny town. The routine was comfortable, and now all that is about to change. Am I really ready to face the future?

After graduation, all the seniors will go their separate ways. Farmers' kids going to college will attend *Cal Poly* in San Louis Obispo. They will dutifully obtain their agricultural degree then return home and work alongside their fathers and someday inherit the farm. Others, unsure of their goals, plan to attend community college affording another two years to decide their future. Still, others could hardly wait to move away, in pursuit of a different lifestyle. Me? I was accepted into a Christian Bible College and made plans to attend in the fall.

That made for a long summer of anticipation. Days seemed to drag by, but looking back, it was way too short when it came to packing my bags and saying goodbye to Mama and Daddy. I promised Katie I would send her a postcard.

I drove my 1955 yellow-and-white two-door Chevy Bel Air three hours toward the coast to Santa Cruz. Taking the long way, I enjoyed the drive that allowed me ample time to think. When I reached San Jose, Mama's breakfast at home was long gone. My stomach began to growl, so I stopped to get a quick bite to eat. I ordered a burger and strawberry milkshake. My meal reminded me of the time I took Katie on a date.

My little sister had never been to the theater, so I took her to Fresno to see a Disney movie. Giddy with excitement, she laughed throughout the entire show. Although I tease her a lot, I love doing little things that make her happy. Watching her watch the movie made me smile. Afterward, we went to McDonald's and ordered a new burger on the menu, the Big Mac. It was so large she was unable to eat it all. I was more than happy to finish it for her.

Leaving San Jose, I headed toward Santa Cruz via Highway 17. With treacherous curves, steep mountainsides, and abrupt cliffs, no wonder it was nicknamed Blood Alley. The road tested my driving skills and my nerves. Not used to mountain driving, I moved into the right lane, allowing seasoned drivers to pass. As I reached the summit and began to descend into the valley, the drop-in temperature was welcoming. The hot air streaming through my open windows became cool and refreshing. I was almost there.

The school, nestled in the Santa Cruz Mountains, and only five miles from the Pacific Ocean seemed the perfect setting for learning and fun. Parking in front of the administration building, I found my way to admissions where I checked in. I received my welcome packet and keys to my second-floor dorm room—which I would share with three other guys.

I climbed the flight of stairs and located my room. With the key pushed into the lock and my hand on the doorknob, I paused, taking in the moment. I realized for the first time, this was the door to an opportunity I thought I would never have, the beginning of a new chapter in my life. I whispered a short prayer of thanks and opened the door.

The room with its white drab walls, linoleum-covered floor, and one lone window seemed to cry out for someone to fill its void. I stepped on in, dropped my luggage in the middle of the room, and looked around.

Strategically placed against each of the four walls is a loft-style bed. Underneath each bed is a built-in desk and small bookshelf, allowing each roommate their own individual space. At the foot of each bed stands a small armoire with a rod for hanging clothes and two small drawers. My roommates had not yet arrived, so I chose my space, unpacked my bags, and made my bed with the sheets and blankets I'd brought from home. Then I decided to take a walk around campus.

I strolled along the sidewalk taking in my surroundings, feeling as though I was in a whole different world from where I had started this morning. The campus is splayed over several acres and surrounded by enormous redwood trees. I came upon a small sign nearly overtaken by brush. Handcrafted from wood, weatherworn, and barely legible, it read "Amphitheater" with an arrow pointing toward the woods. I immediately abandoned the sidewalk and followed the path.

The sunlight, filtered by the canopy of trees, caused the air to cool, and I wished I'd worn a sweatshirt. Wild ferns covered the damp ground and encroached upon the narrow trail as though hiding it from passersby. It's obvious few people explored this path, and I began to question if I should turn back. Then I vaguely remembered a Bible verse about a small and narrow road that leads to life. If those words apply to this path, then something amazing must lie ahead. I continued to a small stream and crossed the moss-covered footbridge leading to a wide-open area. There, I found a makeshift stage with tree stumps for seating. I sat near the stream and listened to the peaceful silence and stared into the rushing water. As though hypnotized by nature, I imagined myself on that stage, preaching a simple message of salvation to a stump-filled crowd, "Enter by the narrow gate, for wide is the gate and broad is the way that leads to destruction, and there are many who go in by it. But small is the gate and narrow the road that leads to life, and only a few find it."

Suddenly, I shivered, and the goose bumps on my arms reminded me of the cool temperature, so I backtracked along the trail, returned to the sidewalk, and welcomed the sun's blanket of warmth.

Located in the center of the campus is a large fountain, a metal globe sculpture that seems to hover above the bubbling water below. Near the fountain, a bronze plaque reads, "Go into all the world and preach the gospel to all creation…" (Mark 16:15). I stood there, staring at the fountain for several minutes, lost in thought. Mentally taking a journey through the various countries, visualizing the people, I realized how different their way of life was from mine. Not speaking to anyone in particular, I questioned out loud, "How many of these people know about Jesus? How many have never even heard his name?"

Yes! This place, this beautiful campus, is where I will learn to be the preacher I was called to be. I felt at peace with my future. My gaze returned to the globe and I wondered, "Where will I go?"

CHAPTER 4

Knowing I shouldn't, I stared. I couldn't help it. Sitting in the corner across the room engrossed in a book, her slight frame barely took up any space on the large cushioned chair. Her long straight auburn hair, creamy complexion, and piercing blue eyes captured my attention. Standing at the end of a bookshelf, caught up in her every movement, I mindlessly grabbed a volume and began to thumb through it, all the while my focus was totally on her.

Suddenly she lifted her head and looked straight at me as though I had called her name. I quickly raised the book, hiding my face, to avoid her gaze. I pretended to read until I couldn't stand it any longer. Slowly, I lowered the book, and those eyes of hers were staring, cutting right through me. I'd been caught. I closed the book, took in a deep breath, and walked toward her.

"Hi," I said. "I'm Richard… I mean Rick. I mean my real name is Richard, but I go by Rick…or Ricky…mostly Rick."

I chided myself for sounding so lame.

She giggled and said, "Hi, Mostly Rick," as though that was my proper name.

"What are you doing here in the library?"

Hmm. Did I not look like the library type? No matter. After seeing her, my mind drew a blank as to why I was actually here. What was happening to me? I could feel myself struggling to get out yet another stammering response.

"Um…research. Yeah, research—for a class."

"You're reading *The Wizard of Oz* for a class?"

"Well, um, I'm researching the physics of how monkeys can fly."

"Sounds interesting. Maybe you can also figure out why the wicked witch is green."

Realizing I was not going to wiggle my way out of this one, I asked, "Do you want to get some coffee?"

She suppressed another giggle, then answered, "I'd love to. And by the way, my name is Anna."

We made small talk as we walked to the dining hall. Without warning, she paused and turned to me, "I've never read *The Wizard of Oz* upside down. How is it?"

"What do you mean?"

"While you were gawking at me—I mean reading—your book was upside down."

She was laughing now. To my surprise, I instantly felt a very real connection with her. I knew this was the beginning of a true friendship.

Anna and I became fast friends, and we soon began to date. When classes didn't demand our attention, we were inseparable. Sunday afternoons meant an ice-cream date at Marianne's, an iconic bright red building with red-and-white checkered linoleum and dancing cow wallpaper. It's the go-to spot for college students and tourists. Anna always ordered fifty-fifty half-vanilla, half-orange sherbet. My usual is a double scoop of strawberry. We always sat at "our table" in the corner, eating our cones and making plans for the upcoming week.

It was one of these Sundays after returning to school that I was reminded of my first day on campus and the amazing walk I had taken that afternoon. As Anna and I lingered on the sidewalk, I asked, "Have you seen the amphitheater?"

"No! Where is it?"

There was a hint of adventure in her voice, which I understood as "Let's go!" We approached the area where I had previously found the sign and I described the details of my earlier trip to that place; the trees, the ferns along the path. I recalled the beauty of the river and the damp, cool air. I imagined myself back there as I told of preaching to the stumps.

I stirred the brush searching for the weathered sign and was unable to find it. She noticed my frustration when I burst out with,

"It was right here! The sign read 'Amphitheater' and had an arrow pointing to the woods!"

This time I drew back the foliage with intent and was met with even more vegetation. I showed Anna where the path should be and tried without success to move toward it, the way totally blocked by gnarled vines—tall, dense, and impenetrable.

There was no denying the concern in her voice, "Are you sure this is the place?"

My frustration showed, and I answered with both arms outstretched in front of me, palms facing up in desperation, "Yes! I'm sure! *It was right here*!"

Her voice, quieter now, almost in a whisper, "Wherever it is, it's not here. Maybe you just had a special moment with God. I believe he speaks to us all the time. We just have to be willing to listen. Maybe that day, you were listening."

I barely slept that night as I replayed the afternoon events over and over in my head. Why couldn't I find that sign? Where was the path? I prayed, "Lord, was the amphitheater real or just in my imagination?"

I tossed and turned, my heart anxious for an answer, until a Bible verse came to mind. "Don't worry about anything; instead, pray about everything. Tell God what you need and thank Him for all He has done. Then you will experience God's peace, which exceeds anything we can understand. His peace will guard your hearts and minds as you live in Christ Jesus."

I prayed again. But instead of questioning God, I thanked Him. It no longer mattered whether the amphitheater was a physical place or not. It was real to me. Anna was right. Maybe that day, I WAS listening!

Sleeping in or waiting for the fog to clear was not on our agenda for this Saturday morning. Eager to spend the day together, Anna and I met at the dining hall, ate a quick breakfast, then headed to the ocean.

According to the traffic, we weren't the only early risers. Beach Street was congested with tourists and locals vying for a coveted parking space along the street. I joined the line of cars circling the block, and just before making another round, a car pulled out in front of me leaving an open parking space. I quickly pulled in. We got out of the car and headed straight for the wharf.

Walking along the weather-worn planks, we often stopped to watch surfers ride the foam-capped waves to the shore. Fishermen poised against the railing waited patiently for a bite, intermittently distracted as they were forced to shoo away the bird's intent on obtaining a meal from their buckets of bait.

The gift shops bustled with tourists searching for souvenirs—reminders of their time at the sea. We preferred the finds that would come later while walking along the sandy beach—an abandoned shell or a sand dollar that had washed ashore. The half-mile trek to the end of the wharf offered spectacular views. A distant boat in full sail skimmed across the water. Sea otters frolicked in the swells while some sea lions dozed on the cross beams below the pier. A few began their characteristic barking. Apparently, our passing above had interrupted their nap. Always mindful of the seagulls circling above, we sat on a bench and enjoyed each other's company as our bodies drank in the warmth of the bright sunshine and the cool ocean air that left the taste of salt on our lips.

Next, we made the trek back to the Boardwalk, stopping along the way for a few pieces of saltwater taffy. Then we spent the afternoon playing arcade games. Spending time with Anna makes me happy. Her smile is generous and her laugh infectious. It wasn't long before my crush turned to love.

The day had begun to fade, displaced by evening. Barefoot, we held hands and walked the sandy beach to the mudstone natural bridge. We crossed and waited for the sun to set. There, we sat mesmerized by the ebb and flow of the small waves licking the sand around our toes and sending sand crabs scurrying to bury themselves in the swash. In the distance, tiny ripples danced across the ocean's surface glistening from the sun's reflecting light. The whole sea slowly rose and fell as though it were breathing, pulsating, taking a breath in, letting it out. And it was in this place we pondered life and made plans for our future.

We watched and waited as the sun gradually slipped away. For a second, like a child extending toes to test the water before jumping in, its glowing edge barely touched the ocean. The radiance of that gleaming medallion transformed the blue sky into a blanket of violet and yellow, setting the clouds ablaze in a fiery orange hue. Finally, almost suddenly, the sun sank below the horizon, its light snuffed, and the clouds returning to their soft silvery gray tone. That's when the lights from the Boardwalk turned the darkness into daytime brilliance. We headed toward the eerie splendor and the loud music like moths being drawn to a flame.

CHAPTER 5

Saturday nights are cheap! Twenty-five-cent rides, hot dogs, cotton candy, soda, and candied apples. We eat hot dogs, share a Coke, then ride our three favorite carnival rides.

The carousel is always first. With seventy-three hand-carved horses sporting real horsehair tails, we each mount a colorful steed situated on the outer edge. Our anticipation grows as the crowd steps onto the platform, filling each empty space. With the ride filled, lights flashing, and music blaring, the carousel begins its slow turn. Gaining speed with each rotation, the horses rise and fall, mimicking a steady gallop. Holding tight to the reigns with our left hands, stretching out our right arms, we reach for the prize—the brass ring. Hoping to hook a ring with our fingers then tossing it into the clown's mouth would earn the reward of a free ride. Painted on the wall just beyond the ring dispenser is the face of the clown. It's blinking, glowing eyes beckon riders to try to toss the ring into the small circular opening of its mouth.

Due to our past carousel-riding, ring-collecting experiences, we were accomplished ring collectors but rarely managed to feed the clown. But tonight, I'm feeling lucky!

With three rings captured, I teased Anna, who had yet to get one. Feeling sorry for her and a little guilty about the teasing, I handed her one of my rings. As the carousel circled, I watched her prepare for the ring toss. Holding the ring loosely between her finger and thumb, waiting for just the right moment, she flung it sideways, as though skipping a rock or throwing a Frisbee. With a loud clink, the brass ring hit the mouth opening, and the clown swallowed the ring. Its eyes lit up, bells rang, and horns blew. Enjoying the applause of everyone on and around the carousel, Anna raised her arms in victory. I noticed a slight smirk as she asked, "Who's the lucky one now?"

Avoiding her actual question, I answered with a sense of pride, "I think we make a great team!" And we each kept one ring as a souvenir.

Next, the world-famous wooden roller coaster, the Giant Dipper! Over and over again, we stood in line, crossing our fingers, hoping to get the front car. And we did! We held hands as the giant chain pulled us toward the peak of the structure. The closer we came, the harder Anna squeezed my hand. As the train crested the top, her hand squeezes were accompanied by a small whimper in anticipation of the turbulent ride ahead. Whimper gave way to a full scream, which continued throughout the ride. It was always the same no matter how many times we got on that coaster. Hand squeeze, whimper, scream, and me having one more reason to tease her.

Our last ride of the evening is the Ferris wheel—the site of first dates, first kisses, and marriage proposals. A bit afraid of heights, this is not my particular favorite. But Anna loves it, so I suppress my fear and board the swinging seat. It always takes me a few minutes to settle in, but as the giant wheel propels us slowly toward the top, I become lost in the moment. The beauty of the lights reflecting on the ocean surface and the smile on Anna's face make it all worthwhile.

CHAPTER 6

Christmas is just around the corner, and my roommates and I decided to play a practical joke before heading home for the winter break. Coming up with something better than what we had pulled off at Thanksgiving would be difficult. We had seat belted pumpkins into the dean's car—like a whole family of jack-o'-lanterns out for a Sunday drive. It was hard to tell if the dean was more irate or embarrassed, but after his "Idle hands are the devil's workshop" speech in the chapel, I imagined wanted posters hung with rusty nails all over campus—dingy brown paper, tattered around the edges, with our somber mug shots above bold letters: REWARD. I almost felt guilty—almost. No, this prank had to be even better!

We sat around the breakfast table in the dining hall, discussing several options. Although the Christmas tree had been there for weeks, it now caught my eye, and I saw it in a different light than I had before. It's an elegant tall deep-green balsam fir that had been placed in front of the ceiling to floor glass window. Tiny white lights twinkled, traditional colored gold and silver glass orbs hung from the sloping branches along with red-and-white candy canes, and a sprinkling of plastic snowflakes. Red cranberries had been strung and loosely draped to encircle the tree. Silver tinsel shimmered from the dense needles.

An angel, poised at the very top, stretched her feathered wings heavenward. White fur trim on her red-velvet robe added to her celestial stature while a halo enhanced her golden hair. All suggested that this cherub's face with a kind, gentle smile, understood the majesty of her position. The tree looked real. The only thing missing was the sweet pine aroma that accompanies a freshly hewn tree. I had plenty of childhood memories of Christmas that would supply me with that last detail until I got home.

It seems almost sacrilegious to entertain the thought, but with a hint of reservation, I presented my idea to my roommates. The vote was unanimous. We would steal the Christmas tree! Only conscience and a collective reminder that we were at a Christian college caused us to modify the plan. We wouldn't actually steal the tree—we would merely relocate it. We put our heads together until the perfect strategy emerged. Once again, my gaze was drawn to the tree. I think somehow it knew our plot because each of those twinkling lights seemed to be tiny eyes, winking and expressing the same message, "I'm in!"

Bzzzz! Bzzzz! Four alarm clocks, each with slightly differing timing, jolted us awake and alerted us to the 2:00 a.m. hour. We quickly dressed in black sweatpants and shirts and stretched black stocking caps over our heads. Tennis shoes completed our attire.

We tiptoed through the hallway and padded quietly down the stairs, careful not to awaken other dorm mates. I slowly opened the exit door to peek outside and ensure there was no other activity.

The private road that encircled the campus was deserted. We slipped into the dark night—a sliver of a crescent moon and dim streetlamps provided just enough illumination that our flashlights were not needed. Amped with excitement, we jogged to the maintenance shack to borrow an extension ladder, one which turned out to be much heavier than we had anticipated. It took all four of us to carry it. Syncing our steps made it easier, but any athletic ability we thought we had was challenged by the slightly uphill trek to the dining hall. Taking a moment to catch our breath, we then propped the ladder against the rear of the building, extending it to reach the flat roof. Our excitement was building, and we giggled like schoolgirls.

The dining hall was kept unlocked at all times, allowing access for students who chose the quieter predawn hours for study. This morning, it was totally empty, a fact that gave credence to our belief that ours was a mission blessed. Following one another in single file, we skirted the building and entered through the double glass doors. We headed to the tree and tilted it over on its side. Somehow, it just seemed wrong to involve the angel in our escapade, so I gingerly removed it from the treetop and carefully placed it atop the indoor fiddle-leaf ficus tree. We then dragged the tree outside and around back to the ladder, leaving a trail of tinsel and fake snow in our wake.

We each had a designated role in this most crucial part of the plan. One on the ladder pulling up on the tree, one on the ground to push from the bottom, the third steadied the ladder, and number four served as our lookout. Several minutes of pushing and pulling resulted in success, the tree was on the roof! Placed in the exact corner of the building where it had previously stood—only higher... much higher.

We descended the ladder, slid down the extension, and carried it back to the maintenance shack. We saved the high fives and boasting until we were safely back in our room. We could hardly wait to see the reactions. Hours later, the campus was abuzz with whodunit speculation, but we four coconspirators silently laughed, bound by this wonderfully kept secret. A few days later in what was probably an attempt to outdo us, another team of jokesters wrapped the huge fountain globe with Saran Wrap and filled it with popcorn. I still think we won.

CHAPTER 7

My first year of college had come to an end. It just so happened that the last day of school was also Anna's birthday. The following day, I took her to Capitola, a quaint seaside village not far from Santa Cruz. We strolled along the narrow sidewalks, checking out menus posted in the windows of the restaurants and enjoyed browsing inside every little shop. Suddenly, Anna proclaimed, "This is what I want for my birthday!"

I noted the trinket in her hand.

"A key chain? That's it?"

"It's not just any key chain! It's for couples. Mine is a heart locket, and yours is a key. We can even add an engraved charm."

It seemed a little high school-ish to me, but it was her birthday, so I agreed. The engraving on Anna's heart-shaped copper disc read "My heart belongs to Ricky." Mine had "I hold the key to Anna's heart" with "1967" on the back.

After switching our keys from the old key rings to the new ones, we continued our walk. The morning of shopping had made us more than ready for a bite to eat, so we ordered lunch at a beachside eatery and sat outside on the patio. The blue sky and ocean air were too perfect to be stifled by eating inside.

I looked across the vast waters of Monterey Bay and watched the seabirds circling above the waves. I turned to Anna. "Did you ever see the movie *The Birds*?"

"Yes! And it scared me half to death. I could hardly sleep that night!"

"You know Alfred Hitchcock directed it, right?"

"Yes…and…?"

I was ready and willing to impress her.

THE WAR WITHIN

"Hitchcock lived in Scotts Valley, just north of Santa Cruz. In 1961, in the early hours of morning, right here in Capitola, thousands of frenzied birds invaded the coastline. They had just feasted on anchovies and became confused by the heavy fog and city lights and began falling from the sky and crashing into houses. Residents startled awake from the clamor, grabbed flashlights, and stumbled into the streets, and found carcasses everywhere. Stunned or still flying, birds began to attack the people."

"And that's how he got the idea for *The Birds*?"

"Yep! Two years later, it was a movie. Turns out the anchovies were poisoned by a neurotoxin in the algae bloom that affects the brain and causes confusion, disorientation, and even death. And that's what happened to the birds."

"*Wow*! I didn't realize you were an encyclopedia of obscure facts."

"You'd be surprised at the treasure trove of useless facts I have tucked away in my brain."

"I'm beginning to realize that."

After lunch, we happened upon a place reminiscent of an old-time photography shop. It was one of those places you could dress up in period clothes and have a sepia tone photo taken. Choosing a western theme, we posed in front of a bar facade with bottles of liquor lining the mirrored shelves. I was transformed into an 1880s gunslinger in black pants, vest, chaps, and cowboy hat. Only the crisp white shirt and red string tie varied the color scheme. I stood there with the long black coat tucked behind the gun belt. My hand rested on the Colt .45. I was poised for action.

Anna was decked out as a saloon girl. Her red satin dress with a fitted bodice was embellished with sequins, and the off-the-shoulder neckline was trimmed in black lace. The waistline was gathered to create a full skirt with a ruffled border at the bottom that ended just above the knee. Her legs were covered in black net stockings, and a lace garter played peekaboo with the hem of the dress. She accessorized with a red feather boa and a black ostrich feather in her hair. I laughed to myself thinking this was definitely not Bible school attire.

She studied the finished photo.

"We look good! I'm a little flirtatious. And you, with those six-shooters on your hip, make a great bad guy! I'm going to frame this."

"It's fun to pretend, but I could never imagine robbing someone, much less at gunpoint! I'll keep this picture in my wallet as a reminder of this wonderful day together."

We each took our copy and then headed back to school to pack.

Saying goodbye was difficult. Anna was going home to Oregon, and I was heading to the Valley—back to the farm. Our plans were to work throughout the summer then return to school in the fall.

Anna cried, and we promised to write and call each other the entire time we were apart. Fall already seemed a long time away.

CHAPTER 8

Completing the first year of college was like jumping the first hurdle in a long race. It feels good. There's a sense of accomplishment, but the finish line is still in the distance. My next hurdle would be to save enough money to return to school in the fall. I made the long drive back home and went to work the following morning.

The sun had yet to rise when Mama knocked on my door. I joined her and Daddy for a breakfast of bacon, eggs, and leftover biscuits from last night's homecoming meal. Katie was the only one who got to sleep in. I donned my old work jeans and long-sleeve white shirt. I lifted my wide-brimmed straw hat, perfect for cotton chopping, from the nail in my room. It was in the exact place I had hung it when I left for college, as though it had waited for me all those months.

Daddy had already sharpened my hoe, which I grabbed from the tool shed. Mama and I joined the rest of the work crew just as the sun began to peek over the horizon. Our workday had begun. An overwhelming sense of déjà vu enveloped me as I walked along the rows of tender cotton plants. I had been away nine months, yet the feeling of familiarity made it seem as though I had never left this place and college was only a dream.

The summer routine would soon become monotonous. Work, eat, sleep, repeat. I squirreled away every penny, but by the end of summer, my savings fell short. Not enough money meant no school. The harsh realization felt as though I had been slammed headlong into a brick wall. I would not be heading back to college in the fall. School was officially on the back burner, and now a reunion with Anna would have to wait as well. My only option was to keep working until I had saved enough for tuition.

Frustrated, I penned a tedious letter, detailing my situation. Now Anna would know every financial roadblock, disappointment, all the confusion and anger, and every emotion that had drawn me into a pit of doubt and self-pity. I had begun to question my future.

"God, do you really want me to be a preacher?"

It wasn't long before I heard from Anna. I eagerly tore open her letter, surprised to find only one page that, when unfolded, revealed a single paragraph in the middle.

> And we know all things work together for good to them who love God, to them who are the called according to His purpose. (Rom. 8:28)

I was filled with doubt, but I bowed my head and pleaded, "God, help me to believe this verse to be true!"

The cotton grew tall, oftentimes waist-high, and when summer turned to fall, it was time to pick cotton. Crop dusters, small airplanes flown by skilled pilots, fly low, just above the fields, spraying defoliant on the plants. This causes the plant's leaves to die and fall to the ground, leaving only the white bolls of cotton ready for plucking. Daddy drove the cotton picker, which was a peculiar-looking contraption. It was a red International Harvester brand with forks on the front and a huge basket on the back. The machine made a clamorous noise as he drove it down the rows of cotton ripping the bolls from their pods and sending them to the basket. Then he would dump the filled basket into the large cotton trailers to be hauled to the cotton gin for processing.

Mama made her eight-foot-long cotton sack out of white canvas-type fabric with a strap that she wore cross-body style. She dragged it behind her, feeling it becoming heavier as she rapidly filled it. Unlike chopping cotton for an hourly wage, picking cotton paid by the pound. Mama was the fastest cotton-picking person I ever saw. Katie had her own little cotton sack and gingerly pulled each bole of cotton from the stalk, placing it into her bag, being careful to avoid scratches on her hands. Contrary to popular belief, raw cotton is not soft. The white bolls, filled with seeds, are cradled in a hard clawlike pod with sharp points like a petrified hand with pointed fingers unwilling to release their grasp. The result for the picker is bleeding scratches on the hands that resembled having had a fight with a cat. And lost!

Picking cotton was work for most of us, but to Katie, it was fun. We didn't have to pick the entire row of cotton, just the first part, maybe twenty or thirty feet in, so the two-row cotton picker Daddy drove could easily make the turn at the end of each row without destroying any unpicked cotton.

When the fields were stripped of the cotton, all that remained were shriveled reminders of the tall stalks that had offered up their white bolls for plucking. Now they waited to be tilled under.

Daddy's boss hired me to drive the tractor, which provided a job for me throughout the winter. It also gave me a lot of time to think as I drove back and forth across the extensive acreage. I now realized that this mundane chore was the very thing my father had devoted himself to doing. Harsher still was now understanding Daddy did this just to eke out a living for our family. Despite the fact that I detested farmwork, it was a means to an end. I would work and earn enough money to return to school and complete my education. Daddy was focused, and he did what he had to do. I could do the same.

It was almost Thanksgiving. There were no more triple-digit temperatures, and the mercury had already begun its descent as the cold, wet winter settled in and blanketed the Valley with Tule fog.

Tule fog (pronounced Tu'lee) is a phenomenon that is difficult to understand unless you have spent a winter in California's vast farming region. Unlike fog that accumulates across the ocean and creeps toward the shore, Tule fog rises from the ground and is particularly common in the San Joaquin Valley, located in the state's Central Valley. This fog is unimaginably dense, and days can stretch into weeks without ever seeing the sun. Some folks call this "pea soup" weather. When driving, visibility is often limited to the car's hood ornament, and accidents are sometimes a daily occurrence on area highways.

Anxiety levels peak even for locals who must venture onto the roads, and skills are tested far beyond many Motor Vehicle

Department requirements. It is not uncommon to see a car pulled up to an intersection, all windows rolled down as the driver attempts to listen for approaching cars whose drivers are equally blinded by the fog. A line of cars will move at a snail's pace, each with the operator's head out the window, trying to visualize his surroundings. Yes, this is winter in the Valley. And like most folks who live here, I was already looking forward to spring.

Today, it was early afternoon when the fog finally lifted. The sun played peekaboo with the low-level cumulus clouds while the air remained chilled and damp. I continued guiding the tractor in its repetitive path, tilling the soil for a few more hours before the evening fog crawled in to announce the end of the workday. Suddenly something caught my eye. I stopped and turned off the engine. I scanned the ground for anything out of the ordinary. Uncertain what I was looking for, my attention was drawn to the slightest movement.

There, I jumped off the tractor to investigate and found two baby jackrabbits. Rabbits tend to be skittish, but these two were huddled together and appeared very scared. I searched the surrounding area suspecting the mother would be nearby, but she was nowhere to be found. The small rabbits began hopping around as though aiding me in my efforts. Suddenly, I was overwhelmed by a sense of dread when I realized there was one place I had not looked. Suspicion became reality when I reluctantly knelt and peered underneath the tractor. The mama rabbit had met her untimely demise, and her babies were now orphans.

What now? I couldn't bring myself to just drive away. These babies could not survive without their mother, so I watched them a while longer. Then I had an idea. I quickly captured them and tucked them into my shirt pocket. I drove the tractor to the end of the field and headed home.

Katie was in her room doing her homework. I knocked on her door.

"Who is it?"

Her question struck me as funny. Asked as if numerous persons dropped by on any given afternoon.

"It's me! I have a surprise for you!"

She slowly opened the door—just barely, the gap only wide enough for me to see one suspicious eye.

"What kind of surprise? You're not going to play a trick on me, are you?"

"Now would I do that?"

"Only every day of my life!"

"Not today! Close your eyes and hold out your hands."

The door opened wide. She clenched her eyes shut and reluctantly held out her cupped hands.

"If you give me something creepy, I'll never forgive you!"

I reached into my pocket, pulled out the baby jackrabbits, and gently placed them in her hands.

She quickly opened her eyes and began to pummel me with questions.

"Where did you get them? Are they for me?"

I had no time to answer before she raced out of the room, yelling for Mama. Katie was begging.

"Please can I keep them? Please? *Please?*"

A thought occurred to me as I listened to my sister's fervent request. I might have crossed the line. Mama didn't care to touch furry animals, and pets were not allowed in the house. This was a farm, and she believed that pets had their place, and that place was outside.

There was no need to worry. Katie's pleas and promises to care for her charges turned the negotiations in her favor. Surprisingly, Mama agreed. The bunnies could stay. I asked Katie, "So how *are* you going to take care of them? It's too cold outside. You'll have to figure out a way to keep them inside and out of trouble. You know, out of Mama's 'hare'."

She immediately recognized the intentional pun.

"Now you think you're a comedian!"

That evening, Katie was still holding the bunnies as she gathered items for their makeshift home. Curious, I asked, "What's all this?"

She could barely contain her excitement.

"I have it all figured out! I'm going to put a towel in the bottom of the laundry basket, heat a big rock on the stove, wrap it in another towel, and put it in the basket so they can snuggle against it and feel the warmth. I have a wind-up clock, and I'll put that in too. They'll be comforted by the ticking. I've heard that works for kittens, so maybe it will work for rabbits. I will have a couple of jar lids for food and water at the other end of the basket. I'm going to cover the top with another towel and set the basket on the floor in front of the refrigerator where the warm air blows out."

"*Wow*! Looks like you've thought of everything!"

She smiled.

"By the way, I've named them 'This' and 'That'."

"Those are odd names!"

"Not really. 'This' bunny is mine. 'That' bunny is yours. But I'm happy to take care of both of them."

She ran to me and gave me a big bear hug.

"Thank you! Thank you! Thank you! This is the best trick ever!"

CHAPTER 9

The United States is involved in a war. All males, ages eighteen to twenty-five were required to register with the Selective Services division of the US government, a.k.a. The Draft. I had registered a year ago when I turned eighteen, fulfilling my obligation. Because I was enrolled in college, I was classified as a 2-D, ministerial student—deferred from military service. That was a relief as I did *not* want to be in the Army.

I had watched the news, seen the protesters, and read the newspaper articles. This was not like World War II, or any other war, where returning soldiers were given a hero's welcome. This was different. Soldiers who made it back from Vietnam were greeted by name-calling, anti-war protesters. So great were the feelings of lost honor and disrespect, many soldiers were too ashamed and embarrassed to even wear their uniforms in public. No! The Army was not for me. After all, I had other plans for my life.

It had been nearly a year since I left college and began working on the farm. My savings grew as well as my anticipation of returning to school and reuniting with Anna. Each passing week and each paycheck brought me one step closer to my goal.

The Tule fog had abandoned the valley. Gray damp air gave way to clear skies and sunshine, the official indication that spring had arrived. The sun, high in the sky, coupled with my growling stomach, indicated the approaching noon hour. I verified the time on my watch and headed home for lunch. Our house was situated in the middle of the farm, adjacent to the fields where we worked, so it was easy to go home, eat, and relax a few minutes before returning to work. When I arrived, Daddy was already seated at the kitchen table, enjoying his coffee. He seldom drank from his cup. Instead, he poured some of the steaming brew into the saucer to cool then sipped from the saucer's edge. A slurping sound followed by an ahh after swallowing indicated his satisfaction. While Mama prepared sandwiches, I walked to the end of the long driveway to collect the mail.

I thumbed through the letters as I leisurely returned to the house. I was hoping to find a pink envelope dabbed with perfume and SWAK written across the back flap. But there was no letter *Sealed with a Kiss* from Anna. Instead, I found an official-looking white envelope addressed to me. Void of an address, the top left-hand corner simply read, "Selective Service, Official Business." I stopped dead in my tracks and stared at the envelope. I didn't want to open it. Frozen, I could feel the beating of my heart. More than beating, it was pounding, a hammering within my chest. With trepidation, I forced myself to tear open the envelope. Bold letters across the top of the page proclaimed the words I never wanted to read: ORDER TO REPORT FOR INDUCTION. Utterly confused, I read it again, still not understanding. Was I being drafted? This time I read the entire letter.

ORDER TO REPORT FOR INDUCTION

From the President of the United States
To: Richard D. Clark

Greeting:

You are hereby ordered for induction in the
Armed Forces of the United States.

I gripped the letter with both hands as the envelope and remaining mail fell to the ground. Shaking my head back and forth, I audibly yelled as though this piece of paper was a flesh and blood person standing right in front of me:

"No! No! *No!* You're wrong! I can't be drafted. I'm in college."

Even as I spoke those words out loud, I realized that I wasn't in college, not officially. I desperately wanted to be in college, but to return, I had to take a year off to work. I was caught up in a vicious circle. It was apparent that now Selective Service got wind of my lapse in education. I had lost my student deferment from the draft. Reclassified as category 1-A meant I was available for military service with no restrictions.

Some folks view a nineteen-year-old as a boy, a child, or a teen, but never a man. He is not old enough to vote or buy a beer, an indication that he lacks maturity and is ill-equipped to make decisions on his own. Uncle Sam's perspective is quite the opposite. Young men or older teens were the preferred candidates for the draft. Most Vietnam War draftees were from poor and working-class families, many from rural towns and farming communities. I met all the qualifications!

I picked up the mail and went inside the house. Mama and Daddy were finishing their meal. I dropped the dusty envelopes on the table and handed my letter to Mama. She knew by the somber look on my face that something was terribly wrong.

"What's this?" she asked.

I could barely speak the words. "I'm being drafted."

She ripped the letter from my hand and read the notice out loud. Refusing to believe it was true, she read it again…and again. Sighing, she passed it to Daddy. He, too, slowly read the notice out loud. I sat down at my place at the table, but my appetite was gone. The sandwich Mama had made me was no longer appealing. We all agreed. I had been drafted. The three of us discussed the reason I had received the notice all the while Daddy repeatedly apologized for not having the means to keep me in school. As Mama stood to clear the table, I noticed a tear pooling in the corner of her eye. Facing away from me, she wiped her face with the back of her hand, trying to hide her emotion.

I had three weeks to tie up any loose ends and report for induction. The first item on my to-do list was to talk with Anna. A letter wouldn't suffice, so I called her and delivered the news. She cried, and we talked for hours. I gave the notice to quit my job and handed over my paycheck to Mama to pay for the long phone calls to Anna. I sold my car to a buddy from high school, and I made an extra effort to spend time with Katie. I treated her to lunch and roller skating afterward. Anything else left undone would have to stay that way. It was time to go.

The drive to the airport was long and silent. Daddy drove with a white-knuckle death grip on the steering wheel, and Mama sat with her eyes clenched shut, willing herself not to cry. Katie, still not fully grasping the seriousness of the situation, just went along for the ride.

We said our goodbyes at the loading gate, and I was on my way to becoming a soldier.

CHAPTER 10

The plane landed. I then boarded a military bus with other soon-to-be soldiers. I would spend the next eight weeks of Army Basic Combat Training at Fort Lewis, Washington. I quickly learned only a few on this ride were volunteers. The rest of us were draftees, and the last place we wanted to be was on this forty-five-minute excursion toward the unknown. I wasn't the only one apprehensive about the future. The same questions weighed heavily on all our minds: Will I be going to Vietnam?

Even more important, Will I make it back home?

I had one question that repeatedly welled up within me in silent bursts of anguish: God, why me?

Our bus driver introduced himself. Eddie, no longer in the military, was a former drill sergeant who still wore Army green fatigues and combat boots.

"I can see you are all eager to get to boot camp, but we have a slight delay. I've been informed there was an accident on base. Any of you hear about it?" He paused as he watched his passengers from his rearview mirror and waited for the reply. In unison, we answered, "*No!*"

We leaned forward as Eddie peered back at us and sighed before speaking again, "Well, a tank ran over a box of popcorn. Two kernels were killed!"

Eddie began laughing, and we all joined in. I wasn't sure what was funnier, his antics or seeing the amusement he found in his own joke. Either way, he managed to lighten the mood and momentarily suppress our anxiety. He managed to insert himself into scattered conversations while continuing to keep his eyes on the road. Along with a few more of his cheesy jokes, we got his rendition of his stint in the Army.

"I put in my twenty and got out. Driving you recruits is just my way of avoiding retirement boredom."

I had never been to the Pacific Northwest, and I was taken aback by the abundance of evergreen trees, the silhouette of the Cascade Mountain range, and the sky-piercing view of Mount Rainier. The towering snowcapped peak bathed in full sunlight commanded the attention of passersby. As we drew near to the base, the surrounding view was interrupted, overwhelmed by the traffic congestion. Fort Lewis is divided by the highway and large brick, military-looking buildings could be seen on either side of the road. Eddie took the exit that led to the base entrance where a guard waved us through the security gate. As he continued driving, all friendly chatter abruptly ceased as our attention was drawn to the various groups of soldiers on the training grounds—some performing drills, marching, exercising, jogging, and some unmoving as they stood at attention. It was at this moment that we knew we were staring at ourselves.

The bus came to a stop at what appeared to be the unloading zone for newbies. We all stood, gathered the bags we had brought from home, and inched our way up the crowded aisle toward the exit. Eddie slowly rose from the driver's seat and used his huge frame to block the door. He faced us standing with feet apart and clenched fists on his hips. His height, close to six feet, wide chest, and slim waist made him an overpowering presence. Suddenly I felt really small. His salt-and-pepper hair was cut short, in flattop style, and his now-stern face and square jaw looked to be chiseled from stone. Several minutes passed as he stood there, glaring at us through his large aviator-style, mirrored glasses. It was as if he was sizing us up and deciding which of us would make it and who would not.

Finally, Eddie took a slow, ominous deep breath. Then he began shouting, "SIT DOWN!" The words came at us rapidly. "Who gave you permission to stand? You don't stand until I tell you to stand! You *do not* exit this bus until I *tell* you to exit this bus!"

"You are sadly mistaken if you think you have any control over what you can and cannot do!"

"You do not make decisions! You are, in fact, incapable of making decisions!"

We stumbled over our bags and each other as we rushed back to our seats. I sat rigid with my back as straight as a plank. My muscles were so tight I felt paralyzed. Hands folded on my lap, my knuckles were white from the intensity of my fingers entwined and clenched into one fist. Sweat popped out on my forehead, and I was afraid to blink. But mostly, I was afraid of Eddie!

Unsure of how much time had passed since Eddie had begun his rant, he continued his roar as he used an abundance of adjectives to describe us and how useless we all were.

"You bunch of nothings should feel lucky that Uncle Sam even considered you to be a part of his team."

Then just as quickly as his persona went from fun-talking bus driver to drill sergeant, his demeanor changed again.

It was as though a switch had been flipped. Eddie slowly removed his sunglasses, leaned back against the dash, and crossed his arms and legs, relaxing his stance. He began speaking in a soft tone and with a crooked grin asked, "Well, how do you like boot camp so far?"

He didn't wait for an answer.

"Thought I would give you a little taste of what's in store for you. This is a drop in the bucket compared to what's ahead, so I've got some advice that might just get you through the next eight weeks and make your lives a little less miserable. Here it is. Keep your eyes and ears open! Keep your mouth shut! Do what you're told, nothing more! Nothing less! Do this, and in no time, you will be on your way to becoming a soldier."

Voice raised slightly, he asked, "Do…you…understand?"

We all vigorously nodded in fearful agreement.

"Now! GET OFF MY BUS!"

We stood, rushed out the door, and quickly fell into line. We were officially in boot camp!

Basic combat training was no joke. It was physically and mentally grueling. Most soldiers are considered infantrymen and are trained accordingly. The drill sergeant's job is to produce a fighting machine, and he aggressively pursued that goal by repeatedly breaking the recruits down, then building them back up. By instilling discipline, physical fitness, and weapons training, each civilian would hopefully transition into a combat soldier.

I had never fired a gun before, so I was petrified when the standard-issue M16-A1 rifle was placed in my hands. I wanted nothing to do with it but suddenly remembered Eddie's advice. I did exactly what I was told: "Nothing more! Nothing less!" We spent several days learning how to handle the weapon and use bullets and bayonets to kill the imaginary enemy. None of that silenced my thoughts:

"I shouldn't be here. My plans have nothing to do with being in the Army, much less being involved in a war."

Sleep was elusive. Like trying to step on my own shadow, it was always just out of reach. When I did doze off, it was fitful and nightmarish, hardly restful. At the end of this day, I was utterly spent and barely had the energy to eat dinner. I choked down a few bites of the chipped beef, creamed, and dropped on toast, and washed it down with a glass of milk. I headed straight to the barracks and collapsed on my bunk.

I was back in college, walking along the path that led to the amphitheater. The cool ocean air, the sound of rushing water, and the majestic beauty of the giant redwoods were relaxing, almost sedative. I felt a peace wash over me like spring rain. I was the dormant seed coming to life. That is until the serenity of the moment was interrupted when I stepped into a hole and came close to falling.

I scolded myself for not being more observant. Now my foot was somehow wedged in the hard clay, trapped in a viselike grip, and being squeezed tighter and tighter. Suddenly, the hole widened, and the hard clay turned into black viscous mud burying both my feet. The more I struggled, the greater the hole became. Then the mud morphed into quicksand and swallowed up my legs. Overtaken by panic and fear, I frantically fought against the downward pull as I was being consumed by the liquid sand. In desperation, I swatted the air grasping for a twig, a vine, anything to hold on to. As I continued to disappear into the abyss, I shouted for help, but my words came out as whispers. No one heard my cry.

I awoke with a start. I was drenched with sweat, my head was pounding, my heart racing, and my hands were shaking uncontrollably. My stomach churned, and I rushed to the latrine. After several minutes of violent heaving, I convinced myself that this terrible night, with everything real and imagined, was a direct result of mess hall food.

A few days passed. I was preparing for an inspection. As I sat on my bed polishing my boots, my hands started to tremble. My head felt hollow, and the sounds around me became distant. I closed my eyes but could still see tiny specks of dancing white light. I barely heard the thud when I dropped my boot. Bending forward, I propped my elbows on my knees and buried my face in my hands. My dog tags dangled in midair between my legs.

"What's wrong with you?" The voice came from inside my head as though it had spoken to someone else. Between sobs, I answered out loud, "I don't know!"

I awoke in the hospital. The front of my shirt was drenched in blood, and the nurse was attending to my broken nose. I began firing questions at her.

"What happened? How did I get here? Where did all this blood come from?"

She grinned mischievously. "You fainted. But lucky for you, your face broke your fall, or you might have been hurt."

I was no stranger to sarcasm, but her humor was wasted on me today.

I had answered a plethora of questions, tolerated the usual tests, and now the doctor sat down next to my bed to deliver the results.

"I have good news and bad news," he began.

I knew what that meant. The good news was seldom good, and people make that statement to soften the blow, so the bad news won't seem so bad. Despite my silent objections, he continued, "You are suffering from anxiety, stress, and depression. In other words, you have had a nervous breakdown. The good news is you lack the coping mechanism to handle stressful situations."

"This is good news? How?"

More unspoken thoughts raced through my mind as he continued, "You have manifested this problem and are considered unstable. You are, therefore, no longer of any use to the Army." My face must have registered my bewilderment because he quickly added, "In a nutshell…you're going home."

This *was* good news!

I wasted no time informing my parents and Anna that I was being discharged. I desperately wanted to ask Anna to marry me, but now I'm not sure if I should. Would she think of me as damaged goods, unstable? Could I be a good husband to her? These questions continued to haunt my mind, then I received her letter:

> Dear Ricky,
>
> I have to admit, upon receiving the news of your illness, I had mixed feelings. First, I was happy you were coming home, but at the same time, I'm concerned for your well-being. I spoke with your parents, and they had some similar thoughts. I just want you to know how much I love you. With open arms, I eagerly await your return.
>
> Love,
> Anna

Weeks went by. All I could think of was going home and getting back to a normal life. I was eager to see my family, but mostly, I longed to see Anna. I was cleared to return to basic training while awaiting my discharge papers. But they never came. I finally surrendered to the fact that I was not going home after all. Graduation came, and I received my orders for advanced individual training. I was going to be a medic. I shipped out to Fort Sam Houston, San Antonio, Texas, where I would receive combat medical training. I was further from home than ever.

CHAPTER 11

"You are not a doctor! You are not here to become a doctor!"

This was the beginning of what was shaping up to be a very long day.

"But upon completion of this training, you will have one of the most important jobs in the Army. The job will be hard..." He paused, and my thoughts wandered to the farm. I realized that I already knew a lot about hard work. He continued, "Your job will also be rewarding. To the discouraged, you will be an encourager. To the restless, you will be the comfort. When all seems lost, you will give hope."

"No, you will not be a doctor, you will be a medic, and your specialty will be saving lives!"

The instructor lectured the entire day. He gave us the lowdown on what to expect from this training and exactly what was expected of us. I felt as though I was back in college. But this time, I wasn't studying to be a preacher.

"Most, if not all of you, will be going to Vietnam. For that reason, everyone in this room will be trained as a combat field medic. You will be the first line of medical assistance during combat. You will be working in a hostile and dangerous environment, and you will have to make split-second, gut-wrenching decisions that hopefully will provide each wounded soldier just enough medical treatment to survive the trip to the hospital.

"Those of you assigned to a hospital will treat everything from the common cold to life-threatening injuries. You will be part of a trauma team and will care for critically wounded soldiers after they are evacuated from the field. You will take vital signs, manage health records, dress and undress patients, change their bandages, and change their sheets. Consider yourselves glorified nurses."

There was no discussion, no question-and-answer time. Just the endless barrage of information. The comparison to college was quickly fading as his next words brought sobering reality.

"It is crucial to the survival of many soldiers that you are good at your job. Not just good, you will prove your skills to be exemplary. You will learn what CPR is and will become proficient in performing it. You will also become an expert at emergency tracheotomy, tourniquet application, and IV placement."

His volume appeared to increase as he labored to make a point. "Here, at Fort Sam, Houston, we strive for excellence. We do not believe in the poke and pray tactic. In critical situations, you won't have time for a do-over. The good news is that we're going to let you practice, and practice, and continue to practice until you can get it right in one try. If you're afraid of needles, my advice is, *get over it*! Because…"

Was that a slight grin we were witnessing as he stretched out his words?

"You…will be practicing…IV placement…on…each other!"

A collective groan voiced our disapproval of his last statement. Then a low growl sounded from the back of the room followed by a boisterous *thud*! Startled, we all turned to see the beefiest, the most muscle-bound guy in the room lying on the floor.

As the instructor calmly walked toward the back, we craned our necks and watched as he cracked open an ammonia vial and waved it under the unconscious man's nose. The soldier jolted awake and sucked in a full breath. He appeared embarrassed and waved off the instructor's offered hand as he struggled to pull himself to a sitting position. He then climbed back into his seat, proclaiming himself to be fine. His ghostly complexion, the tears in his eyes, and sweat on his brow all said otherwise.

The instructor returned to the front of the room. Reaching into his pocket, he pulled out several more of the ammonia vials, called smelling salts, and tossed them onto the desk.

"Anyone else feels faint?"

Our answer was emphatic "No, Sergeant!"

The lesson continued, "See! I came prepared!"

"Whether you are in the hospital or the field, you will learn to be organized, equipped, and prepared to handle any situation."

"You hope for the best, but prepare for the worst."

"Remember, your comrades in arms depend on you."

It was here in San Antonio I met Danny. He was from Arkansas and spoke with a thick Southern drawl. Like me, he had spent his entire life in a small town in the middle of nowhere. I looked up to him—literally—as his lanky six-foot-five frame seemed to tower over and dwarf my meager six feet. His curly, copper-red hair accentuated the light-brown freckles spattered across his long face and pale skin, revealing his Scandinavian heritage. He had one blue eye and one brown eye caused by a condition he could barely pronounce, but which, he said, made him a chick magnet. We quickly became friends.

In the classroom, I hurriedly scribbled lecture notes, and each evening, I pored over the study material and tried to make sense of my illegible scrawl. It wasn't easy for me, and I had to work at it, but I actually began to enjoy the medical training. Danny, on the other hand, was a natural. Even though he rarely took notes and spent even less time studying, he aced all the tests. It didn't seem fair.

What little spare time we had, Danny and I went to the local bar to shoot pool and socialize with fellow soldiers. It was there that Danny introduced me to my first beer.

War films were an integral part of our medical training. But these were not Hollywood simulations of past wars. This is on-the-scene coverage from Vietnam. We watched soldiers, many who had only recently passed through combat training just like us, who were now succumbing to fevers, flu, dysentery, and malaria. Some had burns, others had infections, and were rife with trench foot or gangrene. We witnessed soldiers with life-threatening wounds, the result of shrapnel, booby traps, and explosives. All begged for help—sometimes calling out for Mom, or God, but always screaming for a medic. We watched these men who just days ago had sat in this very classroom, now struggle to save those who could be saved, and ignore the cries of those beyond help.

My mind could not relinquish the horror of what I was seeing. It was like trying to breathe underwater. How could anyone survive in such an environment? Could I? Midway through training, we were instructed to fill out our living wills. We documented our burial instructions and what we wanted done with our remains—in case we didn't make it home. Just a few more classes and I would be there. No more films—I was on my way to experiencing this war firsthand.

Danny and I were taking a well-deserved and much-needed break from relentless studying. We went out to grab a burger and a beer. Danny looked up from his plate and commented on my pensive mood and lack of conversation.

"What's wrong with ya?"

My response was more than a bit defensive. "What do you mean what's wrong with me?"

Danny refused to be put off by my attitude.

"Well...," he drawled, "fer one thang, ya ain't yoursef! Yur heads ahangin' and ya cain't even look me in the eye." He was almost apologetic when he added, "Yur usually more talkative. Taday ya ain't said nuthin'..."

His voice dropped off, and I whispered my answer as though sharing a secret, "I don't think I can do it."

"Whatcha mean ya cain't do it?"

I slowly raised my head and looked Danny straight in the eyes. No longer whispering, I answered, "Look at me! I'm from a small town. Just a wide spot in the road where everyone knows everybody's business. The most exciting thing I've seen is when Mr. Miller's silo caught on fire. The volunteer fire department attempted to extinguish the flames, but it spread too fast and burned down his house and barn. The whole town turned out to watch."

I paused...

"Now I'm being thrown into the middle of a war. And I'm expected to save lives."

I repeated, "I just don't think I can do it!"

Danny had waited patiently while I struggled. Now he jumped in:

"Why cain't ya do it? Cuz ya ain't smart anuf? Ya ain't strong anuf? Ya ain't brave anuf?"

I had made him understand, or so I thought. I almost shouted, "*Yes*! *Yes*! *Yes*! All the above!"

He continued, "Ya mean if'n a soldier wuz hurt, ya wudn't try to hep 'em?"

"That's just it! What if I tried and failed?"

His next words struck home. "Ya only fail if'n ya don't try. Let me tell ya sumpthin'. Yur smart. Yur strong. An' yur brave! I'd be proud ta fight next ta ya. An' if'n I wuz ta ever git hurt, I'd want ya ta fix me up!"

From that moment forward, Danny became my pillar of strength. I knew we would be friends for the rest of our lives.

CHAPTER 12

I soon became all too familiar with summertime weather in San Antonio. Heat and humidity were the expected norm and made for a miserable August in Texas. Storms rolled in quickly and transformed the blue sky into ominous black clouds. The sudden darkness became a showcase for brilliant bolts of lightning spidering across the skies. Heavy raindrops soon joined the spectacular light show with booming thunder dominating this symphony of nature's fury. The powerful percussion rattled windows—and my nerves!

Even as the rain from the earlier downpour subsided, and the clouds gave way to sunshine, the humidity began to soar. The large canopy erected to shade the graduates offered no help in taming the temperature. Steam rose from the ground and created a saunalike atmosphere with air so thick and damp I could taste it. I could hardly wait for this part of the day to be over.

The graduates were decked out in our formal dress uniform and seated on metal folding chairs. This was not my idea of a relaxing afternoon. From my vantage point, I could actually see the heat radiating from the blacktop and appearing like quivering ripples across an ocean's surface. I closed my eyes and momentarily pictured myself standing on the beach, enjoying the cool breeze, and breathing in the refreshing salt air. My mental reprieve was interrupted when the scorching heat from the pavement penetrated the soles of my shoes, causing the uncomfortable sensation of my feet being on fire. Sweat now ran down my neck and soaked my shirt collar, and my underwear was stuck to me like a splattered bug on a windshield. I desperately longed for a drink of cold water and a cool breeze.

My family was unable to attend the graduation. Daddy had always joked that, with his luck, the plane would have a flat tire mid-flight and he would have to get out and change it. I envisioned the scenario and had to chuckle. I knew the long drive from California to Texas was not a possibility, and airfare on Daddy's income was also not feasible. Although I missed them being here, Mama and Daddy sent their best wishes. I could feel the pride they expressed for my hard work and accomplishment.

I was so happy to see Anna. She had worked throughout the summer and had saved enough money to book her flight and hotel room well in advance of this weekend. As soon as the ceremony ended, I grabbed her and rushed to introduce her to Danny. She immediately fell in love with his accent and wasted no time in telling him so. He, in turn, winked his one brown eye and insisted that it was she who had the accent, not him.

Anna and I spent the next day as typical tourists along San Antonio's famous River Walk. We rode a river taxi, explored the Alamo, indulged in ice cream, and shopped for souvenirs. We walked among the crowds and stopped to hear several street musicians who had set up in the open-air venue. There were gospel, jazz, country, and rock artists, each drawing a share of those passing by their particular spot. We tossed a dollar into the open guitar cases that welcomed donations and usually received a nod of thanks from the musician who kept right on playing as we turned to move on.

We continued our stroll and came upon a preacher who had chosen a concrete bench as his venue. Dressed in a suit, his tie was loosely knotted and his coat unbuttoned. He stood on the bench and paced back and forth. Sweat dripped from his nose as he spewed the words of his faith. One hand held a worn Bible that he waved toward heaven. He stabbed a pointed finger at the passing tourists with the other.

He spoke each stern word with conviction, "Sin? Or forgiveness?"
"Heaven? Or hell?"
"Eternal life? Or eternal damnation!"
He was shouting now!
"It's...your...choice!"
"Turn...or burn!"

Anna and I lingered, but at a distance, as we watched the preacher and the passing tourists. His audience was visibly absent, a stark contrast to the many musicians who never failed to capture their listeners' attention. Here. they never even paused but seemed instead to pick up their pace as they hurried to distance themselves from the harsh truth and the preacher who spoke it.

I inwardly placed myself in that man's shoes. I was the preacher pacing back and forth, fervently pleading the message to a crowd of unbelievers who refused to listen.

Suddenly, I see myself standing behind a pulpit. I'm preaching in a crowded sanctuary filled with doubters—all disregarding the truth. One by one, they stand and hurry their steps to leave.

"Was it the message or the delivery?"

I silently pondered before convincing myself it was neither.

"*No*! It was me!" My self-argument continued. "I had no business thinking God actually chose me to be his spokesperson!"

My thoughts shifted to that first day at college and the amphitheater. I had stood on that makeshift stage and preached to the imaginary crowd of unbelievers, each one a weary soul longing for words that would fill their own emptiness. I had been so sure of my calling that day. Mentally, I scolded myself for allowing these thoughts to overtake me but continued the silent back and forth monologue.

"The amphitheater was just a dream! No! I was there! I found the sign. I followed the narrow path…the moss-covered bridge…the amphitheater…the preaching…"

"Who do I think I'm kidding? I'm not a preacher, and I never will be!"

It was at that moment I was elbowed in the side and nudged back to reality.

I wondered if I had spoken out loud. Anna turned to look at me. I wasn't sure if I was detecting sincerity or jesting as she asked, "Is that the kind of preacher you want to be?"

My response was curt. "If I was meant to be a preacher, I wouldn't be here! I wouldn't be in the Army or in Texas! I definitely would not be on my way to Vietnam!" I paused, astounded at the words formulating in my mind, then spoke, "I don't know who got it wrong, me? Or God!"

Anna's mood was now solemn as she gently took my hand and led me to a bench situated under a huge cypress tree. We sat in silence for several minutes before she spoke, "Ricky..."

She somehow knew I was desperate to hear words of encouragement. Her tone was now soft and gentle. She paraphrased a familiar Bible verse as she replied to my frustrated rant, "No matter what you do or where you go, God is always in control. Trust him with all your heart. Don't rely on your own understanding but acknowledge God in everything you do. And he will direct your path."

My response reflected my doubts. "I know what the Bible has to say, but sometimes I have difficulty believing it. I know it's true. I just don't feel like it's true."

"Ricky, you can't always trust your feelings. You have to believe in what you know. It's called faith. You will never experience God's peace until you are first at peace with God."

She had managed to dispel all my negative thoughts. I finally began to relax and focus on the short time we had left to be together. We continued sitting in the shade of the tree while we discussed anything and everything including my upcoming yearlong deployment to Vietnam.

The sun had already begun its descent into the horizon, a reminder that the day had passed all too quickly.

CHAPTER 13

Lunch had been hours earlier, and our stomachs let us know we were ready for dinner. We were near the Alamo, so I suggested we have Mexican food. Anna, however, had a craving for pizza. The torturing heat of the day had subsided just enough to make the temperature somewhat tolerable, so we searched for an Italian restaurant with outdoor seating. The short walk brought us to a place near the river.

The host led us through the restaurant onto the patio and seated us at a round bistro table with two tall chairs that provided us with a perfect view.

The patio had a living canopy of wisteria. The dangling purple clusters from the pergola above filled the dining area with their sweet scent. The soft glow from the small white patio lights and the soothing music streaming from the background created an ambiance that was no less than romantic. We ordered a traditional Italian pizza topped with mozzarella, provolone, artichokes, Italian sausage, olives, and fresh basil. Neither of us wanted this night to end.

"Anna...do you remember the first time we met?"

I didn't wait for her reply.

"We were in the college library. You were tucked away in the corner, sitting in a wingback chair, reading. I couldn't take my eyes off you. Your brow was furrowed, and the corners of your mouth were turned downward as you closed the book and wiped your eyes with the back of your hand."

I paused and glanced her way. She began twisting her hair around her fingers, and I knew she was listening. I continued, "It was at that moment I knew I had to meet you. I remember slowly walking across the room, trying to muster enough courage to ask if you would like to join me for a cup of coffee. Somehow, I got the words out, and to my surprise, you said yes. We walked to the dining hall and spent the next few hours sipping coffee and getting to know each other. I knew then that this was the beginning of something really good!"

Anna sat there. Quiet. Listening. The restaurant was quiet as well. It was as if we were the only two people in the universe. I stood and reached into my pants pocket and pulled out the small velvet box I had been guarding all day. I knelt on one knee as the next words began to come from the depths of my soul.

"Anna, I love you. More than that, I'm in love with you! I can't imagine my life without you in it." I opened the box and held it up as an offering, a token of my love. "Would you be my bride, my forever girlfriend?"

She stared down at me, her expression stoic. She took the tiny box from my trembling hand and examined its contents: a ring. A solitary diamond that held so much promise. I remained kneeling as I eagerly anticipated her joyful reply.

Anna's voiceless response spoke volumes, and I felt as though I had been frozen in time…waiting. Gone was the smile from my face and my heart. The resounding silence was ear-splitting and no less deafening had she screamed. Questions raced through my mind:

Why doesn't she answer?
Should I keep kneeling?
Should I stand?

I didn't know what to do. I continued kneeling, but after several awkward moments, I decided to pull myself up and return to my seat. I was keenly aware that from the time I had first knelt, people at other tables had been watching this drama unfold. Now I could barely stand on my shaking legs, and I felt the loud beating of my heart could be heard by every other diner on that patio. Had I misread Anna's feelings for me? She slowly lifted her head, and our eyes locked.

My excitement turned to dread, and I prepared for rejection. Instead, she answered my question with a question, "Are you asking me to marry you?"

Now I was confused. What had she not understood? Had I stammered? I knew my frustration was showing:

"Yes, that's exactly what I am asking! I believe they call it a proposal!"

She picked up her glass and took a sip of her Dr. Pepper. She returned the drink to the table but continued to stir it with the straw. Her demeanor was markedly one of contemplation. Was she weighing her options? Or could she be deciding on the best way to decline my proposal? I opened my mouth to speak, but words escaped me, so I just pressed my lips together and remained silent. Anna suddenly snapped the box shut and set it down on the table. Every ounce of hope I had been desperately holding onto was now gone, trapped inside that little velvet case. I exhaled a nervous breath and slumped further down in my chair.

I watched Anna pick up the box once again. Had she reconsidered? I waited…a renewed sense of anticipation within me. This time, she opened the lid and gingerly removed the ring. She passed it from one hand to the other, slipping it on and off her finger, toying with it…and with me! Was this all a game to her? I hadn't spoken out loud, but she must have understood my frustration. She quickly slipped the ring on her finger and kept it there. She jumped up, ran around the table, and threw her arms around my neck. Her excitement was now obvious as she spoke, "Of course, I'll marry you! What took you so long to ask?"

I was so happy, but still very confused as I replied, "What took you so long to answer?"

Her mischievous smile was obvious now.

"My answer was always going to be yes! You are always the master prankster, so I thought this would be the perfect opportunity to get one over on you."

Relieved and just a little indignant, I finally spoke, "Jokes are meant to be funny! In case you didn't notice, I wasn't laughing."

Anna continued to giggle.

We decided to get married when I returned from Vietnam and set the date for September of the following year.

CHAPTER 14

Year 1968

I wasn't looking forward to this next year. We were beginning our descent into the unfamiliar and hostile world of Southeast Asia. It seemed like a lifetime had passed since Danny and I and other soldiers had boarded this plane and left the US. In reality, it had only been twenty-four hours. I peered out the window and watched as the landscape came into focus. There were no horror scenes, only serene countryside. I was keenly aware that the beauty of the densely forested mountains was a facade. And the endless coastline caressed by golden sand and the turquoise blue waters of the South China Sea was only camouflage for the turmoil below. For the next 365 days, I would live here. But I would never call this place home.

We landed at Bien Hoa Air Base near Saigon. The door was opened, and within seconds, the cool air that had kept us comfortable inside the plane, at least physically, was displaced by a rush of sticky heat and an odor that could only be described as a mix of rotting garbage and garlic. I hoped this odor was not typical of Vietnam because I knew it was something I could not, would not, get used to.

We exited the plane and were bombarded by the furnace-like atmosphere, the intense tropical heat, and accompanying humidity. Within minutes, our uniforms were drenched with sweat. The only thing worse than the heat was the overabundance of mosquitoes, each one seeking fresh blood. This was Vietnam, known as in-country to US soldiers. Every other place was referred to as the world. I believed we had arrived at the gateway to hell! We hefted our duffel bags onto our shoulders and walked across the pavement to the terminal.

There was barely enough time to use the latrine before a military police, MP for short, was directing us to the Army buses that would take us to our next destination. Danny and I immediately noticed that the windows of every bus had been replaced with bars and were covered with chicken wire. As we stepped inside, I couldn't resist commenting to the driver, "Is this a bus or a prison?"

His reply was swift and without humor, "Could be both!"

The driver didn't speak again until everyone was on board. We were packed in like sardines—soldiers, sitting shoulder to shoulder. Duffel bags littered the aisle, and the raunchy smell of sweat added to the garbage odor. He turned now and addressed his less-than-comfortable audience.

"You all seem to be concerned about the windows. You can see that the glass has been replaced with chicken wire. This is a security measure. It will hopefully prevent grenades and homemade bombs from being thrown inside the bus by locals who are not so eager to see us."

This was not a joke! I envisioned women, children, and grown men chasing the bus as we traveled along the road. They were lobbing their devices, which bounced off the windows and exploded in the air. I even thought I heard them yelling in a language I couldn't understand. The meaning was clear—*go home*!

How I wished I could. This time, I spoke only silently to myself, "Some welcoming party."

Although this scene was just my imagination, the fear of sabotage was real.

The short trip to the Ninetieth Replacement Battalion was incident-free. We were here for in-processing and assignment. The first thing that caught my eye as I stepped off the bus was a large red, white, and blue sign posted above the out-processing area: Going Home? Report Here. USA Bound!

I was immediately homesick. I envied those soldiers who had already put in their time. I wanted to be one of them entering that building—tour over. Instead, I was the new arrival looking at a year of living in Vietnam, a year away from my friends and family, and Anna. My heart rate suddenly quickened as I realized there was a possibility I might never make it back to enter into that building with the "Going Home" sign. We were given a bunk assignment and issued our bedding. Would I ever be USA-bound? Going home? There seemed to be no definitive answer as to how long we would be here. It could be hours or days. Right now, it was time for orientation.

This complex, known as Long Binh Post, is a hub for US soldiers entering and leaving Vietnam. Similar to a small city, it had everything to meet the immediate needs of those who spent time here: medical facilities, post office, laundry, barbershop, movies, a bowling alley—and the Ponderosa. The Ponderosa Club offered sandwiches, pizza, soda, ice cream, and served beer after duty hours.

The staff sergeant continued to ramble on for a half hour or so. He had given the same spiel before and would do so again: why we were here, the Vietnamese culture, and the film *A Nation Builds Under Fire*. Some of the troops called it propaganda, but most of us were just doing our best to stay awake during the documentary blather. When we at last finished, we were required to surrender all our American dollars in exchange for military payment certificates. American cash was not allowed in-country, and to have greenbacks in Vietnam was both illegal and punishable by court-martial.

We proceeded to dinner at the mess hall and afterward were given our temporary assignments. Danny was off to guard duty, and I ended up with kitchen police, KP for short. It was not my first choice to wash dishes, but it was better than latrine duty. I was dog-tired when I finally crawled into my bunk, but falling asleep was more of a wish than an action. I tossed and turned searching for that right spot. I fluffed and punched my pillow and rolled from one side to the other until I was totally entwined in the thin blanket. My restless thoughts carried me back as events of the last year played across my mind. It was as though I was watching a movie, one with an annoying glitch that continued to play the same scenes over and over. It seemed like hours of willing myself to sleep before mental and physical exhaustion allowed me to drift into a semiconscious state…

I was standing in the midst of long rows of freshly planted cotton. The warmth of the sun on my skin and the musty smell of dirt were familiar and comforting. Mama and Daddy waved from the end of the field. Katie stood there with them. Her excitement was evident as she jumped up and down. Their smiles were like beacons guiding me home. I waved back as I began to walk toward them. The more I walked, the greater the distance between us grew. I hurried my steps as I struggled to get closer but to no avail. Out of breath, I stopped running. The smiles on their faces had vanished. Katie was no longer jumping up and down. Mama was crying. I stood there and helplessly watched as the gap between us continued to increase and my family faded out of sight.

I was startled awake by the blaring sound of Reveille, our wake-up call. I was relieved my dream had been interrupted. It was time to shake off the night even though I felt I had not slept at all. I dressed and joined Danny and others heading to the mess hall for breakfast. I asked him, "How did you sleep?"

His reply was typical "Like a rock! I wuz sound asleep afor ma head hit the pilla!"

"Yeah, me too!"

I lied. I just wanted to forget about my dream. After all, it was only a dream…

There was no time for small talk. We shook hands and said goodbye. Danny had received his orders. He was assigned as a combat field medic and was immediately being transferred to his unit. I watched as he departed and was reminded of the war films we had seen during training. I now pictured Danny on the battlefield as he responded to the cries of the wounded: "Medic! Medic!"

Some cries grew louder as my friend rushed to patch the injured and get them loaded into the air ambulance. Other voices became quieter…then ceased altogether. I envisioned Danny continuing his vigil as the helicopter carrying the wounded to the hospital faded into the distance. It was heart-wrenching to think of my best friend in that environment. The question raced through my mind, Will my orders be the same as Danny's?

It would be three days before I had an answer!

I was tired of waiting and worrying about the unknown. My muscles tensed as I heard my name called. The nauseous taste of bile formed in my mouth as my stomach churned. All were a direct result of the nervous anticipation of bad news.

"Would I be assigned to the field?"

I didn't want to be here! I didn't want to be in the jungle! I didn't even want to be in the Army! But here I am, waiting for someone else to decide my fate. I was not in control! The familiar sense of doubt haunted my mind.

"I don't think I can do it."

Then I remembered Danny's words of encouragement: "Yur smart! Yur strong! An' yur brave!"

I was unaware that I had held my breath as I waited to hear my orders. My muscles relaxed, and I finally exhaled a grateful sigh of relief. The burden was lifted when I got the news that I would not be going to the jungle. I finally knew where I was headed. I had been assigned to the Eighty-Fifth Evacuation Hospital in Qui Nhon. Now things moved quickly. I was leaving the Ninetieth for my final in-country destination. It would be twelve months before I would return to the replacement battalion to be processed out of Vietnam and on my way back home. A year seemed like an eternity.

CHAPTER 15

Danny was never far from my mind. I hated that he was in such a volatile environment. Maybe it was guilt at the relief I felt when I realized I wouldn't have to join him. I visualized the hospital as a tall brick building like stateside hospitals or maybe a large Army tent erected in the middle of a dirt field. I didn't know what to expect. Either was preferable to what my friend would face.

The Eighty-Fifth Evacuation Hospital was neither a brick-and-mortar building nor a tent. Instead, I arrived to see over fifty separate Quonset huts splayed across several acres, each one designed for a specific function. Emergency room, x-ray, lab, and others were all connected by wooden slat walkways to avoid having to trudge through thick mud during the monsoon season.

Unlike the corrugated metal construction of the Quonset huts, the barracks were two-story buildings built of wood. I was assigned to barracks no. 2. Inside was an open bay, one large room with rows of metal bunks lining the walls, each bed in close proximity to the next. I located my bed, unpacked my duffel bag, and neatly placed my things into the adjacent locker. I stepped back and took a long look at my new living quarters. I couldn't help but notice how my life had been reduced to this tiny space. All my belongings, everything I would need for the next year, were now stored in a three-foot army-green locker. After settling in, I was given a tour of the base. The inside of the hospital was similar to the barracks—an open bay with iron beds lining the wall, only a few feet separating each one.

I immediately went to work and soon became familiar with patient care. I changed bandages, monitored vitals, and started IVs. These soldiers with their various needs reminded me of orientation back in San Antonio. The instructor had lectured about Vietnam's dangerous mountain terrain, dense brush, and razor-sharp elephant grass. He told of an abundance of virulent vipers, malaria, and dengue disease-carrying mosquitoes, redheaded centipedes, giant spiders, unbearable heat and humidity, and the torrential rain. But mostly, he talked about the jungle covered with booby traps and land mines just waiting for an unsuspecting soldier to fall prey. Now I was seeing the resulting destruction. Again, I thought of Danny and hoped he would be okay.

Most soldiers who were brought into this hospital suffered from shrapnel, bullet, and burn injuries. But many incurred wounds from the overabundance of booby traps hidden throughout the hostile terrain. The punji stick was a simple trap. It was not intended to kill but to inflict bodily harm great enough to slow the American advancement—one wounded soldier at a time. Each trap consisted of bamboo sticks sharpened on one end and often smeared with poison from plants or animal venom, human feces, or urine, and planted in a pit that was then camouflaged with leaves and grass to blend in with the surrounding terrain. The unsuspecting soldier would step on the thin cover and fall prey to the spikes below. Even if the initial injury was not life-threatening, it likely led to poisoning or infection.

Jerry had encountered such a trap. The bamboo spike had pierced the sole of his boot and skewered his foot. The field medic had removed both spike and boot and packed the large hole with antiseptic and gauze. By the time he reached the hospital, Jerry's foot had already turned red and was swollen to twice its normal size. X-rays confirmed he had no broken bones, but the infection had already begun to spread. I changed his bandage, hung a new IV bottle of antibiotics, and kept a vigilant watch for any change in his condition.

Although it had only been a few days, Jerry was already showing progress, and I knew he would be all right. Each time I checked on him his question was the same "Can I stay one more day?"

He wasn't the only one to make that request.

Most recovering soldiers were desperate to postpone the inevitable trip back to their unit and the jungle. I soon realized this war was not just about the physical. It was a psychological battle that instilled fear and destroyed morale and thus inflicted wounds that did not easily heal. This hospital seemed to be nothing more than a revolving door of affliction. Nevertheless, Jerry's infection was gone, and he was temporarily assigned a desk job until his foot completely healed. Soon he would rejoin his unit.

Soldiers come and go. The only variation is their faces. Some, like Jerry, are treated and eventually sent back to the jungle. Others have extensive wounds that render them no longer capable of performing their duties as soldiers. These men were discharged from the Army and sent back home where they attempt to resume a somewhat normal life.

There was one more group. Those soldiers who had given their all. They were sent home in a box draped with an American flag. I wondered how my family would deal with such a tragedy. What would Anna do? With each passing day, it became harder to remember a world beyond this war.

There weren't many options for recreation. We sometimes played cards or hung out at the beach or the bar. I spent most of my free time at the bar, drinking and relaxing with other soldiers as Armed Forces Radio blared our favorite songs from Creedence, The Doors, Steppenwolf, Three Dog Night, Joplin, and Hendrix. The songs about home, drugs, and war somehow helped block out the workday.

Drugs were widely used among the soldiers, especially marijuana. Vietnam was a hothouse for the popular drug. It grew everywhere. It was inexpensive and readily available for purchase from locals, including children. All were happy to trade a pocketful of weed for a few military dollars. I bought my first joint from a ten-year-old boy and became his regular customer. Marijuana quickly became the common tool for soldiers to temporarily escape the horrifying reality of this conflict. When that wasn't enough, they turned to a harder drug…heroin.

Occasionally, movies were shown on base. Tonight's feature was an epic John Wayne western. I preferred comedy, but tonight, I didn't care. I was ready for any mindless activity. I thought about how Daddy watched westerns whenever he got the chance. He would sit in his favorite chair then fall sound asleep no more than ten minutes into the movie. When his snoring became unbearable, Mama would nudge him awake and suggest he go to bed.

The movie began with the title and opening credits rolling across the screen. I settled back in my chair and propped my feet up on the chair in front of me. It quickly became apparent that something was wrong. The movie had been dubbed. John Wayne speaking Vietnamese made it hard to take it seriously. Soldiers began making up dialogue until everyone in the room was laughing. The movie turned out to be a comedy after all, and I think we all forgot where we were—but just for a moment.

Qui Nhon is a small city a few miles from base. It is close enough to go visit the shops, experience the Vietnamese culture, and sample the Asian cuisine. On my first trip there, I immediately knew there was a sharp distinction between my lifestyle at home and life here. The dusty streets of the residential areas were lined with houses constructed of corrugated tin, bamboo, and concrete. Downtown was more industrial with a Catholic Church, railroad station, banks, hotels, and restaurants. Motorized carts and bicycles clogged the narrow streets as their operators taxied passengers back and forth. Men and women wore black silk pajama-style pants, long-sleeve shirts, and conical hats handcrafted from leaves and bamboo.

I passed a vendor selling sandwiches. The aroma called to me, and my mouth began to water, so I ordered the sub. It was delicious. In fact, it was the best sandwich I had ever eaten! I had to know what was in it. Since there was a definite language barrier, I pointed to my sandwich and shrugged my shoulders to indicate my question. The cook understood and quickly answered with a simple word *con khi*. I had picked up a few words since I had been in-country and the translation of *con khi* is "monkey." To verify my suspicion, I bent my elbow, pawed my armpit with my fingers, and made the sound of a chimpanzee. The cook grinned a toothless smile and nodded.

Suddenly, the sandwich was no longer appealing or delicious. I could only think of monkeys playfully swinging from tree to tree. They were minding their own business and, without warning, became lunch. I immediately lost my appetite and vomited the best sandwich

I ever had. The taste did not leave me as quickly. It lingered in my mouth as I continued my self-guided tour of the town and purchased a few gifts for Katie.

CHAPTER 16

Dedicated, Unhesitating Service to Our Fighting Forces.

Dustoff—the call sign for the army air ambulance perfectly describes the integrity of the pilots and crew risking their own lives to save others. Flying into the middle of battle, defying treacherous conditions, inclement weather, mountains, jungles, and marshy plains. Risking exposure for a hostile ambush to pluck sick and injured soldiers from combat and transport them to the hospital. In my opinion, they are the heroes of this war.

I was sound asleep when, all of a sudden, I jolted awake. I immediately felt an aura of uneasiness surrounding me...a haunting awareness of dread. Frozen with fear, I didn't even want to make the slightest movement. But at the same time, I felt the need to hide. I slowly pulled my blanket up, covering my mouth and nose. Without moving my head, my eyes darted from side to side, fully expecting to see someone, or something, standing by my bed, staring down at me. But no one was there. I wanted to blame this ghoulish presence and the rapid throbbing in my chest on a nightmare, but I don't remember having such a dream. With my eyes wide open, I continued to lie motionless for what seemed like hours. Finally, Reveille sounded, and everyone in the barracks began to stir. I welcomed the hint of daylight and the rousing of soldiers. Friendly chatter began, but I didn't join in. I wasn't about to mention my awkward morning to anyone. I quickly dressed and headed to the mess hall for breakfast.

I was barely able to choke down my toast and eggs. I couldn't stop thinking about the frightening episode. I washed down my meal with a couple of cups of coffee then headed off to work. As I walked toward the hospital, I couldn't shake the eerie feeling that left me looking over my shoulder as though something was lurking in the shadows. I quickened my steps, hoping to get to work, forget about the episode, and resume a normal day.

I entered the hospital, quickly closed the door behind me, and exhaled a deep sigh of relief. My reprieve was short-lived as talk among the medical staff revealed that they, too, sensed an atmosphere of eeriness. To my surprise, I wasn't the only one who had experienced this early morning terror. I don't know whether to be relieved or afraid.

By midmorning, ominous black clouds covered the sky. The angry roar of thunder applauded the brilliant jolts of power as ragged clouds released a tumultuous downpour. In a matter of minutes, the dusty roads transitioned from hard clay to viscous mud.

The storm hammered down onto the metal Quonset hut sounding more like a hailstorm of rocks than rain and was unlike any we'd previously experienced. It had us all on edge. Then as quickly as it had begun, it passed, and the black clouds made a hasty retreat unveiling blue sky and sunshine. The moisture in the air joined forces with the blazing sun, causing the humidity to soar. The metal Quonset hut had no air-conditioning and was akin to working in a suffocating tin can.

We all agreed. This morning's dismal feeling could be blamed on the impending storm. Now that the storm had passed, so had the menacing atmosphere of oppression. We all went about our daily routine.

I took a late lunch and was relaxing when I heard the distinctive *whomp-whomp-whomp* of the Huey helicopter, a warning that something had gone terribly wrong. Soldiers had been wounded, and the Dustoff crew was bringing them to the hospital. I immediately headed to the emergency department.

The pilot settled the skids onto the helipad and shut down the engine. The rotors began to wind down as several of us ran from the emergency room toward the chopper. In the belly of the Huey were three soldiers strapped onto stretchers and two sitting in jump seats. We quickly transferred them inside and began our triage routine.

My job is to take vitals, cut off their uniforms, and clean them up so their injuries could be assessed. Next, I would check their dog

THE WAR WITHIN

tags, note their name, rank, and serial number in case they went unconscious…or worse. I began the process when I heard the alarming *whomp-whomp-whomp* once again…then again. The barrage of helicopters seemed endless. The emergency room plunged into chaos, and all off-duty medical personnel were ordered back to work.

The battered soldiers covered in mud, blood, and leaves, quickly filled the beds. We gathered every gurney and wheelchair in the hospital and lined the hallways with wounded soldiers, each one waiting his turn to be treated. The scene was horrific and chaotic. I ran from one bed to the next, trying my best to avoid the sticky scarlet pools on the floor. After ridding the soldiers of their saturated fatigues, I covered them with a blanket and began taking vitals. With the earpieces in place, I firmly held the stethoscope's bell on the inside of the soldier's arm, over the brachial artery, then I repeatedly squeezed the rubber bulb, pumping air into the blood pressure cuff. To hear the pulse amid the din of commotion that surrounded me, my focus had to be absolute. With the cuff taut, I gently turned the air-flow valve, gradually deflating the cuff as I listened hard for the tapping sound of blood as it flowed through the artery.

Then I heard it—not the tapping but a whisper. I quickly removed my earpieces. Now all I could hear were doctors shouting out orders for x-rays, IVs, and meds, mingled with the cries and moans of the wounded soldiers. It took only a moment to disregard the notion that I could make out a single word in all that noise, let alone a whisper. Then I heard it again. This time, I was positive. Someone had called my name! But Rick is a common name, and maybe this was just a coincidence. I focused, listening as I scuffed my way through the refuse of human misery that littered the floor. I continued to follow the sound as I wove my way around doctors and nurses and more gurneys. I reached the area designated *critical*.

His voice was barely audible as he continued to whisper my name. I approached the bed and held his trembling hand as I watched the life leaking out of him. The all-too-familiar smell of copper permeated the air. It was the smell of blood—a lot of blood. I wanted to vomit. Fighting back the bitter taste of bile, I swallowed hard and finally choked out a few words:

"It's Rick. I'm here!"

He appeared eager to speak. His lips were moving, but I could no longer hear his words. I continued talking, trying to calm him down as I peeled off the dried mud and washed his face. He opened his eyes, and I saw one blue eye and one brown eye staring up at me in desperation. It was Danny!

"Danny! What are you doing here?"

His breathing was labored as he struggled to speak. I leaned down and placed my ear next to his mouth. He took short, intentional breaths. His voice raspy as he whispered:

"Toed…ya…hurt…fix…me."

His speech was broken, just like his body. But there was something familiar about his words. Today's fractured request was part of a speech he blasted me with during our medical training in San Antonio. I was discouraged and doubting my ability to become a good medic. He sensed I was struggling and nagged at me until I confessed, "I just don't think I can do it." Now his words of encouragement replay in my mind: *Let me tell ya sumpthin'. Yur smart. Yur strong. An' yur brave! I'd be proud ta fight next ta ya. An' if'n I wuz ta ever git hurt, I'd want ya ta fix me up!*

He had banished my doubt with his words of encouragement. They were all I needed to not only believe I *could* do it but that I *would* do it.

I could no longer blink back my sadness as hot tears spilled from my eyes and fell onto Danny's face. Our sorrow mixed together and ran down the side of his cheek dripping onto the blood-soaked sheet. I continued holding his hand while the doctors assessed his injuries. Then I said goodbye as they wheeled him off to surgery. I exhaled a ragged breath as my shoulders quivered from silent sobs. The nearest wall became brief support as I slowly sank to the floor and hugged my knees to my chest. Silently, I cried out, "God! Why? Why Danny?"

My question directed toward God was definitely not a prayer but a statement of anger.

The storm of helicopters continued throughout the night. Finally, as the sun peeked above the horizon, the last helicopter was emptied and the last soldier treated. I went into the latrine, splashed cold water on my face, and ran my wet fingers through my hair. I looked in the mirror, and staring back at me was an unfamiliar face of a man who had aged overnight. I now realized the ominous presence that overwhelmed me yesterday morning was a warning. Not of a storm of nature's fury but a human storm of casualties and pain. For me, this war is not fought in the jungle or against the Viet Cong. It is fought right here, inside this hospital—a war against time. Each soldier's clock ticking away the few precious minutes between life and death. This was my war.

    I haven't had a decent night's sleep since Danny and several of the other soldiers succumbed to their injuries. Each night, fully exhausted, I collapse onto my bunk and quickly fall sound asleep, but my rest is soon interrupted with visions of that fateful night. I picture the emergency room packed with wall-to-wall soldiers, each one crying out in despair. I peer out the door, and the long line of gurneys waiting to enter the hospital is endless. I hear the continuous whirring of the helicopter rotors, like a never-ending staccato beat of a drum—*whomp-whomp-whomp*. The wheels of gurneys squeak as they continually pass by. The sound echoes off the walls as they carry their wounded. And I smell the blood, that sickening stench of copper.

    I blink. The chaos is suddenly muted. The whomping noise is quieted. The cries silenced. I look around the room, and each soldier is now fully covered with a white sheet. There are no names. There are no faces…only sheets. Every doctor, nurse, and aide is now standing motionless, slumped shoulders, heads bowed in defeat.

    I jolt awake and struggle to emerge from the blanket I have unknowingly thrown over my head. My eyes are swollen, and my pillow is wet with tears. Tears for myself and for all of us who live and work in this nightmarish reality. Tears for the wounded and the dying. And tears for my best friend. I now realized I would never see Danny again. He had gone home in a box.

    Each evening after work, I headed straight to the bar to hang out with other soldiers. We would have a few beers, shoot some pool, and indulge in a little weed. Still, my nightmare continued to haunt me. Adding pain pills to the mix became a way to chase away my demons and escape the cruel reality of this war. Was I the only one haunted by that night? I didn't ask…and they didn't tell.

The only semblance of normality is mail call. I looked forward to hearing from Anna and my family. The letters were uplifting but at the same time disheartening. They were no substitute for the warmth of a hug or face-to-face conversations.

Each month, I received a care package from Katie filled with homemade cookies, Butterfinger candy bars, and a simple note with a hand-drawn heart. But this time, she had written a letter:

Dear Rick,

Mama and Daddy never talk about you, at least not with me. I ask how you are doing, and the answer is always the same: "He's fine." But I get the feeling you aren't fine. Once, I woke up in the middle of the night thinking about you. I had a feeling that you were in trouble, so I prayed. I hope it's true, that you *are* fine, and I don't have to worry.

I can hardly wait for you to come home. Anna asked me to be in the wedding, and Mama is making my dress.

I miss you.

Love,
Katie

I made a special effort to send Katie postcards for her scrapbook, noting everything *was* fine on my side of the world. I knew Mama and Daddy didn't provide Katie with answers. They wanted to protect her from the same heartbreak they felt. I lied to them, and they lied to her.

Mama always wrote about everything going on at home and said she prayed for me every day. I'm glad she prayed, if it made her feel better. The last time I prayed was in college when attending chapel was a requirement. Since then, I was highjacked from a plan that I thought was from God. If there is a God, he didn't come here with me. Or maybe I just left him behind. I'm not sure. My mind is filled with too many questions and not enough answers.

Days, weeks, even months, have passed and the nightmare has nearly subsided. I still think about Danny, but now my focus is on leaving. Only a few more months and I will be going home.

CHAPTER 17

I arrived at the replacement battalion for out-processing, and the first thing I noticed was the red, white, and blue sign: Going Home? Report Here. USA Bound!

It was the same sign I had seen a year ago. This time, instead of facing the unknown, I'm looking back on my year in Vietnam. I watched as another bus unloaded "fresh" soldiers for in-processing. The wide-eyed look on their faces would not last. Their innocence would soon be lost in the harsh reality of war. In a year, they will be physically and mentally beaten. I wanted to warn them of their plight, somehow offer words of encouragement and hope, but how could I? I turned away with deep-felt empathy and headed toward the sign.

The road from the replacement battalion to Bien Hoa airport had not changed. It was the same distance as a year ago when I first arrived in-country, but somehow, the bus ride seemed longer this time. My mind wandered back to that first day we landed in Vietnam—me, Danny, and a plane full of soldiers, all with a sense of foreboding. Mostly teenagers, each hoped he would be one of the lucky ones to return to this airport for the flight back home. Little did I know back then Danny would not be joining me on this trip.

We arrived at Bien Hoa where the Freedom Bird was waiting to take us back to the States. We climbed the steps and took our seats inside. This should have been the happiest day of our lives. We were eager to leave, but we all sat in silence, paranoid that something would happen to keep us here. Many soldiers sat staring out the window, keeping a vigilant eye for enemy collaborators or a rocket aimed to annihilate the plane and all on board. Even now, something could still halt our efforts to leave. Finally, the engines came to life and we began taxiing down the runway. The plane lifted from the ground, and we all held our breath as it began its steep climb into the air.

I peered out the window and watched as the rugged mountains and lush green jungle of Vietnam began to diminish in size. I thought of the hospital, the helicopters, the booby traps, and the soldiers that remain camouflaged below the canopy of trees trudging through the muck of war. I thought of the wounded I helped heal, the wounded I couldn't heal, and I thought of Danny.

This trip was bittersweet. I was happy to be leaving Vietnam, but I couldn't help but think of the soldiers I came here with that were not on this plane. I could hardly wait to get home. But at the same time, I harbored a deep sense of guilt for leaving my fellow soldiers behind in this godforsaken hellhole. It wasn't until we reached the high altitude above the South China Sea that the celebration began. Cheers erupted, and the smiles on our faces were evidence that we were actually on our way home.

It was the middle of the night when we landed in Seattle. By the time the plane had come to a complete stop, we had already crowded into the aisle. We were more than ready to set foot on American soil. The door opened, and the fresh, damp air filled the cabin. We breathed it in and wasted no time rushing down the steps. Unlike the torrential monsoons in Vietnam, the soft rain was slow and steady. Most soldiers ran to the building to avoid the drizzle. I welcomed it. The tiny droplets gently rested on my shoulders before some fell to the ground sounding out a pitter-patter of applause. Others danced on top of the puddles in celebration of my return. I lingered a few more moments taking in the reality that I had come full circle. I made it back to the US.

I took my time walking to the terminal. I knew my connecting flight to Fresno was not until tomorrow, and I was not looking forward to spending the night in the airport. I entered the building, took off my rain-soaked jacket, and shook off the water. When I looked up, Anna was waiting for me with a big smile and outstretched arms. My heart leaped with joy. I dropped my coat and ran toward her. Our embrace was so tight that I could barely breathe. She felt good in my arms. I don't know how long we stood there, but I didn't want to let her go.

"Anna, what are you doing here?"

"I couldn't wait to see you. I found out when your plane was coming in and took an earlier flight to surprise you."

We held hands and strolled through the terminal so I could stretch my tired legs after the long flight. Anna gestured to a bag she brought from home and asked, "Are you hungry? I brought food."

She had filled the bag with sandwiches, sodas, and homemade cookies.

"No! I'm not hungry. I'm starving!"

After a year of mess hall food, a simple meal looked good. I reached inside the bag and pulled out a sandwich. It was a foot-long sub. Suddenly, I was reminded of the monkey meat sub I had in Vietnam. I remembered the aroma of the spicy meat and pictured the smile of the toothless vendor as he handed over my meal. My stomach churned and rumbled in protest. I relayed the story to Anna, and she assured me there was no monkey in this meal.

"I made it myself. It's French bread loaded with salami, ham, turkey, cheese, and lots of tomatoes, lettuce, and those little peppers you like."

We sat in a couple of seats at one of the unoccupied loading gates for a makeshift picnic. I enjoyed every bite of the sandwich. More importantly, I enjoyed the company.

We talked throughout the night. Anna asked questions about Vietnam, but I didn't want to talk about me…or the past twelve months. I was more interested in the future—our future. I had yet to tell anyone about my next assignment. I wanted to tell Anna face-to-face, and our airport rendezvous was the perfect place to break the news.

"Anna, I know this past year has been difficult for you. We were a world apart all the while you were planning a wedding, knowing the uncertainty of me making it back home."

Her face suddenly showed concern as in preparation of bad news.

"I've received my orders, and again, I will be going abroad."

"What are you saying? We're getting married, then you will be leaving me for who knows how long?"

This conversation was not going like I had planned. Somehow, Anna thought I was about to deliver bad news when, in fact, the news was good—very good.

She continued, "I don't want our relationship to only exist by mail."

"I don't either, but—"

I couldn't complete my sentence before she interrupted, "Ricky, what are you saying? Are you calling off the wedding? Are we breaking up?"

Her wrinkled brow and down-turned corners of her mouth were an indication of the sadness welling up inside her. I had to tell her, "Anna, I have to ask you an important question."

Tears began to well up in her eyes.

"Well, what is it?"

"How do you feel about living in Europe?"

"Europe? What do you mean?"

"I've been trying to tell you. My next assignment is Germany. And you're coming with me!"

The worry on her furrowed brow vanished, and her big smile was all the evidence I needed to know she was happy.

"Germany sounds wonderful! Actually, any place is wonderful as long as we're together."

"I couldn't agree more."

"I have a month of leave before heading to Germany, and I have it all planned out. First, I'll spend a couple of weeks with my family. Then our wedding and honeymoon. Then I'll leave for Germany. I will get everything squared away, then you will join me in a couple of months."

The hours with Anna went by all too quickly. It was difficult to say goodbye, but we held onto the promise to see each other soon.

*****

Anna stared out the window as the airplane taxied down the runway. Surprising Ricky at the airport had been incredible. She cherished those few short hours of their reunion. But deep inside, she was troubled, unable to shake the nagging sense of uneasiness. *He seemed different.* She shook her head in an effort to erase the disturbing thoughts as though her mind was an Etch-a-Sketch. She convinced herself he just needed time to adjust to being back home.

*****

Finally, the last leg of my flight. I settled into my seat and closed my eyes, hoping to get some sleep before arriving in Fresno. But I couldn't sleep. I kept thinking about Anna and our time at the airport, our upcoming wedding, the Army, Vietnam, and how things turned out differently than I had once planned. I shouldn't have been drafted. But I was. I shouldn't have gone to Vietnam. But I did. Now I just want to forget about the past twelve months and live a normal life.

A normal life? What is normal? I'm not sure anymore. The only thing I am sure of is I'm about to marry the love of my life and I don't want to mess it up.

Mama, Daddy, and Katie were at the airport anxiously awaiting my arrival. When I entered the terminal, Mama began crying. Katie was enthusiastically waving, and Daddy approached me with an outstretched hand. I swatted his hand away and embraced him with a heartfelt hug. I'm reminded of the day they brought me to this same airport, sending me off to boot camp. That day seemed like a lifetime ago.

I watched the turnstile for my duffel while Daddy went out to the parking lot to pull the car up to the curb. I retrieved my bag, and we headed toward the exit. Suddenly Mama stopped walking.

"What's wrong?"

She turned to face me, and I noticed tears welling up in the corners of her eyes. Once again, I asked, "What's wrong?"

"There's a group of people outside. Don't look at them and don't talk to them. Go straight to the car. Just ignore them."

THE WAR WITHIN

We stepped outside and were met by a mob of anti-war protesters. Expressing their disapproval, the group held signs displaying the peace symbol and banners that read: *Make Love, Not War.* They called me a *baby killer* and other derogatory names all the while chanting, "Hell no! We won't go!"

Suddenly, I felt ashamed. Now I remember the warning we all got before leaving Vietnam: *When you get home, take off your uniform and don't put it back on until you report back to duty. By doing so, you will avoid public ridicule and embarrassment.*

Public ridicule? Embarrassment? I didn't grasp the depth of that warning…until now. I wasn't happy about being in the Army, but at the same time, I was never ashamed of my uniform. I hurried to the car, tossed my bag into the trunk, and sat with Katie in the back seat.

We all talked nonstop for the half-hour drive to Tranquillity. Everyone had a lot of questions, but mostly, we were just happy to be together. It was late afternoon by the time we got to our house. I opened the door, and the sweet aroma of home invited me in like an old friend, greeting me with open arms.

Mama had a pot of pinto beans and ham simmering on the stove. She poured me a tall glass of ice-cold sweet tea then immediately began peeling potatoes for dinner. Katie pulled out all the ingredients from the cupboard for corn bread, mixed it together, poured it into a hot iron skillet, then popped it into the oven.

"Wow, Katie. When did you learn to cook?"

"I've been practicing the whole time you've been away. I even baked you a 'Welcome Home' pecan pie. Your favorite!"

I could hear the crackle and pop as Mama poured the potatoes into the sizzling skillet. The aroma of this home-cooked meal filled the entire house, and I could hardly wait to dig in. I ate a double portion of everything, including Katie's pie. After dinner, I realized how exhausted I was. I had barely slept on the long flight back to the States, stayed up all night at the airport with Anna, the flight home, then the protesters. It was all catching up with me now.

My old room was waiting for me. I took off my uniform and collapsed onto my bed. I exhaled a grateful sigh to be home and fell hard asleep. It was early afternoon the following day when I awoke.

It took me a few minutes to recognize my surroundings and understand I was not in my bunk in Vietnam. I was home. The house was quiet. Daddy had gone to work, Mama was outside hanging laundry on the clothesline, and Katie had informed me last night that she had planned to ride her bike to town to a friend's house.

I stood in the shower until the hot water ran cold then dried with a ragged towel that had seen better days. I put on a pair of old jeans and a T-shirt. I went straight to the kitchen, poured myself a large glass of cold milk, and finished off Katie's pie. Everything about home felt good! At least when I was in this house…

The mob at the airport continued to haunt my mind. Were all soldiers returning from Vietnam treated this way? By no means did I expect a marching band, balloons, and confetti to welcome me home, but I had no idea I would be seen as the enemy. I couldn't keep quiet. I had to voice my opinion. I sat down and penned a letter to the newspaper:

> Dear Editor,
>
> For months and months, I have looked forward to returning home from Vietnam. All that I wanted to do was to come home to the "world" and be with my own kind of people again. Instead of being met by my own kind of people, I was met by a strange creature that calls himself a human being.
> This strange creature has long hair and a beard. He dresses in rags and smells far worse than I ever did while I was in Vietnam.
> He looks upon me in my uniform as if I'm some sort of an animal.
> Why? What did I do?
> For twelve months, I have seen nineteen and twenty-year-old men lose their arms and legs and, in some cases, their lives for these strange

creatures. Was this done in vain? I am glad that these strange creatures aren't in Vietnam.

Because they would surely get killed. Not by the VC but by us animals in uniforms.

SPEC 4 Richard Clark
Tranquillity

There, I said it!

CHAPTER 18

It's finally here! I've waited for this day for over a year! Now it looks like it will be jinxed by rain. I know it's not unusual for the Pacific Northwest to see precipitation, but today's forecast is for nothing less than a downpour. It figures. Some consider rain on your wedding day the same as breaking a mirror or walking under a ladder or a black cat crossing the path in front of you—it's all bad luck.

I quickly scolded myself for the negative thoughts. Today Anna and I begin our future together—rain or shine!

The old country church is situated just outside Portland and is the church Anna and her parents regularly attend. Once a one-room schoolhouse that doubled as a church on Sundays, the building has retained some of its rustic charm despite remodels and modernizations. The original tall narrow structure wrapped in whitewashed clapboard siding still stands as the entrance to a larger sanctuary. A fenced cemetery adjacent to the church honors young and old that lived and died in an era long past. Names and dates carved on their headstones are no longer legible having succumbed to years of deterioration. But the fresh-cut grass and meticulously groomed shrubbery remain as a testimony to the love and care taken to preserve the historical past of this place.

The wedding was set for noon. I arrived at the church an hour early and climbed the steps to the entrance. I opened the double doors to find the pastor of the church waiting to greet me. He was also the minister who would officiate the wedding. I stepped into the lobby, and we shook hands. After hurried exchanges regarding what would soon transpire, he excused himself and rushed off to deal with what I imagined to be last-minute ceremony details.

I knew Anna and her bridal party were hidden away in one of the church's rooms fussing over her makeup, hair, and dress. I could hear the giggling and celebration echoing down the hallway. I desperately wanted to knock on the door and get a sneak peek of my bride, but I had no intention of seeing Anna in her dress before the ceremony. I never regarded myself as superstitious, but today, I didn't want to take any chances. I didn't want to add one more piece of negative wedding folklore to the rainy-day forecast.

This entryway was bright and inviting. A large bulletin board on one of the walls contained pictures of the pastor and his family, announcements for upcoming events, prayer requests, and the number of attendees at last Sunday's service. Situated in one corner was a small round table stacked with Bibles. The accompanying sign indicated they were free.

I headed toward the main part of the church and noticed the words painted above the arched entrance: "When life gives you more than you can stand…kneel."

I used to feel a soothing comfort in church, but now it seemed awkward and foreign.

I walked down the center aisle to the stage. The simple arbor draped with greenery and purple wisteria reminded me of the restaurant in San Antonio where I asked Anna to marry me.

Instead of traditional piano or organ, Anna had chosen to use a string quartet for the wedding music. The ensemble was situated off to one side just below the platform. The two violins, viola, and cello could be heard as the musicians began tuning their instruments. The photographer moved about, capturing several unsuspecting human subjects as he deftly snapped pictures of the decorations. I joined the groomsmen in a room adjacent to the platform and pinned the white rosebud to the lapel of my tux.

Anna's older brother, Paul, was to be my best man. We had met a couple of times before, and I genuinely liked him. Now he looked at me sternly before he spoke, "Don't forget! You're marrying my sister. You know how brothers feel about their sisters!"

I nodded.

"Yes! I know exactly how brothers feel about their sisters. I happen to have one."

He continued, "I just want to let you know that I have friends." He paused.

"You know, the kind of friends that take care of business."

I was a little confused. Where was this conversation heading?

"What do you mean, *friends that take care of business*?"

"All I'm saying is…" He stepped closer. His brow furrowed as he looked me straight in the eyes then continued, "You had better make sure Anna is happy!"

Was this a threat? Some best man! Now I'm not quite sure what to think of my soon-to-be brother-in-law. What have I gotten myself into?

It didn't take long for him to notice my confusion. Possibly it was the look of terror I now imagined to be on my face. He slapped me hard on the shoulder and, along with the other groomsmen, began to laugh.

"I'm just kidding! Anna told me you were a practical joker, so I thought I would get one over on you."

"On my wedding day? You could use a lesson on timing."

He was quick to respond, "I look forward to it."

Relief washed over me. Instead of being the jokester, I now know how it feels to be the victim.

The smile on his face faded. His tone was warm but serious. "All joking aside… If Anna loves you, so do I. Welcome to the family."

That day was the beginning of a good friendship.

Paul and the other groomsmen made their way back to the lobby to prepare for the processional. The quartet began playing preceremony music. I opened the door just enough to see that guests had arrived and were being ushered to their seats. I hoped the soothing music could somehow calm my jitters, but the sweat on my palms proved otherwise. It didn't take long for the pews to fill. Katie was a bridesmaid, so my parents were the only familiar faces out there in the midst of Anna's friends and family members. Tranquillity was just too far away for anyone else to make the trip. The minister took his place on the platform and motioned for me to join him. It was time.

The bridal party began their slow walk down the aisle. I had forgotten how much Katie had grown. She was no longer a little girl. She was a teenager, and she was obviously enjoying her role in this day. The ring bearer followed, carrying a white satin pillow with fake rings tied in place. He was only four years old, and Anna didn't trust him with the real thing. The flower girl entered just before the bride and tossed handfuls of white rose petals. There was a slight pause in the music…then the quartet began playing the "Bridal Chorus." Everyone stood and faced the back of the room in anticipation of the bride's entry.

Anna stepped into the distant doorway. I drew in a sharp breath, almost a gasp. She was beyond beautiful. Her dress was traditional white satin and lace, embellished with tiny pearls. The neckline, shaped like the top of a heart, framed the blue sapphire and diamond necklace that had once belonged to her grandmother. Her cascading bouquet of white roses, lavender, orchids, and baby's breath looked like a waterfall of flowers.

She began walking down the aisle toward me, her pace slow and steady as the chapel length train trailed behind. Her hair was pinned atop her head with auburn ringlets gently falling to her neck.

Suddenly the music seemed to fade and with it the congregation, bridesmaids, and groomsmen. I was so focused on this amazing woman who had actually said yes to me that I had lost sight of everyone else. Even now as she drew near, I could see she was wearing the same beautiful smile that had first drawn me to her in that college library. How long ago was that?

Anna reached the platform, and I snapped back to reality. It was then I noticed the tears welling up in her father's eyes. Were they tears of sadness or joy? I imagine a little of both. He kissed Anna on the cheek and handed her over to me. I suddenly felt the weight of responsibility. Now it was up to me. I was her provider and protector. She passed her bouquet to her maid of honor, and we collected our rings from Paul.

Anna had chosen her ring. A dozen tiny diamonds circling the larger diamond set in white gold. I took it but was unable to tell if my trembling hands were the result of excitement or nerves. I gazed at her as I expressed my love and spoke my vows. Then I took her hand and slid the ring onto her finger. The minister cleared his throat and whispered, "Wrong hand."

I glanced down and saw that I had indeed placed Anna's ring on her right hand. I quickly made the switch in hopes that no one had noticed. Now it was Anna's turn.

She held my hands, looked deep into my eyes, and spoke in a soft, melodious tone, "I, Anna, take you, Rick…"

As she vowed to stand by me for better or worse, richer or poorer, in sickness and in health, my chin began to quiver.

She paused and whispered, "Are you okay?"

I could only nod.

She continued, "To love and cherish always."

That's when I lost control. The tears I had been holding back spilled from my eyes and ran down my face. I felt like a blubbering fool.

The minister handed her his handkerchief. She dabbed my eyes and dried my wet face then stuffed the cloth into my pocket.

"I don't think he wants this back," she whispered.

She correctly placed a simple gold band on my left hand and the minister pronounced us married. I lifted her veil and kissed my wife.

The reception was held in the fellowship hall of the church. White linen tablecloths covered a dozen round tables, each one adorned with a small vase filled with a simple bouquet of white roses and sprigs of lavender. The triple-tier cake was elegantly decorated with fresh flowers—almost too pretty to cut. Anna and I shared our bites of cake, mingled, and danced. We celebrated our day and toasted our future. It was time to say our goodbye to friends and family. We thanked them for sharing our special day then changed clothes and made a beeline for our getaway car. We stuffed our luggage then ourselves into Anna's tiny car. It dawned on me as we pulled away…the weatherman was wrong—*it never did rain*!

CHAPTER 19

The long string of tin cans tied onto the rear bumper made a loud clanking sound as we drove away. The clatter announced to everyone within earshot that we were newlyweds. I stopped a couple of blocks down the road, removed the cans, and stuffed them into the small trunk. Anna's ice-blue 1966 Austin-Healey Sprite convertible was a graduation present from her parents a few years ago. It suits Anna's personality to a T. But for me, it's a little too cramped for my long legs.

I merged onto the freeway then headed toward the coast where we would spend our honeymoon. We were listening to the radio while discussing our plans for the following week when I heard a strange noise coming from the rear of the car. I turned off the radio and listened. Anna heard it too.

"Is that noise normal?" I asked.

"No, is something wrong?"

It sounded like the tin cans were still tied to the bumper, but I knew that wasn't the case. I had to check it out, so I pulled into the next rest area and executed a walk-around inspection. I raised the hood. I peered into the trunk. And I kicked the tires. I found nothing unusual. But how would I know? I don't know anything about cars and have no interest in learning. I got back into the driver's seat and assured Anna everything was okay. Back onto the freeway, the noise continued. Now I am worried. The last thing I want is to be stranded alongside the road. I drove to the nearest gas station to have it checked out.

The sign read Mechanic on Duty, so I pulled in and stopped in front of the open garage door. The mechanic met me as I was getting out of the car. I noticed the name Carl embroidered on the tag of his dirty coveralls. Carl was an older gentleman, and everything about him was gray: his hair, his beard, even his eyes. Under all the oil, dirt, and grime, I imagine his coveralls to also be gray. I secretly hoped that Carl's age equaled his expertise in mechanics.

"Congratulations on your wedding," said Carl.

"Thank you. We were married just a few hours ago. But how did you know?"

"Well, I was in the shop, minding my own business when I heard this god-awful racket. Of course, I quit what I was doing and took a look out the door. And here you come, pulling right in, racket an all. That's when I saw the 'Just Married' sign on your window."

"Anyway…what can I do for you?"

I explained to Carl the noise and where I thought it was coming from.

"This is not how I imagined our marriage would begin, with a broken-down car."

Although Carl had a bum leg and walked with a limp, he efficiently performed a walk-around inspection. He raised the hood. He peered into the trunk. And he kicked the tires.

"I already did that!" I explained. "I didn't see anything wrong."

Carl just stood there, staring at the car. And I stared at Carl. Silently, I questioned the expertise of this mechanic. I crossed and uncrossed my arms in frustration while I waited for his diagnosis. Finally, I just crammed my hands into my pant pockets. Carl reached around and pulled a greasy red rag from his back pocket and began wiping his hands. After several minutes, his hands appeared to be no cleaner than when he had started. He stuffed the rag back into his pocket and, without speaking, turned and slowly limped back into the shop. I looked at Anna and shrugged my shoulders.

"What now?" she asked.

Just as I was opening the car door to leave, Carl returned. He was carrying an awkward-looking tool.

"Follow me," he instructed.

I followed as he suggested, and we walked to the rear of the car. He carefully knelt by the wheel, jimmied the tool under the lip of the hubcap, and pried it off. All of a sudden, a dozen or so small rocks spilled out onto the ground.

"It's a common wedding day prank," explained Carl.

"Friends of the bride and groom will fill one of the hubcaps with rocks. As you drive, the noise will imitate a car problem."

"So are you telling me there's nothing wrong?"

"That's exactly what I'm saying. You're at the receiving end of a practical joke."

Carl replaced the hubcap and didn't charge for his services. He congratulated us one more time and even offered to dispose of the string of tin cans taking up space in our small trunk. I bought a couple of sodas and a bag of chips from the vending machines, and we continued on our way.

It was getting late, and we were exhausted and hungry. Due to our late start and unexpected detour, we wouldn't make it to the coast at a decent hour, so we decided to stop for the night.

The Roadside Inn was neither a lavish hotel nor did it look like a roach-infested dive. Each room, twelve in all, was a separate cottage, simple and inviting. Adjacent to the inn was a mom-and-pop diner that served breakfast all day. We decided to have a bite to eat before checking into a room, so we walked over to the restaurant.

"Table or booth?" she asked.

We both answered in unison, "Booth."

She wore a pink waitress-looking dress that buttoned in front. Around her waist was a white apron tied in back in a perfect bow. Her blond hair, which according to the roots, used to be brown, was secured in a high ponytail. Her red lipstick had begun to fade from a hard day's work, and the scent of Avon's Sweet Honesty was like an aromatic fog stealing our fresh air.

She pulled out a double-stick of Juicy Fruit from her pocket and began chewing vigorously. She grabbed two menus, led us to a secluded seat in the corner, and introduced herself, "I'm Julie. But everyone calls me Jewels. What brings you in tonight?"

Anna began describing our day from start to finish.

As she listened, Jewels seemed antsy, shifting her weight from one foot to the other, saying, "Uh-huh," and nodding throughout Anna's story.

"And that's how we wound up here," sighed Anna.

"Well...," began Jewels, "congratulations on gettin' hitched. Sorry for your car trouble, but you're here now, and boy, oh boy, are you in for a real treat. Our cook, Leon, who prefers to be called Chef, can do amazing things with an egg. But of course, if you like flapjacks, they're good too, so fluffy they just melt in your mouth. The soup of the day is homemade chicken noodle. It comes with homemade rolls or oyster crackers, your choice, and it is de-lish-us. We only use happy chickens, except they're not so happy when it comes to the soup part.

"We have burgers so juicy you'll need a bib. We don't have bibs, but you can just tuck a napkin in your shirt. My favorite is the chicken fried steak, and I'm gonna let you in on a little secret."

Jewels glanced around the room to ensure no one was in earshot then leaned over the table and whispered, "Did you know it's not really chicken? Its steak! It's called chicken fried steak 'cause it's fried up the same way chicken is fried." She straightened up. Her face beaming with pride of this classified knowledge, then she continued, "Man, oh man, the gravy Chef slathers on top is to die for. It comes with potatoes, fried, or mashed. Then there's dessert, and it is *all* good. We have—"

"Jewels!" I said, halting her dialogue.

"I'll have a three-egg Denver omelet with hash browns and toast."

Anna followed with her order, "I'll have some of the fluffy, melt-in-your-mouth pancakes with a side of peanut butter, banana, and real maple syrup."

"Okey dokey," replied Jewels as she scribbled on her notepad then headed off to the kitchen.

We looked at each other in amazement.

Anna commented, "I don't think she took a breath during that whole spiel. I know I didn't."

We devoured our breakfast-for-dinner meals, and Jewels was right—it was *all* good. We were enjoying our second cup of coffee when Jewels and Chef approached our table, each carrying a cupcake decorated with heart-shaped Red Hots candy and a birthday candle.

"Congratulations," said Chef. "Julie informed me you two are newlyweds, and I just wanted to wish you all the best."

"Thank you. This has been an unforgettable day *and* an unforgettable meal."

Saving our cupcakes for later, we left a generous tip and headed back to the Inn.

The green neon sign displayed in the office window flashed "Vacancy," so we entered the small office to pay for a room. The attendant looked to be in his teens, barely old enough for a work permit. Leaning back in his chair with his feet propped up on the desk, he was sound asleep while the TV blared an episode of *Mission Impossible* in the background.

"I really hate to interrupt his nap," I whispered to Anna. Then I double tapped the call bell on the desk.

Startled awake, he jumped to his feet, knocking over the rollaway chair he previously occupied. Embarrassed he'd been caught napping, he stammered the usual question, "C-can I help you?"

"I hope so. We would like to get a room for the night."

"Sorry, but we're full up."

"But your sign in the window states otherwise."

"Actually, I have one room left, but it's the *Honeymoon Suite*. We save it for honeymooners."

"Perfect!" said Anna. "This just happens to be the first night of our honeymoon! See…," she continued as she pointed to the cupcakes. "Chef and Jewels gave us these to celebrate our day."

He seemed unconvinced we were telling the truth, and I was starting to feel frustrated. "C'mon, man, It's late. What are the odds of another couple renting that room tonight? Don't you want to turn on the 'No' to your Vacancy sign?"

He began chewing his lower lip and drummed his fingers on the countertop as though contemplating the consequences of renting the room to unqualified guests.

Once again, I pleaded, "Just let me pay for the room."

Then I tucked a twenty-dollar bill into his shirt pocket. Hesitant, still deciding, he looked beyond us to the parking lot where he noticed the "Just Married" sign on our car. I don't know if it was the sign or the money in his pocket that afforded us a room for the night. I signed in, paid the kid, and he handed me the keys to the honeymoon suite.

I unlocked the door, and we stepped inside. To our surprise, this was not your typical run-of-the-mill, standard motel room. It had a comfortable, homey feel. Instead of lingering odors from chemical cleaners, it smelled of lavender. On the table was a basket of fruit, chocolates, fresh flowers, and a bottle of wine. It had all the amenities for an overnight stay: fresh linens and plenty of hot water. I noticed the absence of a TV, and the first thing Anna noticed was the bed. She ran to it and gently passed her hands across the colorful blanket

"Look at this quilt! It's a double wedding ring pattern! My grandma was a quilter. She made a quilt just like this one for Mom and Dad when they were married. It's still on their bed to this very day. Grandma took some of her old dresses and Grandpa's shirts, cut them into tiny pieces, and sewed them together in an interlocking arch pattern just like this." She traced the colorful arch with her finger as she explained.

"Old American folklore suggests that if a couple spends their first night together under a double wedding ring quilt, their marriage is blessed. I don't think it's a coincidence that our first night together will be under this quilt. Do you?"

"I don't believe in folklore or wives' tales, but this time, I think you're right."

Morning came early, and we were eager to get to the beach. Although the diner served excellent food, we didn't have time for Jewels's rendition of the breakfast menu, so we ate our cupcakes and headed for the coast. We were looking forward to a week of fun and relaxation.

CHAPTER 20

The hotel was situated on a bluff overlooking the ocean. Anna couldn't wait to get her feet wet, so we tossed our luggage into our room and headed toward the water. The path from the hotel to the beach was long and steep. We began our descent, and I already dreaded the return climb. Luckily, the trail had switchbacks. We zigzagged our way to the bottom until we reached the sand. Anna kicked off her sandals and ran toward the surf. I followed suit. My shoes soon accompanied hers, and I, too, bolted for the tide.

The water of the Pacific Ocean along the northwest coast is cold. We sucked in a sudden breath as our feet first touched the water. We turned to run but decided instead to defy the sharp bite of the sea. Soon acclimated to the chill, we examined rocks and searched for unbroken sand dollars while the ebb and flow of foam and salt water continuously washed over our toes.

Anna cried out, "I can barely feel my feet!"

"Feet? What feet?" I teased.

I knew exactly how she felt. We had spent too much time wading in the water and our feet were going numb. Retreating from the surf, we walked along the dry sand and soon felt the tingle as the blood flow slowly returned and warmed our extremities.

Continuing our walk, I spotted something sticking out of the sand. I took a closer look and began to dig. I gradually uncovered a child's toy—a red-and-yellow sand pail. The broken handle and cracks along the bottom revealed it had once been well used before being abandoned by its owner. We kept the small bucket and used it to gather rocks and washed-ashore seashells.

Then Anna had an idea, "Let's build a sandcastle!"

Only kids play in the sand, I thought. Nevertheless, I agreed.

We smoothed out a section of dry sand for the base of our castle. We picked out suitable rocks, dried pieces of driftwood, broken shells, and pieces of seaweed, setting them aside to use later. Then doused the sand with water and packed it down for a firm foundation. Now acting like children, we ran back and forth from the tide, gathering wet sand, packing it into the bucket and dumping it onto the foundation. We must have repeated this action a hundred times. At least it felt like it. After the construction of several towers, we fortified the castle with a wall and decorated it with the saved rocks, shells, and seaweed. The perfect piece of driftwood served as the drawbridge. We dug a moat, filled it with salty water, and dared savages to penetrate our fortress. We stood back and admired our work, pretending to be the king and queen of our very own acropolis. Suddenly, an unexpected wave bowled us over, tossing us into the surf. The frigid water washed over us while liquid sand settled in our hair and underwear. We jumped up as quickly as cats being thrown into a pool of water and hastily abandoned our castle. Running to the path leading to our hotel, we retrieved our shoes and began the steep climb up the hill.

A long hot shower and dry clothes revived us. Then we went to the hotel restaurant and enjoyed a bowl of steaming, hot clam chowder. Exhausted from the events of the day—the building project and run-in with the tide, we agreed tomorrow would be a good day to sleep in. Waking around noon, we decided to take a tour of the tiny coastal town. We visited the heritage museum, toured the famous creamery, sampled several varieties of cheese and ice cream, then strolled through a grove of ancient coastal Douglas firs. The next few days, we did exactly what we set out to do—relax. Most of our time was spent lying on the beach and combing the shore for the perfect shell or rock suitable for a souvenir.

The week had gone by all too quickly. With only one night left, I asked Anna, "If you had to choose, which you do, what would be your choice for tonight's dinner?"

Anna thought for a few moments, then answered with excitement, "Hobo dinners!"

"Hobo dinners? Where do we get those?"

"You don't *get* them. You *make* them. When I was a kid, our family vacation was often spent at the beach. At least one of the nights, we had hobo dinners."

She continued to fill me in on the procedure of compiling this exquisite meal. Then we found a small grocery store and purchased all the ingredients: potatoes, carrots, onions, corn on the cob, spices, and ground beef.

"Don't forget the aluminum foil," she reminded me, "and the stuff for s'mores."

"And the beer," I said matter-of-factly.

"Beer? Since when do you drink beer?"

"Since I've been in the Army," I answered.

"Oh yeah? What other bad habits did you pick up?"

"Oh, nothing to worry about."

I didn't want to ruin our honeymoon with the details: the fact that I had smoked marijuana, took pills, and tried heroin. Disregarding the pang of guilt, I felt for hiding the truth, I kept silent.

We went back to our hotel room and started assembling our hobo dinners. Working together, Anna guided each step.

"First, we mix together the spices and meat. Then form the mixture into a log, like a mini meat loaf, and place it on a triple sheet of foil. Next, shuck the corn, cut up the vegetables, and place them next to the meat. Wrap it all up in the foil and seal it tight."

After the foil packets were completed, we stuffed them into a bag with the rest of our dinner goodies then headed down the path to the beach.

Walking along the sand, we searched for the perfect place to roast our meal. I spotted a large log that had long ago washed ashore. We dug a small pit in the sand near the log, gathered pieces of dried driftwood, and built a fire. I continued adding wood until a hotbed of coals formed at the base of the blaze. Then we buried our dinner in the glowing embers. We sat on the sand and leaned back against the log. The heat from the fire felt good against the evening chill. We recounted the events of the past week: our wedding, the frustrating car trouble, Carl, Jewels, the sandcastle, and our unexpected swim in the sea. I popped the cap off Anna's Dr. Pepper then pulled the tab on a can of beer. We toasted to the past, present, and future.

Watching the sun as it seemingly sank into the ocean, the sky's vibrant colors reminded us of our evenings at the beach during our year in college. Today was not unlike those days: sitting on the sand, watching the sunset, and making plans for our future. Only the thought of that cold ocean water could dampen our memories and once again cause us to shiver. We wrapped ourselves in the blanket I had brought from our room and watched the stars appear.

"There it is!" Anna shouted, pointing heavenward.

"Where, what is?" I questioned as I looked toward the sky.

"Don't you see it? It's the Big Dipper!"

"I wasn't really looking for the Big Dipper, but yes, I see it. Isn't there a Little Dipper as well?"

"It's harder to spot. Just look for the North Star…you know…the bright one. When you find it, you've found the Little Dipper. The North Star is the last star in the Little Dipper's handle."

We found the bright star and were trying to visualize the Little Dipper when our thoughts were interrupted by a hissing sound coming from the fire. The steam escaping from the foil packets was an indication that our buried meals had begun to cook and also served as a reminder that several hours had passed since we last ate.

"I'm starving," announced Anna. "I can't wait for dinner. How about we have dessert first!"

She didn't have to ask me twice! I wasted no time retrieving the marshmallows, graham crackers, and chocolate bars from the grocery bag. Anna unwrapped the candy and broke the crackers in half while I straightened out a couple of wire clothes hangers I had brought from our room. I knew they would make perfect roasting sticks. We skewered the marshmallows onto the hangers and edged them close to the fire. Suddenly, Anna's marshmallow became a blazing torch of sugar.

"I told you to hold it *near* the fire, not stick it *in* the fire!"

"Great advice," she said sarcastically as she jerked her roasting stick from the blaze. Her sudden movement hurled the little ball of fire into the dark sky.

"Look!" I yelled. "A shooting star!"

"Very funny." Anna got my joke, and we laughed while watching the blazing marshmallow fly through the air until it landed somewhere on the beach. Still laughing, Anna pointed to *my* marshmallow. It was now ablaze and dripping off the end of my hanger into the fire. I had been so enamored with Anna's burnt marshmallow that I forgot to pay attention to my own.

"Let's start over," I suggested.

This time, carefully watching as our marshmallows turned golden brown. Anna handed me her roasting stick and constructed the base of the s'more. She placed a chunk of chocolate candy on one of the graham cracker squares and held it out to me. I rested the steaming marshmallow on the candy. She held it in place with another cracker square while I removed the skewer. We repeated this process, then we each squeezed the crackers together until melted chocolate and fluffy marshmallow oozed from the edges. We clinked our s'mores together as though they were glasses of wine then savored every sticky bite. Then we retrieved our hobo dinners, tore open the steamy packages, and ate until we were stuffed.

With our bellies full, we settled back against the log and covered ourselves with the blanket. I wrapped my arm around Anna's shoulder and pulled her close to me. She rested her head against my chest and exhaled a contented breath. We both agreed—tonight was the perfect end to a perfect week!

CHAPTER 21

Once again, I said goodbye. Leaving Anna and my family behind has become an all-too-familiar part of Army life. But this time is different. Instead of dreading my destination, I look forward to it. Anna would soon join me, and we would begin our new life together.

My flight took me to Los Angeles, New York, then on to Germany: Frankfurt, then Munich, where the Army bus was waiting at the airport. I walked toward the bus and was reminded of Vietnam: the buses with bars and chicken wire for windows, the stifling heat and humidity, the rancid odor, malaria-infected mosquitos, and the hostile locals. To my relief, this place had none of those things. As we stepped inside the bus, the young driver smiled and greeted each one of us in German: "Willkommen in Deutschland" ("Welcome to Germany").

Dachau, Germany, is located approximately ten miles northwest of Munich. An abandoned munitions factory from WWI was the inaugural concentration camp opened by the German Nazi regime in 1933, just five weeks after Hitler took power as German chancellor. Liberated by US soldiers in 1945, one week before the end of WWII in Europe, the camp soon became a base for US Army soldiers.

We arrived at the base, and I collected my duffel bag. I walked toward the entrance that had formerly been used as a gatehouse. I stopped and stared at the wrought-iron gate bearing the slogan: *Arbiet Macht Frei*. I felt a sudden pang of sorrow for the people who had long ago passed through here and suffered the atrocities handed them. The sign, meaning *Work Sets You Free* was the stark reminder that I had arrived at Dachau.

I proceeded to check in and received my assigned housing and started the paperwork for Anna to join me in a few months. After a quick tour of the base, I was transported to my new living quarters.

THE WAR WITHIN

My base housing is simple: a one-bedroom, one-bath, no-frills, furnished apartment. I entered the front door and could see that the living room, kitchen, and dining area were one continuous room. The sliding glass door off the kitchen leads to a common grassy area shared with neighbors. Beyond the grass is an alleyway. I was informed that the alleyway is used by the garbage trucks to pick up trash from the dumpsters located a short distance from my back door. Off the living room are a hallway, bathroom, and bedroom.

I unpacked my bag and hung my clothes in the small bedroom closet. Then I imagined Anna's clothes hanging there, taking up the entire space while my clothes hung on a hook over the back of the door. I smiled at the thought. I would gladly give up my closet space to have her here with me. I made a mental note of things I needed to buy, and one of the first items on my list was a car.

After a week of walking to work, I bought an early model Mercedes from a soldier that was returning to the States. I don't love it as much as my '55 Bel Air, but it is reliable and gets me from point A to point B. When I leave Germany, I'll do the same—sell it to an incoming soldier.

I settled into my job and quickly made some new friends. We would often meet up at the bar after work, hang out with the other soldiers, and enjoy a couple of beers. It turns out I'm not the only one here fresh out of Vietnam. Those of us that spent the last year in Southeast Asia have plenty to talk about. We all agree. Compared to Vietnam, life in Dachau is easy. The absence of patients losing life and limb from booby traps, shrapnel, and disease is a welcome change.

Now I work in a clinic and help with routine exams and treat soldiers with common ailments and minor injuries. Most soldiers tend to avoid going to the doctor, but there are a few that we see on a regular basis. Randy is one of them. I met him the first week I was assigned here and have seen him every week since then. His visits to the clinic have been like clockwork. He is a big, burly black guy with unnatural bulging biceps and a short, thick neck. He beams with pride as he declares himself to be "custodian of commons" but admits his job of keeping the mess hall clean and tidy is stressful. He alleviates the anxieties of duty by spending an excessive amount of time lifting weights at the gym. Each weekly visit to the clinic, he describes symptoms of an unknown disease that threaten his mental health and physical well-being. I always look forward to Randy's visits.

Today I'm administering influenza vaccines. Instead of soldiers having to go through the clinic, I'm using an overflow room adjacent to the clinic waiting room. This way, soldiers don't have to check in. Instead, they enter through an outside door, receive their shot, and are on their way. I set the room up by placing several rows of folding chairs just inside the entrance, leaving an aisle down the middle. My table is positioned at the front of the room with a large stack of medical files on one end. A stainless steel tray at the opposite end of the table held my supplies: syringes, needles, rubbing alcohol, cotton balls, Band-Aids, vials of vaccine, and a few ammonia ampules, also known as smelling salts, for those with an overly sensitive fear of needles.

Soldiers begin filing in and reluctantly fill the chairs. I stand in front of my table and address the hesitant crowd, "Each one of you will be receiving a flu shot. I'll do my best to make it quick and painless. It's a simple procedure, really. I will use a syringe like this one…"

I held up a syringe equivalent to the size of the cardboard tube inside a roll of toilet paper.

"Then I attach the needle."

I had found an extra-long needle in the supply closet prior to my demonstration. My hope is that by exaggerating my show-and-tell presentation, they will be relieved to know the actual syringe and needle dwarf in comparison.

"Then I draw the liquid from the vial."

I have a five-hundred-milliliter bottle of saline, nearly seventeen ounces, for effect. Inserting the needle into the rubber cap, I slowly draw an enormous amount of liquid into the syringe.

"Next, I'll rub your arm with alcohol and administer the vaccine."

Holding the huge syringe and needle into the air for display, I depress the plunger, which caused a long stream of water to shoot toward my audience. Several of the soldiers recoiled to avoid the squirting liquid.

I laughed but then apologized for the dramatic demonstration. "I'm just kidding! I won't be using anything this large. Like I said before, I'll do my best to make it quick and painless."

"Now that I have your undivided attention, we'll get started."

I pick up a folder from the top of the pile, verify the written orders for the vaccine, then call my first patient, "Private First Class Bailey, Charles."

Although Chuck or Charlie are common nicknames for the name Charles, everyone knows him as Beetle. He received his nickname in boot camp from an overzealous drill sergeant intending the moniker as an insult in disguise. Charles had the unfortunate coincidence of having the same last name as the inept and lazy comic strip character, Beetle Bailey. The nickname does not adequately describe this soldier, and his work ethics are far from the reputation of his cartoon namesake. Nevertheless, the name stuck.

He slowly stood and walked toward my table, all the while regretting his was the first name called. After swabbing his arm with an alcohol-soaked cotton ball, I fanned the wetness with my hand. He gritted his teeth and clenched his eyes shut in anticipation as I proceeded with the inoculation. The whole procedure took only a few seconds. "All done," I said, as I placed a Band-Aid on his arm.

"What? That's it?"

He turned to the crowd and pumped his arms in triumph.

I had administered several of the vaccines when the door slowly opened, and Randy peered into the room. Cautiously, he stepped in, quietly closed the door behind him, and stood in the back of the room. Each time I called out a name, Randy ducked his head as though he were hiding. His weekly visits had shown him to be the anxious type, and he admitted he had a terrible fear of needles. As each soldier before him received their vaccine, he watched with a guarded eye and grimaced with each poke of a needle. I could see that his anxiety level was escalating. He was now pacing back and forth across the back of the room and I knew I had to get him out of here. I sifted through the pile of folders and found Randy's file. I called out his name, and he jerked his head as though taken by surprise. He stared at me with a dumbfounded look like we were playing hide-and-seek, and I had announced, "Tag! You're it!" With his head bowed and shoulders slumped, he began walking toward me, scuffing his feet. Then he hesitated. Several times, his eyes darted back and forth, from me to the door.

I knew what he was thinking. "Don't do it!" I silently ordered.

Resisting the urge to bolt toward the door, he continued toward me at a snail's pace. By the time he reached my table, beads of sweat had formed on his brow, and his lip began to quiver. I reminded Randy to breathe, but when he saw the needle, he let out a loud whimper and fell to the floor. I knelt beside him and quickly gave him his shot. Then I cracked open an ammonia vial and waved it under his nose. The strong vapor of the smelling salts caused him to wake with a start.

I helped him up and whispered in his ear, "We'll just skip the shot today, and I won't tell anyone."

Randy thanked me, slapped me on the back, and headed off to the gym. I'm sure, at some point, he will wonder why he has a Band-Aid on his arm.

I called the next soldier, and just as he approached my table, the door suddenly burst open, and in stormed Sergeant Havoc. He bypassed all the other soldiers and bullied his way to my table, shoving aside the soldier standing in front of me. His nickname couldn't be more fitting. He took pride in creating havoc and distention among the soldiers. He had no friends, not even among his peers. He removed his shirt and rolled up the sleeve of his tee. With his feet spread apart and firmly planted, he placed both hands on the table and leaned forward into my face until I could see that he had only one steel-gray eye. With contempt in his voice, he barked out an order, "Get this over with Band-Aid! I have better things to do besides watching you play doctor. This is a royal waste of my time!"

I didn't reply. Instead, I took a step back and slowly filled the syringe. He was unaware that I had dulled the needle tip by slightly tapping it on the table. When the needle tore through his skin, he screamed out loud and began spewing expletives and spit. The room quickly fell silent. I knew he could feel the glaring stares drilling into his back. He spun around and shouted, "What are you looking at? You're all just a bunch of spineless, little sissy girls that have to squat to pee! Without me, you would be nothing! In fact, you *are* nothing! Just a bunch of useless, sniveling cowards that want to go home to Mommy!"

Every head turned as he stomped across the room. He slammed the door with such force that it broke the jam. As though their movements were synchronized, all heads quickly turned back toward me. After an awkward moment of silence, the soldiers began clapping. When the applause subsided, I admitted to nothing, took a bow, then called out the next name.

CHAPTER 22

The weather had gone from bad to worse. The temperature plunged to a record-breaking low for December, causing the snow on the ground to turn to ice. I walked out into the ice-laden wind, and it was like being on the receiving end of a hard slap on the face. This bone-chilling, breath-stealing weather is not like anything I have ever experienced. I wasn't looking forward to driving in these conditions, but today is the day I've been waiting for—Anna is arriving!

I cautiously scuffed out to my car and forced open the frozen door. I jumped inside, slammed the door shut, and hurriedly inserted my key into the ignition. Wearing a warm coat and gloves seemed to be of no use as my body began to shiver. I could hardly wait to get the heater going. I turned the key but heard only a sluggish moan from the engine. I tried again and got the same result. "Oh, c'mon!" I shouted at the car as I bashed my hands against the steering wheel. "Don't do this to me! Not today!" Frustrated, I sat there in the freezerlike atmosphere, watching my breath escape into puffs of fog. *Now what do I do? The car won't start. I'm half frozen. And Anna is expecting me to pick her up at the airport.*

I haven't been much on prayer lately but now seemed like a good time to ask God for a favor. I cranked the key once more and prayed, "Please, let the car start." The engine continued to struggle but finally came to life. "Thank God," I said. Just as I heard my own words, I realized they were not a prayer of thanks but a mindless acknowledgment of getting what I wanted. Feeling a bit ungrateful, I looked up to the roof of my car and said, "Thank you, God. This time, I mean it."

I sat there for several minutes before the blast of cold air from the vent turned warm. Then I headed for the airport.

Back home in the Valley, I was used to driving in the dense fog, but driving in these icy conditions had my nerves on end. The last thing I wanted was to end up in a ditch. The angry clouds spit down tiny ice pellets at such a rate the windshield wipers were nearly useless. The trip to the airport took three times as long as it should have, and now I'm late. I parked in one of the designated spaces for loading and unloading passengers. Hurriedly, I stepped out of the car and locked the door with my spare key, leaving the engine running so the car would be nice and warm when I returned with Anna. I rushed toward the entrance and momentarily savored the warmth of the indoors before I hightailed it to baggage claim.

The area was nearly vacant as most passengers had already retrieved their luggage and moved on. I immediately spotted Anna near the turnstile, sitting on one of her suitcases. She was staring at her watch, undoubtedly checking to see how late I was. I headed toward her. It was in that moment she lifted her head, caught my gaze, and stood. We ran toward each other and collided with a long-awaited kiss and embrace.

"Sorry I'm late, but the weather…"

She cut me off in midsentence, "I began to think you weren't coming. I kept hearing announcements about the dangerous road conditions. I was afraid you wouldn't be able to get here."

I had a valid excuse for being late, but I wanted to make light of the situation. "A little bit of snow could never keep me from you. I'm like the mailman, neither snow nor rain nor—"

"Okay, okay," she interrupted. "Let's get out of here."

I collected Anna's luggage, and as we walked through the terminal, I noticed she was dressed in comfortable traveling clothes: jeans, tennis shoes, and a short jacket covering a tee.

"I hope you brought warmer clothes," I said.

"I brought what I had in my closet. You know, it doesn't get this cold in Oregon."

We reached the exit and walked to the car as fast as possible without slipping on the ice. I unlocked the passenger side door so she could get out of the cold, then I placed her luggage in the trunk, and hurried to join her inside. I drove straight to the PX to buy Anna some suitable European winter wear. She picked out a couple of outfits, boots, coat, scarf, and gloves.

"That should do it," she said.

"Nope, your wardrobe is not quite complete."

"What do you mean?"

"You need a hat. Everyone in Germany wears a winter hat." I pointed to the wool stocking cap on my head.

I paid the clerk then waited outside the dressing room while she changed into her new clothes…and I waited. I whisper-yelled toward her room, "Aren't you done yet? What's taking so long?"

Silence…

Jokingly, I called out, "Do I need to send in a search party?"

Again, silence. Now I'm worried. Was she so exhausted from the flight that she had fallen asleep? Just as I was about to go in after her, she emerged from the dressing room. Strutting like a runway model as she showcased her new look. Her smile and tilted head emphasized her big fur hat.

I immediately sounded out a wolf whistle then said, "Du bist wunderschön." ("You're beautiful.")

"Danke" was her quick reply. ("Thank you.")

"What? You speak German?"

"I've been learning a few words."

We gathered up the shopping bags then headed straight to the car. I turned the key in the ignition, and to my surprise, the engine instantly jumped to life. After the short drive to our apartment, we parked, grabbed all the luggage, and shopping bags to avoid another trip to the car, then we headed to the front door. I inserted the key into the lock then hesitated. "Wait here."

"Are you kidding me? You want me to stand out here in the freezing cold while you go inside?"

I ignored her question, unlocked the door, and tossed everything inside. I quickly turned to her, swept her off her feet, and carried her over the threshold. She wrapped her arms around my neck and began giggling like a little girl. I shoved the door closed with my foot as I continued holding her in my arms. Then I kissed her and whispered in her ear, "Welcome home."

CHAPTER 23

One of the deadliest weapons during WWII was food—or the lack of. People in Germany were starving. Mothers wandered the streets, rummaging through the garbage, hoping to find a scrap of food to feed their children, praying they survive one more day.

Since Anna and I are fairly new to Dachau, my coworker, Ryan, invited us to his house for dinner so Anna and his wife, Sarah, could get acquainted. We were enjoying our meals and conversation when Ryan mentioned *the white lady*.

"Who?" I asked.

Ryan looked surprised. "You mean you haven't heard of *the white lady of Dachau*?"

"No, who is she?"

"She's only seen at night," explained Sarah. "She appears at the dumpsters, dressed in white, searching for food."

Anna caught Sarah's gaze, "You mean this white lady is a ghost?"

"I don't believe in ghosts," I said. "I think people that claim to encounter ghosts just have overactive imaginations. Have either of *you* seen the *white lady*?"

"Um, not personally, but I've heard stories of others who have seen her."

"That's just it. They're only stories. Like I said, I don't believe in ghosts."

"Whether you believe in ghosts or not, just be sure to lock your doors at night."

"I always do, but should I ask the reason behind your concern?"

"Because sometimes after a door has been locked, it is later found to not only be unlocked but ajar."

"Are you expecting me to believe there's a ghost wandering around base, opening locks and sifting through garbage in search of food?"

Ryan and Sarah looked at each other then back at Anna and me, both their heads nodding.

"I'm quite aware of the horrifying history of Dachau. I'm not superstitious. I'm not afraid of the dark. And I don't believe in ghosts. I guess you could say I don't scare easily. This would be a great story if we were sitting around a campfire, drumming up ancient legends about ghosts and goblins. Next, you'll be shining a flashlight under your chin to exaggerate the spookiness of your tale. But since we aren't camping and there's no bonfire, don't be offended if I don't believe you."

"Look, Rick, all I'm trying to say is check your doors, make sure they're locked, and don't go out after dark…alone."

Anna and I left their apartment and headed back to ours. We discussed our dinner conversation and shrugged off the ghost story as just that—a ghost story.

Several weeks passed since our ghostly conversation with Ryan and Sarah, but I couldn't stop thinking about *the white lady*. Could there really be some truth to the legend? I began to question my unbelief. Although I had seen no evidence of this rumor, I still took precautionary measures. Each night, I make it a point to check the doors to ensure they are locked. I even cut the handle off an old broom I found in the closet. Placing it on the track of the sliding glass door served as a secondary locking device, making it impossible for the door to be opened.

This evening, we had just finished watching a movie, and Anna went into the kitchen for a drink of water before bed. I turned off the TV and headed toward the bedroom when I heard her call out, "I thought you locked the door."

"I did. You know every night after dinner I take out the trash, and when I return, I lock the door."

"Well, tonight you forgot."

"No, I didn't forget. It's my normal nightly routine. I lock the door and place the broom handle in the track."

I joined her in the kitchen to investigate. She was right. Not only was the stick out of place, but the door was also unlocked and slightly ajar.

"I'm *positive* I locked the door! Anna, is this a trick?"

She looked at me, and her expression suggested she was not joking. Our gaze was quickly drawn back to the open door. Again, we looked back at each other then back at the door. At that moment, a real sense of eeriness came over us as we both recalled our dinner conversation with Ryan and Sara—*because sometimes after locking a door, it's later found to not only be unlocked but ajar.*

I slammed the sliding door shut and quickly turned the lock. Anna yanked the curtains closed while I placed the broom handle in the door track. Then we raced to the bedroom. Anna made a flying leap into bed and yanked the covers over her head. I slammed the bedroom door shut, jammed the back of a chair under the doorknob, and joined Anna under the covers. Our hearts were pounding in unison as we whispered to each other most of the night. Finally, we drifted off to sleep until the alarm jolted us awake a few hours later.

I was hoping last night's scare had all been a bad dream, but when I peered at the bedroom door, the chair was still lodged beneath the doorknob. I slowly sat up on the side of the bed. I didn't want to open the door, but I knew sooner or later, I had to.

Anna still had the covers pulled up overhead. Slowly, she lowered them just enough to expose her eyes and whispered, "You're not going out there, are you?"

I quickly turned to Anna, put my finger over my pursed lips, and lightly said, "Shhhh." Then I quietly tiptoed across the room and gently removed the chair, being careful to not make any noise. I slowly turned the doorknob and opened the door just enough to peek into the hallway beyond. I halfway believed I would come face-to-face with the intruder, but no one was there. I exhaled a nervous breath then crept out of the bedroom and cautiously tiptoed through the apartment until I reached the kitchen. Not sure what I was expecting, but nothing was out of place. To my relief, the door was still locked, curtains drawn, and the broom handle in place. I called out to Anna, "All clear."

The following day, I mentioned the previous night's disturbing event to a few coworkers, hoping they would not think me crazy. Ryan wasted no time chiming in, "I thought you didn't believe in ghosts."

I noted a little sarcasm in his tone. "I don't. At least I didn't. I'm not sure what I believe. I just know from now on, I'm triple checking my doors at night."

Several weeks passed with no further incidents. I convinced myself I had indeed forgotten to lock the door that evening. Our self-inflicted fear was the result of our own imaginations. Anna and I concluded that the *white lady* was only a mythical legend that lived in the minds of believers.

Tonight, I made dinner. I replicated our honeymoon hobo dinners, but instead of burying them in a beach bonfire, I baked them in the oven.

"Since you cooked, I'll take out the trash," offered Anna.

She tied up the bag and headed to the dumpster. Halfway there, she stopped dead in her tracks, dropped the bag, and ran back to the apartment. I was finishing up the dishes when she burst through the door, quickly locking it behind her.

Out of breath, she shouted, "I SAW HER!"

"Who?" I questioned.

"I SAW HER!" she repeated. "THE WHITE LADY! I was walking across the lawn when I saw something moving about the dumpster. At first, I thought it was someone tossing trash into the bin. Then I realized it wasn't a person at all. It was the *white lady*! She was dressed in white, translucent really. It was a weird sensation. I could **see** her, but at the same time, I could see *through* her. It was only for a few seconds, but I know it was her."

"Anna, I thought we had decided the *white lady* was just a myth, a silly ghost story. And what about the garbage you dropped? Are you just going to leave it out there on the ground?"

"Yup, that's exactly what I'm going to do."

I couldn't pass up this opportunity to tease her a little.

"C'mon, go on out and finish your job. I'll go with you and hold your hand. I'll protect you from the big, bad boogeyman."

Anna was not amused and refused to go back outside.

Once again, I joked with a hint of sarcasm, "I guess I'll have to clean up your mess all by myself."

I stepped outside and slid the door shut behind me. I immediately heard the lock click. I turned back to look at Anna through the glass just as she yanked the curtains closed.

"Scaredy-cat," I mumbled. "There's no such thing as ghosts." I leisurely walked across the lawn, retrieved the abandoned bag of trash, then headed toward the dumpster. As I drew near, an overwhelming sense of eeriness surrounded me. I felt a prickly sensation at the nape of my neck, and the skin on my arms turned to gooseflesh. I stood still and studied my surroundings. Although I didn't see anyone, or anything unusual, my fight-or-flight response kicked in, urging me to run.

With all my might, I threw the bag at the dumpster, hoping it landed inside then ran back across the lawn to the apartment. When I got there, the door was still locked and the curtains drawn. I vigorously hammered on the glass until Anna finally opened the door. Then I slipped inside, slammed the door shut, and threw the lock.

"Why didn't you watch for me and open the door when I got back?"

She ignored my question. "Did you see it? I mean *her*. Did you see *her*?"

I did not want to reveal my hair-raising experience, so I tried to answer in a calm tone. "No, I didn't see her or anyone else."

"Then why are you out of breath and have goose bumps on your arms?"

"Well… I…uh…from now on, let's just take out the trash in the morning."

Months have passed since that incident. That was the first and last time we encountered the white lady. But now I have bragging rights and a reason to taunt the newbies just arriving at Dachau.

CHAPTER 24

The snow finally melted. Winter is over, and the warmth of spring has us itching to do a little exploring. We decided on a weekend getaway to our neighboring country, Austria. Staying the night in an expensive hotel was not in our budget, so we opted for a camping trip. Neither of us are experienced campers, but it seemed like a fun way to visit another country. We packed the car with all the essentials: food, two army-issued sleeping bags, pillows, a flashlight, soda, and beer.

We spent part of the day enjoying the scenery as we drove along the winding backroads of Austria. I spotted a meadow with a clump of maple trees and pulled off the road to a clearing. We got out of the car and explored the area. It wasn't a campsite per se, but an ash-covered fire ring was evidence there had been previous campers.

"This looks like a good place to camp for the night. How about it, Anna? Are you ready to sleep under the stars?"

"As long as we can snuggle and have a fire to keep us warm."

We gathered sticks and deadwood and placed them into the abandoned fire ring where previous campers had left a bed of partially burned charcoal. I built a blazing campfire, then we skewered hot dogs onto long sticks and roasted them over the fire. I grabbed a couple of beers and handed one to Anna. She pulled the tab and took a big swig. She immediately spit the mouthful into the fire and wiped her face with the back of her hand. "Yuck!" she said. "Beer tastes just as nasty as it smells. How can you drink that stuff?" She handed me her opened can.

"Just remember, Anna, we are in Germany, and the drink of choice is beer."

"Well, Rick, according to the amount of beer you drink, you must have German in your blood. But I think I'll stick with my Dr. Pepper."

We spent the rest of the evening relaxing next to the fire. We toasted marshmallows and made plans to visit other European countries while we were stationed in Germany. It was now dark, so we rolled our sleeping bags out on the ground next to the car and crawled inside. I tried to stay awake while Anna was talking, but my eyelids slowly drooped, and I fell fast asleep. It wasn't long before she shook me awake. In a loud whisper, she asked, "Did you hear that?"

"Hear what?" Groggy from sleep, I tried to listen, but I couldn't focus.

"I don't know. Maybe a bear or something."

This time, I opened my eyes and listened hard. "I don't hear anything. Just go back to sleep." I dozed back off, and once again, Anna shook me awake.

"There it is again."

I sat up in my sleeping bag, rubbed my eyes, and tried to concentrate on the noise she was so worried about. This time, I heard it too—a rustling sound accompanied by a faint clanging. I couldn't identify the noise, and I didn't want to scare Anna, so I casually said, "It's nothing. Just go to sleep."

Lying back down, I slid into my sleeping bag as far as I could, covered my head, and pulled the zipper up until it stopped. Meanwhile, Anna continued her argument, "We don't know what's out there! It could be someone snooping around, or a bear, or some other kind of animal looking for food. And that food could be us!"

"Anna, I think you've watched too many scary movies. I'm sure we'll be fine. We'll wake up in the morning, right here, next to the car, in our sleeping bags."

No longer whispering, Anna replied with a tone of determination, "Well, you can stay out here if you want, but I'm sleeping in the car."

She quickly stood, gathered up her sleeping bag and pillow, then crawled inside the car.

I began thinking about what Anna had said. Animals could be looking for food. We were unfamiliar with the area, so maybe I, too, should sleep in the car. Then I heard the lock on the door click.

"That's just great. If there *is* something out here, I can't even get inside the car!"

Darkness now blankets the clearing, and I am wide awake. I uncover my head and stare upward. The dazzling twinkle in the moonless sky is mesmerizing, like a baby being rocked to sleep. It wasn't long before I forgot about the would-be intruder and closed my eyes.

Aroused from a deep sleep, I had that feeling—the feeling that I'm being watched. I was afraid to move but forced myself to slowly pull my sleeping bag up over my head—hiding. Was Anna right? Maybe something was out there. I tried to calm my breathing, but my anxiety grew as a sound like footsteps drew near then stopped next to my sleeping bag. I could hear labored breathing. Sniffs and snorts. Something poking at my bag.

"Be still." I told myself, "Just. Be. Still."

Suddenly, something grabbed the foot of my sleeping bag and began dragging me away from our camp. All I could think about was Anna. Could she help me? Just then, I heard her voice call out, "Ricky! Where are you going? Throw me the car keys. How will I get home without them?"

I cried out in desperation, "Aaaannnaaa..."

My muffled cry faded away as the distance between us grew.

The slamming of the car door jolted me awake, and I sat bolt upright.

"Ricky? Did you call me?"

Realizing my harrowing experience was only a dream, I calmly answered, "No, I was asleep until you got out of the car."

"Sorry to wake you, but I thought I heard you say my name. Are you sure you didn't call me?"

"I'm positive. Let's get our sleeping bags put away."

We were rolling up our bags when I heard Anna mumble, "Well, at least you didn't get dragged off by a wild animal."

I muttered under my breath, "If you only knew."

I was still trying to shake off last night's experience while Anna made peanut butter and jelly sandwiches for breakfast. After eating, we packed everything back in the car and went for a hike. We walked through the trees near our camp and entered a large open field carpeted with wildflowers. The backdrop of snowcapped Swiss Alps and the flowering meadow looked like a painting. Anna picked a bouquet and stuck an alpine rose in her hair. We could hear the faint sound of trickling water, and it wasn't long before we came upon a small stream. We followed the water as it cut a path through the wildflower meadow leading to a fenced pasture that contained several heads of Brown Swiss cows. A bell dangled from each cow's neck and clanked as they walked. Anna and I looked at each other and started laughing. This was the scary sound we heard last night.

After a little more exploring, we walked back to our campsite then headed out to our next destination, Innsbruck. We hiked to a mountain village, toured an old castle, and visited several gift shops. We bought a few souvenirs then headed back to the car and the trip home to Germany.

I usually maintain a driving speed of 80 miles per hour, nearly 129 kilometers, but today I was feeling adventurous. I pressed my foot on the gas pedal and watched as the needle climbed to 85… then 90.

"What are you doing?" asked Anna.

"I'm driving."

"I can see that. But why are you speeding?"

"I'm not really speeding. We're on the Autobahn, and the speed limit allows you to drive as fast as your car will go."

Anna kept watching the speedometer. When it reached ninety-five, she blurted out, "Ricky! Do you *really* have to go this fast?"

"Of course, I do. I have to see what the ol' girl is made of."

"Well, when the ol' girl reaches one hundred, you'd better slow her down."

The speedometer continued to climb 95…100…105.

"Ricky!" she shouted.

"Anna, where's your sense of adventure?"

Our back-and-forth exchange was interrupted by a loud knocking sound coming from the engine. The speedometer gauge began to decline, and smoke now poured out from under the hood. I quickly steered over to the side of the road and hit the brakes. The car barely came to a stop before Anna flung open her door and ran to a grassy area next to the road. Fearful of a car fire, I joined her. Her arms were crossed as she tapped her foot. It was obvious she was upset.

"I told you to slow down! But no! You had to push it! And look where we are now. I guess now you know exactly what the ol' girl is made of."

I opened my mouth to retaliate with my own bit of sarcasm but stifled my response when a car pulled up and parked a safe distance behind our crippled ride. A young German couple joined us on the grass. In broken English, they asked if we were okay. I had no chance to answer.

"Of course, we're not okay!" Anna's words spewed forth like an erupting volcano. "Five minutes ago, we had a car. Now we don't. We were on our way home. Now we're not. Five minutes ago, we weren't stranded, and now we are." Her eyes glared back at me. "Thanks to someone with a lead foot."

The couple wisely ignored the tension and offered us a ride to the nearest petrol station. I called Ryan and Sarah, and they were happy to come and take us back to base. Then I called for a tow truck to have the car taken to a scrapyard.

After the incident with the Mercedes behind, I bought a 1963 Volkswagen Beetle with a canvas ragtop. It was a far cry from the luxury car, but it was affordable and fun.

CHAPTER 25

Throughout the following year, we visited several of our neighboring countries. The VW had turned out to be our touring car. Each destination was an excuse to shop. I bought souvenirs for the family: Katie, a hand-painted glass-beaded necklace from Italy; Daddy, a Bavarian German beer stein; and Mama, an authentic cuckoo clock from the Black Forest region of Southern Germany. Anna also bought gifts for her family. We packed them all away until we could gift them in person.

Switzerland, Italy, and France were all wonderful. But Spain was by far our favorite. We stayed there an entire week and loved every minute of it. We were in awe of that country's natural beauty and admired its astonishing architecture. The people were so friendly they already had us yearning for yet another visit. The soft golden sands of the Mediterranean were at the top of our list. We waded in the turquoise waters and basked in the warm sunshine. Anna's skin turned a nice shade of bronze, and I went home with a sunburn.

My stint at Dachau was coming to an end and we would soon be leaving Germany. I wanted to have a special night with Anna, so I asked her out on a date.

"What do you mean, a date? We're married. Married people don't date."

"Really, Anna? What rule book did you find that in? The 'Married People Don't Date' rule book?"

"Don't be silly. There's no rule book. I just assumed that dating was…you know…for dating. The thing you do before getting married."

"Well, if there is such a rule, I'm breaking it. But if you're too married to go on a date—"

She quickly interrupted, "I accept! What do you have in mind?"
"How about dinner and a movie?"
"Yes! I want to see *Love Story*."
"You mean *Love Story*, the movie?"
"Yes, I've heard it's really good."
"Well, I was kind of thinking about M*A*S*H, a comedy."
"Oh, come on, Ricky, I know you'll like it."

Watching a romantic drama is not my idea of a good time, but I wanted to make it special for Anna, so I agreed.

We drove into Munich and found a hole-in-the-wall restaurant that served Flammkuchen: A German pizza on cracker-thin crust with creamy sauce, topped with smoky bacon and caramelized onions. Of course, the drink of choice in Germany is beer, so I ordered a couple of popular drinks. For Anna, I ordered Radlers (beer and lemonade). For me, Colaweizen (beer and cola). Our dinner was a true German experience. Halfway through our meal, I noticed Anna hadn't touched her Radlers.

"Aren't you going to drink your beer?" I asked.
"Why would I drink it? You know I don't like beer."
"I only ordered it for you to experience a true German meal."

I knew Anna had never acquired a taste for beer and that she didn't approve of the amount of brew I kept in the fridge. I called the server and ordered her a lemonade, without the beer, leaving the Radlers for me. Then I handed her a small gift-wrapped box.

"What's this?" she asked.
"Just a little something I picked up in Belgium. I wanted you to have a special souvenir."

Anna tore off the paper, revealing a small velvet box.
"Remember the last velvet box I offered you?"
"Of course, I do. It held a promise ring and an offer of marriage. Ricky, I still feel bad about teasing you that day."
"It's okay. I'm sure I had it coming."

Anna slowly opened the hinged box. Staring back at her was a solitary diamond necklace.
"I know it isn't big...or expensive...or—"
She cut me off midsentence, "It's perfect!"

Immediately, she clasped it around her neck then began to dig into the giant bag she called her purse.

"It just so happens I have a little something for you as well."

She pulled out a gift-wrapped box, larger than the one I had given her, and handed it to me.

I ripped off the paper, opened the box, and found a glass bottle. Inside was an impressive sailing vessel. "A ship in a bottle? How did you ever buy this without me seeing it?"

"I picked it up at a little shop in Hamburg. I saw it on the shelf and knew you would like it. When you were in the restroom, I bought it and stuffed it into my big purse."

"You were right. I love it. Now all we need is a mantel to put it on."

I wrapped up the leftover pizza to take home for tomorrow's breakfast. We drove around Munich and found our way to the cinema. Inside, the overwhelming smell of sweet popcorn caused our mouths to water. We were still stuffed from dinner, but the aroma tempted our senses. We had to have some. We entered the darkened theater and chose our seats. Anna wanted to sit right up front. I wanted to sit in the back. We split the difference and sat in the middle.

The movie was originally filmed in English, but here, it is dubbed in German with English subtitles. Uninterested, I kept nodding off during the movie and woke just in time to see the credits roll across the screen. I glanced over at Anna, and she was wiping her eyes with the sleeve of her shirt.

"Why are you crying?" I asked.

"Because I hated that Jenny died."

"So you didn't like the movie?"

"Oh, I loved it."

"You mean you hated it *and* loved it?"

"It's a girl thing. You wouldn't understand."

"Well, despite all the crying, I hope you enjoyed the evening."

"I had a great time! We'll have to break the 'Married People Don't Date' rule more often."

"Sounds good to me. Only next time I get to pick the movie."

We held hands as we walked through the parking lot. Anna wasted no time teasing me about sleeping during the movie. As we drew close to our car, I stopped midstride.

"Ricky, what's wrong?"

"I'm not sure, but I think our car has been vandalized."

As we approached the VW, we could see that the ragtop had been cut and torn open. I peered inside to see what had been stolen. Everything was just as we had left it—except the steering wheel—it was missing. I yelled out loud to no one in particular, "Are you kidding me? Who steals a steering wheel?"

A couple walking to their car heard my rant. They approached and asked, "Was ist falsch?" ("What is *wrong*?") I point to the inside of my car, and they immediately started laughing. Their laughter was so infectious that Anna and I caught the humor of the situation and joined in. When the couple caught their breath, the man slapped me on the back and said, "Tut mir leid." Then continued to their car, giggling the whole way.

"It was nice of him to say he was sorry, but what do we do now?" asked Anna. "How will we get home?"

I walked around to the front of the car, rummaged through the trunk, and found a pair of vise grip pliers, obviously left by the previous owner. I clamped them onto the bolt where the steering wheel used to be, folded down the torn roof, and began the drive home.

Although I didn't plan on putting the ragtop down, the ride home in our little convertible was an adventure all its own. I looked over at Anna and couldn't help but laugh. Her long hair, whipping with the wind was slapping her in the face. In turn, she laughed at me as I maneuvered the car through traffic and around corners with a pair of pliers.

When we got home, I reached over to the back seat to retrieve our leftover pizza and discovered it had also gone missing. I looked over at Anna and showed her my empty hands.

"Apparently, stealing a steering wheel creates quite an appetite. I don't know which disappoints me most, the car being vandalized or not being able to have pizza for breakfast."

Anna just kept laughing.

I received orders for my next assignment. We will be heading back to the States—to Fort Stewart, Georgia.

That's just great! I thought. *Humidity, and mosquitos!*

CHAPTER 26

Anna and I moved into our assigned housing. We immediately realized that August was not the best time to relocate to Georgia. There was no time to acclimate to the hot, sticky weather, so we spent most of the next couple of months indoors, grateful for air-conditioning. I settled in to my job at the hospital and quickly became friends with a few of my coworkers, Jay in particular.

Jay and I discovered we had a lot in common. We are both from California. He was drafted between college semesters and went to boot camp at Fort Lewis. He was then selected for medical training and went to Fort Sam Houston, Texas…then to Vietnam. Turns out we were even in Southeast Asia at the same time but were stationed at different bases. Our paths had never crossed until now. Now we see each other nearly every day. The difference between Jay and me is that he had never married. He was engaged, but when he returned from Vietnam, his fiancée called off the wedding. She said he wasn't the same person she fell in love with. After a couple of years of bachelor life, he is now engaged to another coworker, Stacy.

Today, Jay and I are assigned to the emergency room. So far, it's been quiet. No real emergencies, just routine checkups and paperwork. We were in the break room, having a cup of coffee when we heard the overhead speaker, "All available medical staff return to the emergency room, *stat*." Jay and I, along with everyone else on break, hightailed it to the ER. There had been a training accident involving three vehicles and several soldiers. I don't know the details, but by the looks of the soldiers being wheeled in, it's serious. One has a fractured wrist, so he is given pain medication and told he would have to wait until the critical patients are tended to first. Others have lacerations, concussions, compound fractures, and burns.

One soldier in particular is severely burned. I start his treatment with an IV and pain meds while the doctors assess the severity of his injury. The putrid stench of burned flesh takes me back to Vietnam. I envision the hospital, the wounded, the maimed, and the unmistakable odor of death. I shake my head in a feeble attempt to clear my mind and refocus on the patient in front of me. But the images are stuck in my head. The sickening smell of the blood-soaked gurneys and burning flesh linger in my nostrils. It's all a stark reminder of a piece of the past I desperately wanted to forget.

All the patients have been tended to, and we finally finished our shift.

"I am so glad this day is over," I commented to Jay. "I'm ready to sit down and relax."

"Yeah, me too. How about you come over to my house? We can have a few beers, unwind, and smoke a little weed."

I was a little hesitant because after leaving Vietnam, I had promised myself I would leave drugs alone. I wasn't proud of the choices I had made, so I never revealed to Anna my Vietnam drug experience.

"I don't know, Jay. I should go on home. Anna will be expecting me."

"Come on, Rick, we've had a rough day. Don't you think you deserve a little relaxation? You can call Anna from my place."

I know I should go straight home but decide an hour detour won't hurt. And Jay is right. After today, I *do* deserve to relax. I followed Jay to his house, and we indulged in a little herb and al, as he fondly called it. This little detour brought back even more memories of Vietnam: how I used marijuana to escape the war, the ten-year-old kid I bought the drug from, the pain pills…the heroin. Two hours passed and the call I intended to make to Anna had slipped my mind. I always call if I'm going to be late, but today I forgot. I know she's worried, so I rushed home and immediately made up a lame excuse why I was late.

"Don't lie to me." Anna's anger was evident in her tone.

"You went to Jay's after work and didn't bother to call."

"Yes, I did go to Jay's. We had a really rough day at work, and he invited me over for a couple of beers, and…how did you know?"

"Stacy was thoughtful enough to call and let me know you were at their house and…"

Anna sniffed the air. "What's that smell? Have you been smoking pot?"

"Anna, it's not a big deal. Everyone is doing it."

"Well, I'm not doing it."

"Well, maybe you should!"

I immediately regretted my sharp remark.

Anna stormed off to the bedroom and slammed the door.

I slept on the couch.

I woke up early and made an apologetic breakfast. When the aroma of bacon and pancakes filled the air, Anna sneaked up behind me, wrapped her arms around my waist, and squeezed. I turned, held her close, and whispered, "I was rude to you last night, and I'm sorry. You had every right to be angry."

"Ricky, you know I can't stay mad at you. But I just don't get it. Why keep secrets from me?"

I knew it was time to come clean. I told Anna about Vietnam: the helicopters delivering soldiers to the emergency room—some wounded, some beyond saving. The soldiers crying out in pain, begging for help. The blood-stained floors and that sickening smell of copper. I relived that awful night when I didn't even recognize Danny and the overwhelming heartache when he didn't make it.

"Drugs were a way to escape, marijuana, pills, even heroin. I did it all."

Now Anna was crying. "Oh, Ricky! I had no idea."

Now that I had dug up the past, the nightmares returned.

It begins in church. I am standing behind the pulpit, preaching to a small congregation. I feel calm knowing this is the place I'm supposed to be. I speak from the *book of Psalms*, chapter 46:

> God is our refuge and strength, an ever-present help in trouble. Therefore, we will not fear…

Suddenly, my sermon is interrupted. The congregation fades away. The room is no longer filled with pews. Instead, it's crowded with gurneys. This quiet place of worship is no longer a sanctuary but a hospital. Gurneys are filled with soldiers. Some wounded. Some lie silent. Danny is on one of the gurneys. His frail arm reaching out to me as he painfully whispers my name. I try running to my best friend, but I'm unable to move. My feet are no longer feet but heavy blocks of cement. I struggle to lift one foot, then the other, and one by one, each soldier's cry fades into silence. I know I'm too late.

I rub my eyes with the palms of my hands in an attempt to wipe away the somber scene. Then I blink. I'm no longer amidst the sea of gurneys but in the middle of the Asian jungle. Alone. The silence is so loud I can't help but wonder if I am deaf. Surrounded by the dank smell of rotting leaves and suffocating heat, I remember this place. It's hell. Suddenly, the quiet is interrupted. In the distance, I hear a soldier's desperate call, "Medic!"

Then I hear another…and another…until the cries for help meld like an orchestra of crickets singing their chorus on a warm summer's evening. Only this is no song. I fall to my knees and press my palms over my ears, but the cries only grow louder.

The pounding in my chest wakens me. I peer at the clock and realize I had only slept a couple of hours. Drenched in sweat and unable to go back to sleep, I get up, take a hot shower, and make a pot of coffee. Anna comes into the kitchen and sits in the chair opposite me. She reaches across the table and takes my hand.

"Ricky, this is the second time this week you've had a bad dream."

"Anna, this isn't just a dream. It's a living nightmare of that horrible night in Vietnam."

"Oh, Ricky, I'm so sorry. I don't know how to help. Maybe you could go to church and talk with the pastor."

"Why would I want to do that? He's just going to tell me that God can fix my problems."

"Well, maybe God can."

"Maybe he can, and maybe he can't. I once trusted that God had a plan for my life, but look where I am now. If there is a God, I don't think he cares."

Anna noticed a change. She came to terms with my marijuana use because of the nightmares, but she didn't know about the pills. As the dreams continued to bring terror to my nights, I did what I needed to do to dull the pain. Spending money on drugs was not in our budget, so I started taking some of the grocery and gas money for my own personal use. I knew it wouldn't be long before Anna would figure out what I was doing. I had to find a way to get extra cash on the side…

CHAPTER 27

Jay acquired a couple of handguns. I don't know how, and I didn't ask. Our strategy was to use the guns for intimidation, for show, not to actually fire them, so he left the ammo at home.

Today is payday. I drive to Jay's apartment, and he is standing on the sidewalk, waiting for me. He opens the car door, sticks his head inside, and asks, "Are you ready for this?"

"Just get in."

He climbs on in and slams the door. I drive to the Post Exchange, our military store known as the PX, and backed into an empty space at the far end of the parking lot. Then we waited. We watched people as they came and went, hoping to spot the perfect person.

"Rick, this is a stupid idea. We've been sitting here for over an hour and still haven't seen anyone that looks promising. It's getting late, and the PX is about to close. Why don't we just call it a day?"

"Just be patient. The right person will come along, and we'll…"

Suddenly, Jay jabbed me in my side with his elbow and pointed. "Look at that guy."

A man was walking across the parking lot, checking his pockets. He pulled out a large wad of bills and was counting his cash. I whispered to Jay, "He's our man. We'll wait until he comes out of the store and follow him to his car."

In preparation, we tucked the guns inside the belted waistband of our pants, pulled our shirts over the bulge to conceal the weapons, and waited. After half an hour, the man exited the store. He tore the wrapper off a candy bar and began eating it while walking back to his car.

"Jay, do you see what I see?"

"Yeah, he's eating a candy bar."

"Not only that, he's not carrying a bag. That means he must still have all that cash in his pocket."

We got out of the car and hurried across the parking lot.

Just when the man was about to unlock his car door, we approached him from behind. Jay jammed his unloaded gun into the man's back.

"Gimme your money!" he ordered.

The man froze. Then he quickly raised his hands in submission as his half-eaten candy bar and keys fell to the ground.

"I-I-I don't have any money," he whimpered.

"Stop stalling!" ordered Jay. "Hand it over before someone gets hurt!"

The man didn't move a muscle.

It was obvious Jay's tone and tactic were less than convincing, so I took over. I tried the gentle approach.

"Look, mister, I'm sorry if we made you a little uncomfortable. We watched as you crossed the parking lot before entering the store. You had pulled a big wad of cash from your pocket and was counting it. So don't try to convince us your pockets are empty. We could have relieved you of your money before you went shopping, but being the kind and considerate gentlemen that we are, we waited. So how about you just hand over your cash and we can all be on our way?"

I must not have been very persuasive because the man continued standing there with his arms raised toward the sky.

Jay chimed back in, "You aren't too smart, are you? What part of 'Give me your money' don't you understand? Maybe I need to speak slower…Give. Me. Your. Money!" The man slowly lowered one arm, reached into his pocket, and pulled out a handful of cash. Then he tossed the money toward Jay. The bills floated in the air like autumn leaves falling from a tree. Jay ran in circles, jumping, and swatting the air as he tried his best to catch the cash and stuff each captured bill into his pocket. Despite the seriousness of the situation, I couldn't keep from laughing.

"Oh, you think this is funny?" yelled Jay.

"Well, it kinda is. You should see yourself…jumping…grabbing…"

"I'm glad I can provide you with some entertainment. How about you stop laughing and get back to the business at hand? What do we do now? We can't just let him drive away. He'll go straight to a phone and call the police."

The man's car was parked next to a patch of grass, holding an old rusty pole. It looked like it had once displayed a small sign but now stood as an eyesore in the parking lot. To keep the man from following us, we positioned his arms around the pole and tightly duct-taped his hands together. Jay picked up the man's keys and threw them as far as he could. Then we hightailed it to my car and fled the scene.

I drove like a bat out of hell as Jay counted the loot. He threw the cash on the floor of the car and yelled, "Forty-seven dollars! Can you believe it? It's payday, and he only had forty-seven dollars—all in ones!"

"Yeah," I replied, "it's payday. That's probably all the money his wife lets him have."

"Stop joking around. I don't know about you, but I was really scared. All that for a lousy forty-seven dollars. Does Anna know?"

"No, I told her I was going to the PX, which wasn't really a lie."

Jay combed the floor with his fingers, gathered up the money, and handed me twenty-three dollars. "Here's your half," he growled.

"What about the other dollar?" I asked.

He glared at me then ripped a bill in half.

"Here!" he yelled as he threw the torn bill at me, "Here's your fifty cents."

I quickly pulled into the nearest parking lot and turned off the engine.

"What are you doing?" Jay was visibly angry.

"I need to think."

"It's a little late for that. You should've done you're thinking before we committed a felony."

"Hey, you can't blame this all on me. You got the guns. Remember?"

"If you hadn't roped me into your cockamamie plan, we wouldn't have needed the guns."

"Yeah, yeah, yeah, we're both innocent."

I pulled out my wallet to tuck away the unearned cash and noticed a piece of paper poking out from one of the credit card slots. Thinking it was a note or a phone number, I pulled it out to get a better look. The scribble on the back was faded and barely legible, but I could see that it was a number…1967. Suddenly my heart filled with trepidation. I slowly unfolded the paper. Staring back at me was a picture of Anna dressed in a saloon girl outfit. I was dressed as a gunslinger. My hand rested on the pistol strapped to my hip. The irony was not lost on me.

I had forgotten all about this photo…until now. I recalled the day we had it taken. It was the end of our first year in college and Anna's birthday. We went to a seaside village to celebrate, and she insisted on the photo as a souvenir. Only a few years had passed since then, but it seemed like a lifetime ago. I studied the picture. The worn fold lines and the years of hiding in my wallet caused the photo to look as though it was fractured. One of the cracks spidered down the picture right between me and Anna, dividing us.

"What's that?" Jay asked.

"Oh, it's nothing. Just an old picture."

I quickly folded it and shoved it back into my wallet. I was angry at myself for disregarding its importance.

"Just a picture? You look like you've seen a ghost."

"Maybe I have."

"Jay, do you ever wish you could go back in time and do things differently? You know, make better choices?"

"Every. Single. Day. Take today for example, a bad decision."

I started the car and slowly pulled out from the parking lot. We rode in silence as I drove to Jay's house. I dropped him off, then headed home.

The following evening, Anna and I were watching TV when the doorbell rang. I answered the door, and two military police officers were standing on my stoop. The MPs handcuffed me and led me to the back seat of their car. As we drove away, I looked back at Anna and mouthed the words, "I'm so sorry."

The image of her standing in the doorway all alone, crying, was almost unbearable. And it was all my fault.

During the court-martial, the victim testified that he had gone to the bank and withdrawn a large sum of money just prior to shopping at the PX. He pointed me out as one of the assailants then described the incident, "While crossing the parking lot, I counted my money to make sure I had enough to buy an engagement ring for my girlfriend. Then I went inside and purchased the ring. I slipped the little box into my shirt pocket and stuffed my remaining cash into my pants pocket, forty-seven dollars."

When asked how he escaped from being tied to a pole, he answered, "The pole was loose, so I just pulled it out of the ground."

Jay and I each received a dishonorable discharge and a sentence of eighteen months of military prison in Fort Leavenworth, Kansas.

Sarah, Jay's fiancé, moved to Texas to be near her sister. Anna went home to Portland to live with her parents until my release. Katie thought I was merely transferred to another military base. Mama and Daddy were heartbroken.

CHAPTER 28

*D*ishonorable. Reprehensible conduct.

That's how I was judged.

The architecture is impressive—apart from the fact that this is a federal prison! Leavenworth was built in the early 1900s by prison labor. The walls stand forty feet above ground, forty feet below ground, and are over four feet thick. The domed top marks the center of the complex with two adjacent wings, each nearly two city blocks long. The illusion was that of a grand palace fit for a king. But one step inside quickly reminds me this is no palace.

The door slammed shut behind me. At that moment, reality set in. I knew without a doubt that my world had changed. I was now confined to the inside of these walls, and my freedom was on the other side of that door. The guard took me straight to the *receiving* and *discharge* area. To my surprise, I wasn't the only one there. Other new arrivals and inmates transferred here from other institutions were each waiting their turn to be processed in. After R&D, we were all escorted to holding cells to be strip-searched. This cell was not a cubical of seclusion as I had imagined, but an open area, disallowing the slightest possibility of privacy. A wooden bench separated officers from inmates, and we were instructed to remove our clothing. I emptied my pockets, removed my wedding ring, took off all my clothes, and placed everything on the bench. An officer looked over my entire body, noting any unusual markings. The scar on my left knee was his first notation. I had nearly forgotten about the accident that had caused that scar.

I received a bike for my eighth birthday. It wasn't new, but it was new to me. I couldn't wait to see how fast I could pedal that bike. I leaned in toward the handlebars and furiously pumped my legs. With each turn of the pedal, my speed increased—faster and faster I rode. That is until my front tire hit a hole and flattened my tire. I went flying over the handlebars and landed on the graveled road, tearing my pants as pebbles ground into my knee. Blood ran down my entire leg, and I cried as I walked my bike back home. Mama washed my knee and dabbed it with mercurochrome. When I cringed in pain, she blew on my wound to ease the stinging effects of the medicine. I thought I would get in trouble for tearing my pants, but Mama just gave me a big hug and said, "It's only a scratch, you'll be fine."

The officer noted my birthmark, a pinkish area of skin on the nape of my neck. *Mama said it was a stork bite. I once asked her why a stork would bite the baby it was delivering, but she never gave me a real answer.* He also searched for hidden contraband and gang-affiliated tattoos. I once thought about getting a tattoo, but now I'm glad I didn't. The last thing he noted was the needle marks on my arm. This revealed my recent past and the underlying cause of why I'm now in prison.

Finally, when the search was over, the officer asked my size. I told him my shirt, pants, and shoe size. He turned, pulled clothes from bins lining the wall behind him, then tossed me a pair of underwear, a T-shirt, socks, slip-on shoes, and my new prison uniform—army surplus fatigues. I dressed as he examined my belongings. He informed me that everything would be sent to the address listed in my file, except for the money he had removed from my wallet.

Oh yeah, the money—the lousy twenty-three dollars from the robbery.

We both signed a receipt verifying the cash amount, then he handed me a carbon copy. He stuffed the original receipt, along with the cash, into an envelope, and scrawled my name and inmate number on the front. Then sealed the envelope and placed it into a lockbox.

"Don't worry about your money," he said. "We'll add it to your account at the commissary. You can spend it there."

After I dressed, I attended an interview with my assigned case manager and counselor. They asked several questions, but there was one that caused me to reconsider my answer: "Do you know anyone in here that might cause you harm, someone that may be vengeful toward you?"

I quickly answered, "No." But then I thought of Jay. *Would he think it's all my fault we are in prison? Surely, he realized he was just as much to blame as me.*

Cell house A, nearly two blocks long, housed an abundance of cells, hence the name cell house. Each cell housed up to twelve inmates. I hated the fact that this small space will be my home for the next eighteen months. I was assigned to one of the two empty beds in my cell, and I secretly hoped Jay would get the other. Two days passed before Jay arrived, and just as I had hoped, he was assigned to my cell. We both had realized it was our own stupid fault we were here and agreed not to blame each other. We would remain friends—at least while we were on the inside.

Admissions and *orientation* was held the following week. The A&O classes informed all new inmates about the rules and regulations, what to expect, and what was expected of us. Then we were instructed to get a job. If we didn't already have a skill that could be used, a test was given to see where we would best fit in. There were several shops to choose from.

One shop made shoes for the Parks and Forestry Service personnel. Another made T-shirts for the military. There was a shop that crafted paint brushes, a woodworking shop, a canvas shop to make wheeled baskets for the US Postal Service, and a mechanical shop where the workers fix anything in the prison that is broken—it could be anything between painting walls and unclogging toilets. And of course, there were always clerical jobs, so an office was provided for that. Since I didn't have any of the special skill sets for the other shops, I considered clerical. After all, I *can* type. The problem with typing is, I'm not very good at it…so I took the test. At the end of A&O, I was informed of my assigned job. It turns out I am best suited for custodial work—a prison janitor. And my pay will be a generous fifteen cents per hour!

I quickly learned that everything in prison is a sequence of structure and rules—what to do and when to do it.

Up by 6:00 a.m., clean our cell, make our bunk, go to the dining hall for breakfast. After breakfast, we had to report to our detail supervisor for accountability and orders for the day's work. If our work was completed in a timely manner, we were allowed to go back to our cell or go out to the yard.

Lunch was at 11:00 a.m. If our assigned work was not completed, we would return to our jobs and work until 3:00 p.m.

After work, we showered then returned to our cell for a 4:00 p.m. stand-up count. Not only have all the inmates been assigned a number, each night we are counted.

Sleep didn't come easy. I tossed and turned throughout the entire night and woke with an uneasiness in my stomach. I know the nervous rumble is because I begin my new job today. All I can think about is working alongside other inmates and how they might treat the new guy. After making my bunk and straightening up my area, I head over to the dining hall. I don't know why I bother. I have no appetite, and the smell of food is nauseating. But I force myself to eat a few bites of toast anyway, hoping the dry bread will settle my stomach. After finishing off my coffee, I head over to the custodial department. The detail supervisor pairs me with another inmate to learn the job.

"Hi, my name is Tiny. My real name is Albert, but 'round here, everyone calls me *Tiny*."

"I'm Rick," I said as I looked him over and tried my best not to snicker. There was nothing tiny about him. My six-foot frame could easily be swallowed up by the bulk of his shadow. His thick arms filled the sleeves of his shirt, and he seemingly had no neck. His lofty stature and robust girth must have earned him the contrary nickname Tiny. I imagine he's called Tiny for the same reason a three-legged dog is called Lucky or a Chihuahua is named Killer.

"Well, Rick, I kin' tell by yur accent, ya ain't frum da South. I'm a guessin' ya cum frum da west."

My accent? I wanted to tell Tiny that he was the one with a drawl, but I kept my opinion to myself.

"That's right. I'm from California, born and raised. But my parents are from Oklahoma."

"Well, at least ya got sum good blood in ya." Then he laughed. "I'm fixin' ta git ta work. Stick close ta me an' I'll show ya what ta do."

When Tiny wasn't giving instructions, he was humming. I recognized some of the tunes—old church hymns. Although I haven't thought about those songs for a very long time, I often found myself humming along. *Maybe he wasn't so scary after all—like a gentle giant. Still, just to be safe, I'm going to stay on Tiny's good side.*

Tiny informed me that Leavenworth is no walk in the park. "But if ya mind yer Ps and Qs, you'll do okay. This place has housed some real bad dudes."

He then proceeded to educate me about some of its prior inmates:

James Earl Ray—prior to his conviction for the assassination of Martin Luther King Jr. in 1968, he had served a four-year sentence in Leavenworth for mail fraud.

George "Bugs" Moran—a Chicago prohibition-era gangster. He was the intended target of the *St. Valentine's Day Massacre* orchestrated by his nemesis, Al Capone. Although several of Moran's men were gunned down, Moran escaped death that day, and Capone, who was in Florida at the time of the massacre, was never indicted for the murders.

After serving a prison sentence in Ohio, Moran was immediately arrested for a previous crime of robbery and sentenced to ten years in Leavenworth. By then, he was suffering from lung cancer and died one month into his ten-year sentence. He had outlived Al Capone by a decade, but cancer had finished the job Capone had botched. Once a wealthy man, Moran died nearly penniless and is buried in the Leavenworth Federal Penitentiary Cemetery.

Robert Stroud—the Birdman of Leavenworth. A psychopath, convicted of murder, and sentenced to life in prison in solitary confinement. He collected birds, performed experiments on them, and wrote about his findings. In 1942, he was transferred to Alcatraz Island, also known as The Rock. Built on an island, surrounded by the chilly shark-infested waters of the San Francisco Bay, Alcatraz was regarded as the toughest prison in America. During his time there, Stroud was not allowed the luxury of birds. The movie *Birdman of Alcatraz* paints an unrealistic, fictionalized version of the life of Stroud.

THE WAR WITHIN

The entire week, I worked with Tiny. He showed me the ropes of the custodial department, taught me how to properly mop, collect the trash, and sanitize the bathrooms. When Tiny wasn't humming, we talked.

"Hey, Rick, did ya know there's church on Sundees? Seein' as tamarra is Sundee, I 'spect ta see ya there."

I nodded. "I'll be there."

Just like I promised, I attended church. I'm not sure if my motivation was to actually get something out of the service or to keep Tiny happy.

The following week was payday, and payday is a big deal. Our earnings go straight into an account at the commissary where we are allowed to purchase items. On my first trip to the commissary, I bought shampoo, a Butterfinger candy bar, a few stamps, paper, and envelopes. I went back to my cell and began to write letters:

Dear Anna,

Here I am, already in my fifth week in prison. With one month under my belt, I only have seventeen to go. I'm feeling a little more comfortable with the daily routine, and my job isn't bad. I do a lot of sweeping, mopping, waxing and buffing the floors, sanitizing bathrooms, and collecting trash. It's almost like the day I faked being sick to get out of going to school. Mama figured it out and put me to work. At least in here, it keeps me out of trouble. Ha! Ha! That's kind of ironic since the reason I'm here in the first place is because I'm in trouble.

Anna, I'm sorry I've made a mess of things. I hope I can make it up to you someday. Please send me a picture of you. I miss and love you with all my heart.

Ricky

SHARLENE LEKER

Dear Mama and Daddy,

    It's not all bad here. We get to watch movies a couple of times a week, and the food here is really good. We have fried chicken day, hamburger day, steak day, and on Fridays, we get fish. Of course, the food here could never match your homemade biscuits and gravy.

    You'll be happy to know that I'm going to church. The prison chaplain holds a service each Sunday, and I make it a point to attend.

    I'm sure you haven't told Katie about the robbery or me being in prison, but I think she's old enough to handle it. I know she's used to getting postcards from me, but I don't think a picture of the prison with bold letters across the top: *Wish you were here*, would send the right message. Use your own judgment—tell her when the time is right.

    Please don't worry about me. I'm okay.

    From the bottom of my heart, I love you all.

Richard

    I tried to be upbeat and paint a picture of prison life as more of an inconvenience than an eighteen-month sleepover with hardened criminals. The truth is, prison is hard. I don't want my family to know that some days I'm scared, and I hate myself for being here.

    How did my life get so screwed up?

CHAPTER 29

My dishonorable discharge crushed my spirit more than my prison sentence. My life came to a screeching halt when I entered the prison system. I had no plans and nothing to look forward to, at least not for the next eighteen months. The one thing I did have was time—time to think about the mistakes I've made and time to think about my future.

The first few months into my sentence, I experienced all five stages of grief. I grieved the loss of freedom, career, friends, and possibly Anna. Not that I ever want to bear arms again, but I was stripped of my Second Amendment right to do so. I can no longer vote, and I've lost any future veteran benefits I would have earned. To top it all off, when I get out of here, no one will want to hire me—I'll be an ex-convict.

Denial: I can't believe I'm in prison. It's not really my fault—if only Jay hadn't gotten the guns...

Anger: God, this is all your fault. If you wanted me to be a preacher, why didn't you make a way for me to stay in college? Then I wouldn't have been drafted, had a breakdown, and gone to Vietnam. I would have never known that I like drugs...from preacher to prison. How can I be so stupid...?

Bargaining: If I promise to change, do what's right, get a job... maybe Anna will wait for me...

Depression: What if Anna doesn't wait for me? Maybe she will find someone else to love her. I love her, but this time, I really messed up. I wouldn't blame her for moving on. She deserves to be happy. I deserve what I'm getting...

Acceptance: I can't go back and right the wrong. I can only move forward. Starting over won't be easy, but in a way, my time in prison allows me to break free from my past. I can leave this place and start over—a new beginning. Yes, a new beginning—that sounds good!

Month after month, I followed the daily routine, did my job, and followed the rules. I distanced myself from the troublemakers—the gangs and wannabe tough guys that have nothing to lose. I didn't want anything to do with those inmates. Unlike many of them, who will spend the rest of their lives behind these walls of stone, my time was short, and I did have something to lose.

My time in prison will come to an end in a few months, and I will go home. In the meantime, I'm working with my counselor to make a release plan for transition from confinement to freedom. This includes my probation, where I will live, how I will obtain work, and a substance abuse treatment plan. The day prior to my release, I will navigate the so-called prison merry-go-round. I will make the rounds to all the departments to get signed off. That means I won't owe anything. All debts are paid. Not only did I pay my debt to society, but I have to pay any debts I incurred while in prison.

CHAPTER 30

I thought this day would never get here—my release! In place of my prison garb, I was given a pair of jeans, a white shirt, one hundred dollars, and a bus ticket to Portland. I have been officially discharged! I walked out the door and climbed into the car, waiting to take me to the bus station. I was surprised to see that the driver of the inmate taxi was an inmate himself. I questioned him about his access to the outside world.

"You mean they just let you drive out the prison gate? How is that possible?"

"I'm trustworthy," he explained. "I have a state driver's license and permission from the prison. I can go in and out…just as long as I return. By the way, I'm Luke. Congratulations on getting your walking papers."

"Thank you. It's been a long eighteen months."

Although Luke is afforded the privilege of driving in and out of prison, he's still a prisoner. Unlike him, I'm leaving this jail and I don't have to return.

Luke dropped me off at the bus station, wished me good luck, and left me standing in the parking lot. I paused for several minutes to look at my surroundings. Somehow, the sky appeared to be bluer, the sun brighter, and the air fresher. It felt good!

The bus ride from Kansas to Oregon seemed endless. The 1,700-mile journey through six states made for a long trip—especially on a bus. Finally, we arrived in Portland and pulled into the passenger loading and unloading area. Before we came to a complete stop, I stood and quickly made my way down the aisle. I wanted to be the first one off the bus. I stood at the door for what I thought was a ridiculous amount of time. I began to think the driver was never going to open it. When he finally did, I jumped off the bus and rushed into the station. Anna was standing near the door, holding a large bouquet of balloons and a sign printed with "Welcome Home." When she spotted me, she dropped the sign, lost her grip on the balloons, and ran to me with open arms. The balloons floated up to the ceiling as we ran to each other. Our colliding embrace and passionate kiss nearly bowled us over.

Anna has been working as a waitress at a local restaurant while I served my time. Now that I'm out, she is taking a couple of weeks off, so we can spend more time together. We stay a few days in Portland with Anna's parents. I enjoy their company, but Tranquillity is pulling on my heartstrings. I'm eager to go to California.

The following morning, I met with my parole officer. We discussed my "get back into society" plan and set up future appointment times to meet with him and attend Alcoholics Anonymous. I expressed my desire to get a job, but first, I wanted to visit my family in California.

He gave me written permission to leave the state and included a warning: "If you decide to stay longer than allowed, it will be a violation of your parole and you will go to jail. Understand?"

I agreed.

Anna and I left early in the morning, hours before sunrise. I drove south, through the entire state of Oregon. We entered the Cascade Mountain range and crossed over the Siskiyou Mountain pass. A few miles past the summit, the sign came into view: "Welcome to California." I smiled. I knew by the end of this long day we would be with my parents and little sister. Throughout the day, Anna and I traded off driving. When we had only a couple of hours left until we made it to our destination, I took over and drove the last leg of our trip.

It soon became evident we were in the heart of California, the San Joaquin Valley, known as the Great Central Valley. We locals simply refer to it as *The Valley*. Central California is a carpet of agricultural fields, one after another, as far as the eye can see. The flat terrain and rich fertile soil contribute to the production of nearly every edible nut, fruit, and vegetable. Beef, poultry, dairy, grains, and cotton are also grown in this area. I was taking in the scenery when Anna broke the silence.

"This place reminds me of a patchwork quilt, like the ones my grandmother used to make. All these different crops, adjacent to one another look as though they are sewn together, like fabric, blanketing the earth with color."

When I didn't respond, she glanced over at me, "Are you okay? You look a little flushed."

"I was just thinking. This valley feels like home. Just seeing all these fields reminds me of Daddy. How hard he works tilling up the ground, planting, irrigating, and harvesting. It also reminds me of all the days I spent walking the rows of cotton, chopping weeds in the summer's relentless heat. Don't get me wrong, it wasn't all bad. It's just that farming is a lot of hard work…"

I remember every summer, after the tomatoes were harvested and sent to the canneries for processing, Mama, me, and Katie loaded the car with boxes, buckets, and baskets, and gleaned the field of leftover tomatoes. Then we spent a week canning.

Once, when the canneries went on strike, we went to the orchard and loaded the car with ripe, juicy peaches. When Katie complained about the canning process, especially peeling all those peaches, Mama reminded her, "We didn't have to pay for any of this food. We just have to put in the effort to preserve it. Maybe you forgot how nice it is to take a jar of tree-ripened peaches off the shelf and enjoy a warm peach cobbler in the middle of winter." For a little while, Katie didn't say anything. She just continued peeling peaches. Then she commented, mostly under her breath, "I love your peach cobbler…especially in the middle of winter."

I turn off the highway onto the main road leading to Tranquillity.

Ten minutes later, I see our old house and the big red barn in the distance. Now we're on our street and I have a clear view of the house. My stomach flutters in a dance of excitement. I can see the long dirt driveway and the pump house that provided us with god-awful tasting water. Over by the barn is the old abandoned outhouse.

I recall the time I locked Katie in the old toilet. *I coaxed her inside, slammed the door shut, and placed a big rock against the outside of the door so she couldn't open it. Then I ran to the back of the house and peered around the corner to see how long it would take her to escape. From inside the house, Mama heard Katie's yelling and banging on the outhouse door. She ran outside, removed the rock, and set Katie free. I was immediately grounded and assigned Katie's chores for a week.*

I turn into the driveway. Mama and Katie must have been watching for us because I can see them standing on the porch, waving enthusiastically. Mama is wearing an apron tied around her waist like she always does when she is cooking. I pull up next to the porch and turn off the car's engine. Mama reaches down, grabs the hem of her apron, then wipes her eyes. I open the car door as she runs to greet me. Katie is right behind her, waiting for a hug. It's not that Mama isn't happy to see Anna. She loves her too, but this visit, I'm the long-awaited *prodigal son*.

We all walked into the house, and I could tell Mama had put that apron to good use that day. The smell of fried chicken and freshly baked pecan pie caused my mouth to water. Katie wasted no time in taking credit for the pie.

"I was going to bake you a cake, but I remembered how much you like pie, so I made your favorite."

"I'm sure it's delicious. I wouldn't mind having a predinner sample."

Katie cut an ample slice of pie and set it on the table in front of me. Anna refused her piece and said she would just have a taste of mine. It was still warm, and I savored every bite, except for the bite I shared with Anna.

"Katie, I didn't know you were such a good cook."

She was beaming with pride as she quickly answered, "Mama taught me everything I know."

It's been a long time since I've been home. I can't believe how much Katie has grown. She is no longer the little girl I endlessly teased but has matured into a young woman. Soon, she will be out of high school, ready to begin a life of her own.

Anna and I sat at the kitchen table while Mama and Katie tended to dinner. Anna offered to help, but Mama wouldn't have it.

"You've had a long drive. Just sit and relax."

Throughout our conversation, it was easy to see that Mama was overjoyed I was home. At the same time, I could sense the sadness she was trying to hide. She could tell I had changed. I was no longer the shy, innocent teen she and Daddy had driven to the airport a few years back. I had picked up some bad habits, made bad choices, and was not the untainted son they had once known.

Daddy had just come in from the field. He was in the garage taking off his work boots, so I went out to greet him. My father is a strong man and firmly believed strong men didn't cry. Today, for the first time in my life, I witnessed tears spill from his eyes. I know he is happy to see me, but I also sense those tears are caused by grief and worry. And it is all my fault. He tried to speak, but his words were broken, as his spirit seemed to be. He pulled a handkerchief from his back pocket and hung his head as he wiped his face. A few moments of silence passed before he lifted his head and looked me straight in the eyes.

"Tell me, son, where did I go wrong? I did my best to raise you right. So tell me, where did I go wrong?"

My head drooped in shame. Now I was the one with tears running down my face.

"Daddy, you can't blame yourself. I couldn't ask for a better father. What I did was wrong. I made bad choices, and I've had to suffer the consequences." He pulled me to his chest, and we wept on each other's shoulders. At that moment, I realized how much my father loved me, and his love was unconditional.

We spent a week at my parents' house. I relished the time with my family, but I knew it was time for Anna and me to head back to Portland and begin our new life together. The long drive back provided ample time for us to reconcile and plan on how to move forward. I must have said I'm sorry a thousand times.

"Ricky, I'm no longer mad at you. I was angry at first—and hurt. I prayed every day for the strength to get through this. Then one night before bed, I was reading my Bible. In the book of Psalms, God says he heals the brokenhearted and binds their wounds. It took me a while to believe it, but I worked through the anger and came through it loving you no less than I ever have. I just want us to be happy again."

I reached over and took Anna's hand and gave it a squeeze. "I can't imagine what I put you through. Thank you for sticking with me."

"Isn't that what marriage is all about, sticking with each other? I married you for better or worse. We've just been through the worst. Now let's make it better."

CHAPTER 31

Rick is my only sibling. He is nearly nine years older than me. I will always think of him as my big brother. But now it's different—we are friends.

I was ten years old when my brother went off to college. That's when I received my first postcard. I was so excited because the card was actually addressed to me. I took pleasure in the fact that I was receiving my own mail. When Rick went into the Army, he continued sending postcards. In all his travels, he took the time to think of me. Even if he was in an airport changing planes, he would pick out a card and drop it in the mail. I could hardly wait to read the handwritten note on the back, commenting on his whereabouts. My brother had a way of making me feel special.

I received cards from Washington, Texas, Hawaii, Vietnam, Georgia, and several European countries. By this time, I had a scrapbook bulging with pictures of various places I could only dream of visiting. When Rick went to Kansas, I thought he was just transferred to another army base. At least that's what I was told. But it didn't take long before I knew something was wrong. After all, the postcards stopped coming.

In those earlier years, my parents thought I was too young to understand what was going on with Rick, so they never told me of the crime he had committed and his time in prison. I now know they were only trying to protect me from the reality that my brother, whom I nearly worshipped, wasn't perfect. I held him in such high esteem that if I knew of his misdeeds, they thought my spirit would have been crushed and disappointment would have knocked him off the pedestal I had placed him on.

Answers to my questions were left only to my imagination, and I never could have imagined Rick's truth. It wasn't until I became an adult that the relationship between Rick and I grew from siblings into a friendship.

Rick and Anna settled in Oregon. I married my high school sweetheart, Mark, and we settled down in California, not far from Mama and Daddy. Although Rick and I rarely saw each other, he often called just to chat. During one of our conversations, I asked, "Rick, what happened to you? Why did you stop sending me postcards?"

"You mean you don't know?"

He couldn't see my head shaking back and forth and that I had bitten my lower lip in anticipation of something I didn't want to hear. My silence was the answer to his question.

Rick took in a deep breath, then let out a long sigh, then he began. He told of how he felt God's calling to be a preacher and his excitement when he entered college to study for the ministry. How he had to skip a year and work on the farm to save enough money to return to school. He told of the day he received his draft notice, boot camp, the nervous breakdown, Vietnam, the hospital, the nightmares, drugs…and prison. While he revealed all those hidden facts, my heart was breaking, and I silently wept. I knew I couldn't change his past, but now I could provide encouragement and support, if nothing more than to lend a listening ear.

He continued, "When I got out of prison, I promised Anna the world. I assured her I would get a job and work hard so we could buy a house, save money for vacations, and start a family. I desperately wanted to fit back into society and live a normal life. Anna continued working at the restaurant, and eventually, we moved into our own apartment.

"Each day I scoured the want ads, filled out applications, and waited. I waited for the phone to ring. I waited for the mail. Finally, when I received a response from one of my applications, I eagerly tore open the envelope only to find a rejection letter. That was the first of many.

"Maybe I shouldn't even try."

"Well, Rick, if you're inviting me to your pity party, I'm not interested. I'm sorry you're having a tough time, but you have to hang in there. Quitting is not an option. The one thing losers do… is quit."

We talked for a little while longer, and when I hung up the phone, I whispered a little prayer, *Lord, please help my brother find a job.*

A few days passed, and I received another call from Rick. I answered the phone and barely said, "Hello" before he interrupted, "Katie, I have finally figured it out."

"Exactly what have you figured out?"

"It's the application. My criminal history! Are you a veteran? I mark yes. Have you been convicted of a felony? I mark yes. And that's the problem. That's why no one wants to hire me. All they see is that I'm an ex-con. Therefore, they think I'm not trustworthy."

His tone was beyond agitated. He was angry.

"No one will even give me a chance! I guess that's what I get for trying to be honest."

He was about to continue his rant until I interrupted, "Rick, you have to stay positive. Something will come along. What does Anna say about your lack of employment?"

"She just keeps telling me to pray for a job."

"To tell you the truth, I shouldn't have to pray."

He hesitated…

"For everything I've been through, God owes me one."

"Rick, you don't believe that, do you? You really think God *owes* you?"

He didn't answer my question. Instead, he changed the subject and talked about the weather.

A few months later, Rick called with good news, "Katie! I got a job!" He was so excited that I had to tell him to slow down and take a breath.

"I filled out the application, went in for an interview, and they said they would get back with me. I thought their response would be like all the others, '*I'm sorry, but the position you have applied for has been filled. We'll keep your application on file and call you if something else comes up.*' Well, this time, they hired me! I'll be working for the city, mowing lawns and emptying trash cans in the parks."

"Congratulations, Rick! I told you something would come along."

Rick and Anna saved their money and after a couple of years were able to buy a small house in Hillsboro, only fifteen miles from Portland. Rick referred to it as their *starter home*. "Eventually," he said, "I want to give Anna the home of her dreams."

CHAPTER 32

"Fired? What do you mean fired?" Anna couldn't believe what she was hearing. "Ricky, what happened? What did you do?"

"They said I lied on my job application."

"Well, did you?"

"Anna, it was the only way. All I did was mark no on the veteran and felony questions. And if you want to know why? Just take a look at my pile of rejection letters...that's why!"

I could tell Anna was disappointed. The look on her face confirmed my own thoughts: *We had a good thing going, and once again, I had to go and blow it.*

Days turned to months, and it seemed every time I turned around, I was flipping a page on the calendar. With each new month came that nagging voice in my head, reminding me to get a job. I haven't been very persistent in my search for work lately. In fact, I hadn't tried at all. The truth is, I didn't want to. I didn't want to face another rejection. So I kept procrastinating, telling myself, *I'll do it tomorrow.*

This morning started like every other day with Anna getting ready for work. I poured each of us a cup of coffee and waited for her in the kitchen. She walked in, bypassed her coffee, and barely glanced my way.

"Ricky, I left a grocery list and money on the counter. We only need a few items. I would like you to pick them up today. That is if you have the time."

I noticed a little sarcasm in her tone, but I politely answered, "Of course I have time. I'll go to the store for you, and I'll even make tonight's dinner."

She grabbed her keys from the hook on the wall next to the door and walked out of the house, not bothering to close the door behind her. I heard the car door slam, then she hurriedly backed out of the driveway, and sped off to work. I stuck my head out the door and yelled into the air, "What? No goodbye kiss?"

Anna usually offers her affection before leaving for work, but today I sensed tension in the air. I finished my second cup of coffee, picked up the money from the counter, and added it to my empty wallet. Then I grabbed the shopping list and shoved it into my pants pocket. Safeway is only a few blocks from our house, which makes a trip to the store easy and convenient. We only have one car, and Anna drives it to work. Besides, walking gives me an excuse to get out of the house, and I can always use the exercise.

I enter the store, grab a shopping cart, pull the list from my pocket, and locate each item: milk, eggs, and bologna. Then I cruise down the aisles looking for dinner ideas. I decide on spaghetti. It's easy on the budget and simple to throw together, so I add pasta, sauce, and a package of ground beef to the cart as well. One other thing I want that is not on the list is my favorite brew. I pass down the beer aisle and add a six-pack to the cart. In the midst of all this food, I feel a pang of hunger and remember I had skipped breakfast, and now I'm craving something sweet. I walk over to the candy aisle, pick up a Butterfinger, quickly unwrap it, and take a big bite. I savor the sweetness while I head to the bread aisle to get the last item on the list. Then I make my way to the checkout. While waiting in line, I finish off the candy bar, and without thinking, shove the wrapper into my pocket. I pay for the food and drop the meager change into my pants pocket.

I picked up the bags and headed home. Carrying the groceries was cumbersome. I had to stop and rearrange the bags a few times, but I made it home without incident. After putting the food away, I pulled the change from my pocket. With it came the Butterfinger wrapper. Suddenly, it dawned on me that I had not paid for the candy. I considered going back to the store and paying but thought that one little candy bar wouldn't make a difference. After all, the store has coverage for lost and damaged goods. Then I realized how easy it was to get away with something I hadn't paid for.

Anna pulled into the driveway just as I finished setting the table. I poured her a tall glass of iced tea and dished spaghetti onto our plates.

"Wow, Ricky, I see you've been busy."

"I told you this morning I would make dinner. After we eat, you can relax, and I'll do the dishes."

"Thank you. This is a big help."

We sat at the table, and I noticed a look of concern on Anna's face. I watched as she stared at her plate. She toyed with her food, winding noodles with her fork, but she didn't eat.

"Anna, what's going on? You haven't been yourself lately."

I took a big gulp from my can of beer and waited for an answer. Finally, she looked up at me.

"Ricky, I'm worried. You haven't had any work for a while, and we are barely scraping by. It's all I can do to pay the mortgage. There's no room for any extras, like your beer. And by the way, I smelled marijuana on your clothes the other day. Where did you get the money for that?"

"Don't worry, Anna, I didn't buy it. I got it from Greg."

"Greg? Our neighbor?"

"I helped him with his yard work. Afterward, we sat in his backyard and drank a cold beer. That's when he offered me a joint. I guess that was his way of paying me."

"Ricky, you know I don't approve of you smoking marijuana. Besides, when you got out of prison, you promised you wouldn't do that anymore. I know you like helping people, and I love that about you, but volunteering to work for free doesn't buy groceries. If you had a real job, we could pay our bills *and* have food in this house."

She was right. I needed to find a job. The following week, I pored over the want ads. The pickings were slim to none, and I didn't qualify for any of them. Anna had spent her last three dollars on gas for the car, and with payday still a week away, the realization finally hit me—we were broke.

I cleaned the house, folded the laundry, and noticed it was already past noon. We had already eaten all the leftovers, so I searched the cupboards for something to eat. I found a package of saltine crackers, a nearly empty jar of peanut butter, and a can of pork and beans. I looked inside the refrigerator, and it was equally bare. We have been eating pinto beans for several days, and even those leftovers are now gone.

I ate the crackers and the rest of the peanut butter for lunch, but that only left the pork and beans for dinner. Remembering the dollar and change in my pocket from my last trip to the store, I knew it would be enough to buy a box of off-brand mac and cheese and a package of hot dogs—the cheap ones, so I headed back to Safeway. Since I was only picking up a couple of items, I had no need for a shopping cart, I walked to the meat section and searched for the hot dogs with the lowest price. I picked up the store brand and noticed the price increase since the last time I had purchased them. Now I wouldn't have enough money for both hot dogs *and* mac and cheese. I had to choose between the two.

I stood in the meat aisle for several minutes, deciding if I should forget about what I came here for and just buy another pound of beans. Then I looked around at other shoppers and noticed most of their carts loaded with food. I only wished to be so lucky. I tossed the hot dogs back into the cold case, quickly walked to the refrigerated cooler, and pulled out a small bottle of chocolate milk. Then I went straight to the snack aisle. I scanned the shelves filled with cookies and picked up a package of Oreos. Then I proceeded toward the checkout. Friday is payday for most people, and the store is usually crowded. I try to avoid shopping on this day, but today, I decided it could work to my advantage.

Instead of standing in line to pay for my snack, I walked out of the store. This was a test. I sat down on a bench near the entrance, drank the milk, and ate my way through half the package of cookies. Just like my previously pilfered Butterfinger, no one seemed to notice. I tossed the rest of the cookies into the trash, stood up, dusted the crumbs from my shirt, and walked back into the store. This time, I would need a cart.

I add items to the cart as I walk up and down every aisle. I even load a large bag of dog food for our neighbor's golden retriever, Deuce. I like that dog. I have been shopping for over an hour, and my cart is nearly full. Now it is time to check out. I push the shopping cart through a closed check stand and park it by the restroom near the front of the store. I use the restroom then come back and retrieve my cart. Instead of going back toward the cashier, I head for the exit. My heart is pounding, and a little voice tells me to turn around. Ignoring the advice, I keep walking. I expect to hear an alarm go off, but nothing happens—just like with the cookies and the milk. That is until I'm halfway across the parking lot.

"Stop!" he shouted.

I knew this demand was directed at me. I complied and turned around to see a man speed-walking toward me. He looked to be in his late thirties, shorter than me, and had a paunch belly protruding far beyond his belt. When he caught up with me, his plump cheeks were bright red. He was out of breath and sweating. The tag pinned to his vest identified him as Stu. Below his name, in bold print, was his title: *store manager*. I looked at Stu in his exhausted state. I'm positive I could outrun him, even pushing a loaded cart, but I'd been caught, and there's no use trying to avoid it. I stood there in the parking lot amid the curious eyes of the many shoppers. They were either heading into the store or returning to their cars with the groceries they had no doubt paid for. Between laborious breaths, Stu questioned me about the contents of the cart. I patted my pockets, pretending to locate my proof of purchase.

"What are you looking for?"

I feigned a smile and said matter-of-factly, "My receipt."

"You're not going to find it. I watched you on the security camera, and you didn't pay for any of these items."

Stu was angry. His tone was less than cordial when he ordered, "Come with me."

He took the cart, and I walked beside him while he pushed it back into the store—into his office.

"Now let's add all this up."

He had already called the police, and soon two officers knocked, opened the door, then stepped inside. I sat in the corner in a metal folding chair as Stu set to totaling the stolen items. Leaning forward, I propped my elbows on my knees, buried my face in my hands, and closed my eyes. I silently asked myself, *Did you actually think you would get away with this? What will you say to Anna?*

I know I'm going to jail. My question is, for how long? That depends on the total. I understand that if the stolen value is less than $500, it's considered a misdemeanor. Over that amount is a felony, and felonies garner more jail time. My mind was racing. I desperately hoped the total would be well below the felony threshold. Then I had an idea—a brilliant idea…so I thought.

I lifted my head and interrupted Stu, "Excuse me."

He stopped adding and looked over at me. "You have a question?"

"Well, kinda. My wife clips coupons and keeps them in a shoebox. Can I run home really quick and get them? I only live a few blocks away, and I'll be right back."

Stu looked at me as though I had three eyes. "Are you kidding me?"

I didn't answer him. Actually, I wasn't kidding.

CHAPTER 33

I rushed to answer the phone. I was expecting to hear Rick's voice on the other end, but to my surprise, it wasn't him—it was Anna. Over the years, Anna and I have become good friends, but she doesn't usually call me. She leaves that up to Rick. I immediately knew something was wrong.

"Katie, your brother's in jail."

I was not expecting to hear this kind of news.

"What do you mean he's in jail?"

"He was caught shoplifting."

"Shoplifting?"

"Yes, shoplifting, and it's all my fault."

"Anna, how can that be your fault?"

"Lately, I've been mad at him for not working, and I told him so. It's been entirely up to me to support us. I can barely pay the bills, and what does he do? He goes out and buys beer. I guess stealing a cartload of groceries was his twisted way of helping out, so now he's in jail."

"How much time did he get?"

"Six months."

I paused before speaking again, trying desperately to quiet my many emotions.

"Anna, I'm so sorry. I don't want to make light of the situation, but for the next six months, you only have one mouth to feed."

"That's exactly what he said."

"Now what are you going to do?"

"What else can I do? I'll just keep doing what I've been doing, go to work and try to keep my head above water."

"Anna, I love my brother, but now I don't know whether to be sad for him or mad at him, probably a little of both."

"Have you or Rick called my parents?"

"No, he doesn't want them to know. He thinks he can keep this a secret, pretending everything is fine. Besides, I'm not going to do his dirty work for him. Rick can call your parents himself and explain to them why he's in jail."

I had barely hung up the phone when it rang again. I picked up the receiver, and before I could answer, I heard a recorded message, asking if I would accept charges for a collect call from Washington County Corrections. I knew this call must be from Rick. I answered yes.

His voice was shaking as he spoke. "Katie, I messed up."

"I know. I just got off the phone with Anna."

"I don't know what I was thinking. I saw all those people in the store with their carts loaded with groceries, and I didn't even have enough money to buy a cheap package of hot dogs and a generic box of mac and cheese. I guess I was a little jealous, so I grabbed my own cart and filled it up. All the while shopping, I envisioned Anna's surprise when she saw the cupboards and fridge full of food. It didn't occur to me that she would question where it all came from or that I would actually get caught. Now I'm stuck in jail for six months. Anna is probably better off without me anyway."

"Don't think that way. She loves you. She's upset right now, but she still loves you."

I knew the answer before I asked, but I questioned him anyway, "Have you called Mama and Daddy?"

"No, I don't want them to know."

"Rick, this isn't something you can hide. Besides, if they don't hear from you, they will think something bad has happened."

"Well, it has."

"You know what I mean. At least let them know you're not dead."

"Katie, how about you give them a call for me, let them know what's going on? You know, soften the blow. And I will call them the next time I can use the phone."

"Really? You want me to be the bearer of your bad news? Anna said she wouldn't do your dirty work for you, and neither will I. Rick, you need to be the one to call Mama and Daddy."

"I know. I was just hoping I could get you to do it for me."

"Why would you think I would do it for you?"

"Because we are siblings. That's what we do. We help each other out. Besides, you're my favorite sister."

"That's not saying much since I'm your *only* sister."

"Well, if I had another sister, you would still be my favorite."

"Rick, you are my only brother, but not so much my favorite right now. You got yourself into this mess, so the least you can do is call our parents and tell them yourself."

"And by the way, don't try to butter me up with the you're-my-favorite-sister tactic. It won't work."

Our call was interrupted by a voice message, letting us know Rick's phone call was about to end.

"Katie, I'm sorry for asking you to call Mama and Daddy for me. I love you. And by the way, you really are my favorite sister."

"Goodbye, Rick. I love you too."

I hung up the phone and sat in silence. Tears spilled from my eyes as I grieved for the loss of the childhood brother I once knew. I remember his relentless teasing, but mostly, I remember the little things. Like the time he drove his teenage friends to the mountains to play in the snow. I desperately wanted to go along, but he adamantly said no. Then he explained he wanted to spend this day with his friends. I was so mad at him for leaving me behind that I vowed to never speak to him again. That is until he came home and called me out to the car. He opened the trunk, and to my surprise, it was filled with snow. He shoveled the snow onto the yard, then we proceeded to build a snowman followed by a snowball fight.

That day, I couldn't go to the snow, so he brought it to me. I reveled in the thought that I could possibly be the only one in the Valley with an awesome brother and a real snowman.

What happened to you, Rick?

CHAPTER 34

The next six months went by slowly for Anna. Time ticked by like a clock in need of winding, the small hand pausing as if struggling to capture the next minute. But today was different.

Anna hummed along with the tunes blaring from the radio as she filled the slow cooker with all the ingredients for stew: potatoes, carrots, celery, spices, and ground beef. *Stew meat*, she thought, *would make a better stew, but buying the bite-size cubes of chuck roast was not in the budget. After all, I already splurged on a carton of ice cream.*

Next, she dumped the cake mix into a large bowl and blended in the extra ingredients. Then poured the batter into two round baking pans, popped them into the oven, and set the timer. As the cake baked, she set to tidying up the house. It was already clean, but she wanted it to be perfect.

While running the dusting rag over the furniture, the timer sounded. She rushed to the kitchen, removed the pans from the oven, and poked a toothpick into the center of each cake to test for doneness. The toothpick came out clean, so she left the pans on top of the stove to cool then went back to finish the dusting and vacuumed one last time.

After the cake had cooled, she placed one of the layers on a plate and spread a hefty dollop of frosting on top, then added the other layer and inserted a few toothpicks from top to bottom to keep the layers together. Tradition says "If you find a toothpick in your slice, you get another piece." She finished icing the cake, washed the dishes, and headed off to the bathroom.

She filled the tub with hot water, added fragrant bath crystals, and stepped in. She slid down into the tub until the water touched her chin. She rested her head against the back of the tub and closed her eyes. The steamy water and lavender scent soothed her body, and her thoughts began to drift…

We were walking along the beach, gathering pieces of dried driftwood and stacking them into a pile. Rick picked out the smaller pieces and stood them together like a miniature tepee. Then he struck a match and added it to the dried wood. The fire rose above the little tent as he kept adding the wood. Soon we had a blazing hot fire. The sun quickly faded, and we sat on the sand and stretched our legs until our toes nearly reached the fire's glowing embers. I nestled into Rick's chest as he wrapped his arm around my shoulder and pulled the blanket around us. The warmth from our bodies, the fire's heat, and the sound of the ocean waves seemed to transport us into a world all our own.

We used a large log as a makeshift headrest as we leaned back and gazed up into the moonless sky. The darkness hung over us like a blanket of black velvet. One by one, the tiny lights appeared until the dark no longer held our attention. Some of the lights were brilliant, some not so bright. Others seemed to fade away then return, while others flickered, as though dancing on the stage of the night sky. Stargazing is no less than mesmerizing—even hypnotic. We must have fallen asleep. The next thing I knew, the fire had died, and the blanket no longer provided warmth against the cool, damp ocean breeze. I was cold, and my body began to shake…

The hot water had turned cold, and she awoke with a shiver. Not knowing how long she'd been soaking, Anna was suddenly filled with panic. She quickly jumped from the tub, grabbed a towel, wrapped it around her, and ran to the bedroom, all the while chanting, "I can't be late! I can't be late!" She checked the clock and realized she still had plenty of time and exhaled a deep sigh of relief.

Anna dried off and pulled a sundress from the closet. Rick had bought the dress for her when they lived in Germany. She had kept it all these years and worn it only on special occasions. She brushed her long hair, applied a little mascara and lipstick, then dabbed a drop of perfume behind each ear. Standing in front of the full-length mirror attached to the back of the bedroom door, she turned from side to side until she was satisfied she had inspected every inch of her appearance.

The butterflies in her stomach seemed to flutter even more with every passing minute. "Anna! Get hold of yourself!" Her words rang through the bedroom as though she had spoken to someone else. "You've been married several years now, and here you are, acting like a teenager going on your first date." But she couldn't help the excitement. The jail was just on the other side of town and she had visited Rick there often, but this time wasn't just a visit. This will be a reunion. Rick is coming home!

CHAPTER 35

I drove to the jail, signed in, and waited. I drummed my fingers on the arm of the chair then stood and paced back and forth across the room. I returned to the chair, picked up a magazine, and mindlessly thumbed through it. I looked at my watch, then glared at the clerk sitting behind a glass window. I tossed the magazine onto the table, walked over, and tapped on the glass. The clerk looked up from her paperwork and partially slid the window open.

"You have a question?" she politely asked.

"Why is this taking so long? I was told to be here at two o'clock, and it's already past three." I knew I had raised my voice, but I didn't care.

"Ma'am, there's no need to worry. It's not unusual for the release of an inmate to take this long, sometimes longer. Just have a seat and relax. He'll be out soon."

Anna walked back to the same chair she'd occupied for over an hour. She plopped down, crossed her arms, and tapped her foot in frustration. She called out to the clerk, "I don't know what's worse, labeling my husband as an *inmate* or you calling me *ma'am*." Fortunately, the clerk had already closed the window and paid no attention to her rant.

Anna, what's wrong with you? You're acting like a child throwing a tantrum. That comment was unnecessary and not at all like you. Regretting her rude behavior, Anna bowed her head. *Dear God, please forgive me for my bad attitude and help me to be kind and loving toward others. Amen.*

I lifted my head just as the door near the clerk's booth creaked open. I quickly stood as an officer escorted Ricky into the lobby. In anticipation of our long-awaited embrace, I ran across the room and fell into his arms. After a few moments, he whispered, "Let's get out of here."

We held hands as we walked toward the car when Rick stopped suddenly and spun me around as though we were dancing.

"I see you're wearing your special occasion sundress. Is there something special about today?"

"Well, I didn't bake a welcome home cake for no reason."

"You made me a cake?"

"Not just a cake, a welcome home dinner."

As soon as we entered the house, the aroma from the stew filled our nostrils.

"I don't know what you're cooking, but I can hardly wait to dig into a homemade meal."

We sat at the table and enjoyed our dinner. But more than that, we enjoyed being together—until the mood suddenly changed.

"Anna, I know I've said it before, but I'm really sorry for what I've done and the grief I've put you through. From now on, I'm going to earn an honest living, help out with the bills, and be a better husband."

"Ricky, I've heard this speech before. How is this time going to be any different?"

"I have a plan."

"You have a plan? What kind of plan?"

"I had six months to think about what to do when I got out. It's been nearly impossible for me to land a job, so I'm going to start my own business?"

"What kind of business?"

"Lawn care. I already have gardening tools and a lawn mower. I could make up some flyers and hand them out to all our neighbors."

I was skeptical but tried not to show it.

"Wow, Rick. You've really thought this through. When do you want to start?"

"Tomorrow."

Rick carried out his plan. He made flyers, went door to door, and acquired a few neighborhood clients. As his clientele grew, he saved enough money to buy an older model, baby-blue Chevy Luv

THE WAR WITHIN

pickup from a friend of a friend. The truck had more than its share of dents, but it ran well, and that's all Rick cared about. Now he could expand his business beyond his neighborhood.

Soon, the workload was more than Rick could handle.

"Anna, I can't keep up. I'm working every day of the week and I'm still unable to finish all the jobs. I never thought I'd have this problem. I need to hire someone to help me out. Tomorrow I'm going to put an ad in the newspaper and see what happens."

The day the ad appeared in the paper, Rick received a call from a man inquiring about the job. After a short conversation, he scheduled a time for an interview. Rick hung up the phone, and I noticed a puzzled look on his face.

"Ricky, what's wrong?"

"I can't shake the feeling that there is something familiar about that caller. He said his name is Dave, but I don't recall knowing anyone by that name. It's a strange feeling, and I can't pin it down, but somehow, I know him."

An hour later, Dave rang the doorbell. He looked to be around my age, medium build with broad shoulders. His long dirty-blond hair was pulled back into a ponytail and mutton chops framed his jawline leaving his chin clean-shaven. He was casually dressed in faded jeans and a sleeveless T-shirt.

I invited him in, led him into the kitchen, and offered him a seat. I poured us each a cup of coffee and joined him at the table.

My eyes were immediately drawn to the tattoo covering Dave's upper arm: a tattered American flag overlaid with a coiled rattlesnake and the words *Don't Tread on Me* inked below.

"Did you serve in Vietnam?" I asked.

"I was *in-country* in '68. Infantry. Six months in, I was wounded and sent back to the States. Lost the sight in one eye, but that's okay, I have a spare."

We both chuckled at his feeble attempt at making a joke.

It was now clear how I knew him and how I felt that connection. It was not just a connection—but a kinship. We are brothers. Not by blood but by circumstance—a cruel twist of fate. I'm reminded of that horrific night in Vietnam: the barrage of Dustoff helicopters transporting soldiers from the bowels of war to the hospital for treatment. I recall the emergency room filled with wounded men and those who could no longer feel their pain. I've tried to forget that night, but how can I? That's the night so many of my comrades perished, including my best friend, Danny. Dave was one of the seriously injured soldiers brought to the hospital that night. After I cut off his fatigues, I wrapped the blood pressure cuff around his arm. It was then I noticed a tattoo on his bicep—an American flag and a coiled rattlesnake.

Our conversation went on for over an hour, and I hired him on the spot.

We stood, shook hands, and I walked Dave to the door. He took a couple of steps then turned back with a puzzled look on his face.

"By the way, how did you know I was in Nam?"

"I recognized your tattoo."

CHAPTER 36

The warm days of summer gave way to crisp air, morning dew, and sweatshirts. Amber and crimson leaves danced their way through the air and rested on the earth below, covering it with a blanket of vibrant color. Anna and I held hands while we walked around the neighborhood. The crunching sound of leaves echoed our every step. We breathed in the musky-sweet aroma of autumn then watched our exhaled breath rise from our lips like a foggy mist.

"I sure love this time of year," commented Anna. "The trees are so colorful, and that little nip in the air is refreshing. It makes me want to go home and have a steaming hot cup of cocoa. How about you, Rick?"

"I'll take the cocoa, but I'm not excited about this time of year when it comes to raking leaves."

Anna and I were in the middle of dinner that night when the phone rang. I didn't want to interrupt our meal, so I just let it ring. Anna looked at the phone then looked at me.

"Aren't you going to get that?"

"No, once they figure out no one is going to answer, they'll hang up."

But they didn't. The ringing continued. I took a long pull from my beer then pushed away from the table.

"Whoever it is, they sure are persistent."

I lifted the receiver from the phone cradle and answered with the customary greeting, "Hello?"

Silence. Again, I questioned, "Hello? Who is this?"

Still, no answer.

I was about to hang up when I heard a trembling voice, "Richard."

I immediately knew something was wrong.

"Mama?"

"Cancer. Your father has cancer. Lung cancer."

She just kept saying that word. I opened my mouth to speak, but my throat suddenly closed in around my voice.

"Richard, did you hear me?"

I swallowed hard and struggled to speak, "Mama, I'm so sorry. How bad is it?"

"The doctor said it is stage four. I just know that means it's bad."

Anna now stood beside me. She whispered, "What's wrong?"

I tilted the receiver, so we could both listen as Mama continued, "In a couple of weeks, he will begin chemotherapy. The doctor explained the process and warned us of the side effects. It's bad enough he has cancer, but now he's sick with worry. The unforeseen future weighs heavy on his mind. He's not afraid of dying. He's just worried if he doesn't make it through this, he will leave me all alone. I told him to focus on getting better. We'll cross that bridge when, and if, we get there."

"Have you told Katie?"

"I just got off the phone with her. She wanted to rush right over, but I told her to wait a few days."

"At least she lives close by. If you need her, don't hesitate to call. Is there anything I can do?"

"Richard, now would be the time for you to start praying. Your father needs all the help he can get."

"Okay, Mama. I'm sure Anna will send up some prayers."

"You know, son, it wouldn't hurt for you to talk to God yourself."

I didn't want to cause her any more pain by telling her that God and I haven't been on speaking terms for quite a while, so I agreed. We talked a little while longer, then I hung up the phone and turned to Anna. Her cheeks were wet with tears.

Daddy began his chemotherapy treatments. I would call and talk with him every week. Each conversation was pretty much identical to the last. I asked how he was doing. He always answered, "I'm feeling okay. I can't wait to get through these treatments so I can get back to work."

I would express my encouragement, but deep down, I knew his answer was only wishful thinking. Sadly, I think he knew that I knew.

Later, in the evening when Daddy was fast asleep, Mama would call and let me know how he was really doing.

"Richard, the chemo is hard on him. He is nauseous, doesn't want to eat, and has no energy. When he started losing his hair, he just had me shave his head. With my help, he can walk to the bathroom. But that short distance wears him out, and he has to lie back down. He is spending more and more time in bed. At first, the chemo treatments looked promising, but his last x-ray revealed the cancer had spread. It won't be long until he is bedridden. The doctors recommend he go into a nursing home. But I let them know that he is not going anywhere. He will stay at home, and I will take care of him."

I knew Mama was not physically strong enough to take care of Daddy. I also knew that neither one of them would ever want to go into a nursing home. Anna and I talked it over and decided Daddy needed me.

I briefed Dave on the situation, and he agreed to work the lawn care business while I was gone. I went to California, moved into my old bedroom, and cared for my father.

Months passed. I was there for Daddy day and night. I watched as he stopped eating. I watched as he lost weight and shrank to nearly skin and bones. I watched as his once-strong voice became a mumble, and his words no longer made sense. The hardest day of all was when he could no longer remember my name.

Today, I sit next to Daddy's bed and gaze at him. I recall how hard he worked to provide for our family. He rarely took a day off work, but every summer, he took an entire week and drove us to the coast. We camped near the beach behind the sand dunes, played in the surf, ate our meals cooked over a campfire, and slept in a tent Mama had rented from *Tent City*—the everything-you-need-for-camping store. I smile as I reminisce about the good times. Then my smile fades.

Daddy is now a shadow of the strong, resilient, vibrant man I remember. I recall all the times I let him down. I was the cause of his worry and disappointment. A pang of guilt washes over me, and I wonder if Daddy knows how much I love him. I'm sure I didn't say it enough. I always assumed he knew. I don't want to admit it, but deep down, I know his time is nearing the end. I spend every day talking to him as I wash his body and change his clothes. I turn him from side to side to prevent bedsores. I crush his morphine pill, dissolve it in a spoon of water, and force him to swallow. After Daddy drifts off to sleep and Mama steps out of the room, I pour another pill from his bottle and pop it into my mouth.

I was fast asleep when Mama rushed into my room and shakes me awake, panic evident in her voice.

"He's barely breathing. I've already called for an ambulance, and it's on the way. Katie will be here any minute."

I jumped out of bed, pulled on my jeans and a T-shirt, then run to Daddy's side. Mama was right. His breathing is labored. I watch his chest, and I can barely see it rise and fall. I speak his name, but he doesn't respond. Mama was pacing back and forth across the bedroom and questioned, "What do we do now?"

"There's not much we can do. When the ambulance arrives, they will take him to the hospital and make him comfortable."

"What you mean is, when he leaves this house, he won't be coming back."

"I'm sorry, Mama, but I'm afraid so."

I drew her into my arms, and we both cried.

I immediately called Anna to let her know Daddy is dying and to get here as soon as possible.

She soon called back.

"I booked the next flight to Fresno. I'll be there this afternoon."

I noted the flight number and time of arrival.

"I'll meet you at the airport."

Mama rode in the ambulance with Daddy while Katie and I followed in the car. Daddy was promptly admitted and given medication through an IV.

"Is he in any pain?" Mama asked.

The doctor placed his hand on her shoulder and calmly answered, "No, he is heavily sedated and is resting comfortably."

He continued, "Mrs. Clark, I know this is hard, but I have to ask. When the time comes, do you want us to provide life support?"

"You mean hook him up to a breathing machine?"

"Yes, I know it's a difficult decision, but..."

"We already discussed this issue. Before he got so bad, he told me...in the end...he didn't want a machine to keep him alive. He said it would only prolong the inevitable. His heart is right with God, and he is ready to go home."

"Mrs. Clark, I'm sorry to say that his illness is terminal. He will not be going home."

"I'm not talking about this home. I'm referring to his heavenly home."

The doctor's face registered his skepticism as he nodded then left the room.

Mama, Katie, and I sat with Daddy in the hospital room. Hours passed while we listened to his labored breathing and watched his chest rise and fall. We talked some, but mostly, we watched Daddy, wondering if each of his ragged breaths would be his last.

Anna's plane was due to land, so I left the hospital and drove to the airport. I parked in the loading zone and headed straight to baggage claim. Anna was standing at the carousel, waiting for her suitcase to make its way around the conveyer. I didn't want to be rude, but this was no time for manners. Excusing myself through the crowd would take extra time—time I couldn't waste. I pushed my way through the crowd and plucked Anna's bag from the roundabout. I grabbed her hand and half yelled, "Come on, we have to hurry!"

We practically ran to the exit. I tossed Anna's luggage into the trunk of the car and quickly drove back to the hospital. We stepped into Daddy's room. Mama and Katie were crying. I immediately knew that Daddy was gone. I couldn't help it. I felt betrayed.

Mama must have known what I was thinking. She wiped her eyes, reached for my hand, and led me to Daddy's bedside.

"Richard, I believe your father was waiting for you to leave."

"Why would he do that? For months, I took care of him. The few minutes I leave to go to the airport, he dies. I didn't even get to say goodbye."

I believe it was his way of saving you from feeling that you couldn't do anything else to help him. You were his caregiver. You did everything you could to make him comfortable…to keep him alive. Maybe, if you hadn't left, he would have somehow felt an obligation to cling to life when, in fact, he just wanted you to let him go.

One week later, my father was lowered into the ground. He had wanted a graveside service.

"Keep it simple," he said. "Nothing elaborate or expensive."

Anna went home a couple of days after the funeral. Katie and I stayed with Mama for another week. Katie helped pack up Daddy's clothes, and Mama asked me to rearrange the furniture in the bedroom. I moved the bed to the opposite side of the room then put the nightstand next to the bed. When positioning it in place, the drawer slid open. There wasn't much inside—a pencil, notepad, and Bible. I pushed the drawer closed and heard something roll to the front. I opened the drawer a second time. This time, I noticed a small plastic prescription bottle. I recognized the pills inside—morphine. The entire time I cared for Daddy, I had never looked inside that drawer. I picked up the bottle and hid it in my pocket.

CHAPTER 37

I returned home, unpacked my clothes, and hid the bottle of pills from Anna. The last thing I wanted was for her to find out I'm using Daddy's prescription for myself.

Little by little, I found myself being drawn back into some of my old habits—drinking and drugs.

Anna often asked why my paycheck had dwindled. I offered my excuses, which were nothing more than lies—"I'm waiting on the customer to pay," "That customer canceled the job," "Their check didn't clear..." The truth of the matter is, I often spent my earnings on feeding my addiction.

I began today's workload early. By noon, I was ready for something to eat. I had been banned from Safeway but took a chance no one would notice I had entered the store. I picked up a sandwich from the deli then decided on cookies and milk for dessert. I pulled out a bottle of chocolate milk from the dairy cooler and headed to the cookie aisle. I reached for the Oreos and suddenly had the feeling of déjà vu. I recalled the last time I shopped for chocolate milk and cookies. This time, I intended to pay for my food.

I picked up the Oreos and noticed a woman had left her cart unattended as she walked farther up the aisle.

She had left her purse wide open in the child seat of the cart. A stack of coupons and a checkbook were in plain view. *Silly woman, you're just asking for someone to take your wallet.* I looked around. We were the only two in this aisle. She was so preoccupied with choosing just the right cookie she paid me no attention. I casually walked by her cart, plucked the checkbook from her purse, and tore off a check. Quickly, I stuffed the checkbook back into her purse and slipped the blank check into my pocket. I calmly proceeded to the checkout, paid for my food, and headed home to eat my lunch. As soon as I got there, I slid the check under our mattress, confident Anna would not discover my hiding place.

The following day, after Anna had left for work, I retrieved the check and decided to pay myself for a job well done. I wrote the amount for eighty-five dollars and signed with the name printed on the top, left corner—Homer Buttram. To make the check appear valid, I scrawled, "Yard work" on the memo line. After all, I do have my own lawn care business.

The check was drawn on a local bank, so I went inside, walked up to the teller, and handed her the check. I put on my best smile and said, "I'd like to cash this please."

She looked the check over, had me endorse the back, and commented, "Since you don't have an account with us, I'll have to get my manager's approval. I'll be right back." She walked across the lobby and handed the check to a woman sitting behind a large desk. The manager studied it for a moment then glanced up at me. I smiled and lifted my hand slightly, offering a friendly wave. She stood, and both women walked back over to the teller's window.

"Hi, Mr. Clark," greeted the manager. "I see here you've done some yard work for Mr. Buttram."

"Yes, I did. He hired me to mow his lawn and trim up some of the bushes. I hope he likes my work. I'd like to keep working for him."

"Eighty-five dollars is a lot of money for mowing a lawn. He must have a large yard."

"It's average. Like I said, I also trimmed some bushes, and he added in a tip."

"Mr. Clark, I'm a little confused about one thing. Maybe you can help clear it up."

"Yes, I'm happy to help."

"Are you familiar with the Columbia River?"

"Of course. It's the huge river between Portland, Oregon, and Vancouver, Washington. It divides the two states."

Why is she asking me this? Anyone living here is familiar with that river. She looks smart, but I guess looks aren't everything.

"Well, Mr. Clark, Mr. and Mrs. Buttram have been longtime customers with this bank, and I'm just wondering…how is it that you were able to mow their lawn when they live on the Columbia…on a houseboat?"

My smile faded. I turned to walk out of the bank and came face-to-face with two police officers who had been standing right behind me.

I didn't get the eighty-five dollars. Instead, I got six months' probation and two hundred hours of community service. As luck would have it, the Portland Rose Festival is going on and I am assigned *pooper-scooper* duty for the Parades. I think to myself, *This is better than jail, but community service stinks…literally.*

CHAPTER 38

I am consumed with my schedule. My lawn mowing business, mandatory community service, and meetings with my parole officer left little time for pleasure. Spending time with Anna had been pushed to the bottom of my list. Our evenings have turned into a boring routine. We come home from our jobs physically exhausted, make a quick dinner, wash the dishes, and attempt to relax a little before going to bed. Anna cozies herself at the end of the couch, opens her book, and begins to read. I sit across the room in my oversize chair, prop my feet up on a footstool, and watch TV. Most evenings are void of conversation. Except when we argue. Our disagreements are usually over trivial things that really don't matter. The underlying truth is *we are growing apart*.

This has to change.

Today, I informed Dave I was taking off work a little early.

"What's up?" he asked. "You have a hot date?"

"As a matter of fact, I do. She doesn't know it yet, but I'm taking Anna out to dinner."

I left work a couple of hours early and stopped by the grocery store to buy Anna a bouquet of flowers from the floral department. Once home, I opened the cupboard under the kitchen sink and pulled out the tall crystal vase. It's one of Anna's favorite wedding gifts.

I snipped the ends of the stems and placed the flowers in the vase, filled it with water, then set to tidying up the house. I washed the leftover dishes from this morning's breakfast, swept the kitchen floor, and vacuumed the living room. I still had plenty of time before Anna got home, so I took a long hot shower, shaved, and put on some of my nicest clothes. I even applied a dab of Anna's favorite men's cologne, which she teasingly called my stink pretty.

I happened to be standing in the kitchen when Anna entered the house. She hung her keys on the hook by the door, tossed her purse onto the counter, and announced, "Whew, what a day! I'm exhausted." She first noticed the flowers on the table then the empty sink. Turning, her eyes raked over me from head to toe.

"Why are you all dressed up? Why the flowers? Ricky, what's going on?"

"Don't bother making dinner, I'm taking you out."

"What's the special occasion?"

"Do we need a special occasion to go out?"

"No, but we normally don't—"

"Anna," I interrupted, "we've been in a rut lately, and I want us to enjoy an evening without going through the same old nightly routine."

"Sounds good to me. Let's go!"

I drove to one of our favorite restaurants, *The Old Spaghetti Factory*. We hadn't been there for a while, so I knew Anna would like it.

We were escorted to a table for two, and the server took our order. Anna ordered lasagna, and I stuck with my favorite—spaghetti. While waiting for our entrées, the server brought us a cutting board with a fresh-baked, out-of-the-oven loaf of sourdough bread. We each cut off a hefty slice, smeared it with creamy whipped butter, and took a large bite. With her mouth full, Anna spoke as she chewed, "This is so good. I don't even need my lasagna. I'll just pig out on this bread."

I laughed at her uncharacteristic table manners and agreed as I cut off another slice.

We talked and laughed while we ate our meal, but it was obvious Anna was a little annoyed that I had ordered more than one beer.

"Ricky, don't you think you've had enough to drink? I didn't bring my purse, and without my driver's license, I can't drive home."

"Don't worry, Anna, this is my last beer. I'm fine for the short drive home."

Topping off our meal, we had the customary scoop of ice cream for dessert. I chose vanilla, and Anna had spumoni. We scraped our bowls clean and moaned about our bellies being overly stuffed. I reached across the table and took Anna's hand. I looked into her eyes, and for a brief moment, I was reminded of the young love we once had. I noticed a tear pool in the corner of her eye.

"Anna, I'm sorry I've let you down. I don't want to be the person I've become. Can we start over?"

"Ricky, I want nothing more than for us to be happy. But your past promises have failed. And honestly, I'm tired of being played the fool. You promise one thing…I take you at your word…then you do the opposite. I know about your lies…and the drugs. I even know about the stealing."

"Of course, you do. I took that woman's check and tried to cash it. That's why I'm on probation."

"Oh, come on, Ricky, I'm not referring to that. It's quite obvious your fingers are a little *sticky*. You bring items home from the store and they aren't listed on the receipt. You think you are so clever, but I know. I have no doubt you want to change, but I'm a little skeptical when you use the word promise. You've said it before. This time, for me to believe you, you'll have to practice what you preach."

Practice what I preach. Those words hit me hard, like ice water being thrown in my face. My memory suddenly trailed back to the dream I once had of becoming a preacher—a time when I thought my life was filled with purpose—the very reason for my existence. Turns out, it was only a pipe dream, an allusion of hope.

"Ricky, what I mean to say is…this is it. Your last chance."

CHAPTER 39

"**W**hat do you mean my last chance?"

"Ricky, I love you with all my heart. But right now, my heart has a hole in it. A hole you once filled with fun, love, and laughter. If you can't get your act together—"

"Anna, this time, I really mean it. From this moment on, I won't lie, cheat, or steal. I'll give up drugs and drinking. Well, maybe not the drinking. I'd still like to enjoy a beer once in a while…if that's okay with you."

I rolled my eyes and shook my head. *Ricky was already revising his own promise.*

We were on our way home when, suddenly, I heard the short blast of a siren and immediately glanced up at the rearview mirror. The reflection of flashing red lights was a sure indication I was being pulled over. I steered the car to the road's shoulder, turned off the engine, and rolled down my window.

"Ricky, what's going on? What did you do?"

"I don't know. I didn't do anything wrong. At least, I don't think I did."

Did I unknowingly commit a traffic violation?

It was then Rick noticed he had forgotten to buckle his seat belt when we left the restaurant. He quickly clicked it into place. The officer approached the driver's side window and asked for his driver's license and registration. It was obvious the officer's no-nonsense attitude had Ricky on edge.

Ricky pulled his ID from his wallet and asked, "Why are you stopping me? I wasn't speeding."

The officer looked over the ID and answered, "I'm stopping you because you weren't wearing your seat belt."

"But *I am* wearing my seatbelt." Ricky pointed to his shoulder harness.

"You weren't wearing it prior to my stopping you."

"Officer, are you suggesting I had put the seat belt on after I stopped?"

"That's exactly what I'm suggesting."

"You must be mistaken. I did have my seat belt on. Just ask my wife…she'll tell you."

I turn to Anna, force a tight-lip smile, and wink, hoping she will get the message and go along with my story. *The last thing I need is a DUI.*

"Okay, Mr. Clark, I'll play your game." He looks over at Anna.

"Ma'am, was your husband wearing his seat belt prior to my stopping him?"

Several seconds pass as she stares at the officer.

Come on, Anna, just say yes.

"Officer, if my husband said he had his seat belt on, he had his seat belt on."

I exhaled a sigh of relief, knowing Anna had backed up my lie. Then she continued, "I never argue with him when he's drunk."

I quickly turn back to Anna, thinking this must be a joke. But she wasn't smiling.

The officer promptly questioned, "Mr. Clark, how much have you had to drink tonight?"

"Oh, not much, only a beer."

"How many beers?"

"One?"

That was another lie.

The officer instructed me to step out of the car. He performed a field sobriety test and determined I should not be driving. He placed me under arrest and escorted me to the back seat of his cruiser, then walked back to our car.

"Mrs. Clark, are you able to drive your car home, or should I call for a tow?"

"Officer, a tow won't be necessary. I'm completely capable."

Ricky was on his way to jail, and I drove the car home…without my driver's license.

The judicial system frowns on DUIs, especially those incurred by someone on probation. Ricky's infraction warranted more than just a slap on the wrist. He got extended probation, a suspended driver's license, a $500 fine, and an order to attend alcohol education classes. That is…when he gets out of jail.

CHAPTER 40

This is not going to be the happy, get-out-of-jail reunion like last time. There will be no home-cooked meal or welcome home cake. In fact, I haven't visited Rick the entire thirty days he was in jail. He is due to walk through the door any moment now. My stress level is high—probably because I had tossed and turned all night, and now the constant churning in my stomach has made me nauseous. My nerves have nearly gotten the best of me, but I ignore the urge to run to the restroom.

The seemingly endless wait is finally over as Rick enters the room escorted by an officer. I force myself to swallow the bile in my throat, walk over to him, and give him a cold hug. I am happy to see him—really, I am—but I can't let my feelings get in the way of what I know I need to do.

The short drive home was void of conversation until Rick spoke up, "Anna, what's wrong? You haven't said a word since we left the jail. Aren't you happy to see me?"

"Of course, I am."

"Well, you have a funny way of showing it."

"I have a lot on my mind…that's all."

"Does it have anything to do with me?"

"Yes, Rick, it has everything to do with you."

"I've been away for an entire month. I thought you'd have cooled off by now. Why are you still mad?"

"Because you lied to me…again. All that talk about you wanting to start over and change your ways. We didn't get a mile from the restaurant when you were pulled over. You lied to the police officer, then expected me to lie for you. It took you no time at all to break your promise."

"Anna, I'm sorry. I prom—"

"Ricky, I know what you're going to say… I'm sorry… I promise… I've heard it a thousand times. Coming from you, those words mean nothing to me."

I didn't expect to have this conversation so soon. I thought we would make it home, but Rick had unlocked all my bottled-up resentment. There was no holding back now.

"You've become cocky, even cavalier, with your attitude of entitlement. You think you can do whatever you want, whenever you want, with no consequences to yourself or others. Did you ever stop to think that each time you pull one of your shenanigans it affects me too?"

"Anna, I'm—"

"I've already spoken with Dave, and he is willing to let you stay with him for a few weeks until you find other arrangements."

"Other arrangements? You mean you're kicking me out?"

"There's one more thing…"

That's just great. What bombshell are you going to drop on me now?

"I just received a foreclosure notice… We're losing the house."

"Oh, Anna, I'm so sor—"

I cut him off before he could say that word I now hated. I continued, "When your drugs became more important than contributing to our household expenses, I couldn't keep up with the payments on my own. I was going to tell you, but then we went to dinner that night, and after our conversation, I had hoped we could get back on track. But you had to go and blow it. I've already secured a small one-bedroom apartment. The current tenants will be moving out in a couple of weeks, then I can move in."

"Anna, is there anything I can say to change your mind?"

"Ricky, I can't believe any promises you make. I will believe you when your actions speak louder than your words."

Rick sat in silence for the remainder of the drive. When they arrived home, he pulled out his old Army duffel bag and stuffed it with his clothes, toothbrush, shaving kit, and a few personal items: Music CDs and his all-time favorite book, *The Grapes of Wrath*. Anna had found the old leather-bound copy at a used bookstore a few years earlier and she had purchased it as a special gift.

Rick paused and stared at the book. He read of the trials, tribulations, and just plain bad luck the Joad family had while migrating to California. Unable to find work in Oklahoma, farmers abandoned the dried-up panhandle and headed to the Golden State in hopes of finding jobs.

Mama and Daddy were from Oklahoma, he recalled. Desperate to find work, they had joined the mass of Midwest farmers who were part of the migration to California.

The year was 1937, during the Dust Bowl, the *dirty thirties*, when my parents said goodbye to their home state of Oklahoma. Daddy wasn't quite twenty years old when his family traveled west, but he didn't meet Mama until years later. Mama was only eleven when her entire family—four generations—packed up their belongings and headed to California. Rumor had it that California was so rich in agriculture it was compared to the garden of Eden. Mama's family thought if the rumor held true, surely jobs would be waiting for them.

They traveled the cement highway of Route 66 through Oklahoma, Texas, New Mexico, and Arizona. They crossed the Arizona border, skirting the Mojave Desert, one of the hottest places on earth. Mama said her papa thought they had all gone straight to hell. Then they entered the town of Needles, known as the *Gateway to California*. They finally left Route 66 at Barstow and headed northwest to Bakersfield. Many migrants ended their trek, settled there, and went to work on the farms. Some worked in the oil fields and settled in the nearby town of Oildale. Mama's family continued, toward the heart of the state—the San Joaquin Valley. Years later, Mama and Daddy met each other while chopping cotton. Daddy would sharpen Mama's hoe, help chop the morning glory from her row, and share his cold water. It seems like an odd way of courting, but when Daddy proposed, Mama said yes.

The book also reminded Rick that it didn't matter how many curveballs life might throw, strength and love could sustain. He blinked hard, trying to keep back a tear, and unknowingly spoke out loud, "I hope our love will somehow sustain us."

Anna's heart ached as she stood in the doorway and watched Rick pack. Had she made the right decision? The last month had been filled with sleepless nights, tear-soaked pillows, and hours of prayer. Her decision had not been made in haste. Although the pain was nearly unbearable, Anna knew this was the right thing to do. She stepped on into the bedroom. Rick turned when she touched his back. Anna gently took his hands in hers, peered into his eyes, and spoke from her heart, "Ricky, I love you, and I always will. But we can't go on like this. I would like nothing more than us to be together. I hope someday we can."

She followed Rick as he carried his duffel bag out to the driveway and tossed it into the bed of his truck. He turned to her.

"Anna..."

Anna placed her finger over Rick's lips, silencing his words.

"Ricky, just because we need some time apart doesn't mean I could ever stop loving you. You will always be my best friend and the love of my life."

Rick reached for Anna and pulled her into his chest. Their arms wrapped around each other in a tight embrace. Rick buried his face in her hair and breathed in the familiar scent of her shampoo. He didn't want to let her go, but after an entire minute, she pulled away and gave him a quick kiss. Rick got in his truck and slowly backed out of the driveway. He wiped the wetness from his cheeks, waved goodbye, then drove away.

Anna went back inside the house and closed the door. She fell to her knees, buried her face in her hands, and wept.

CHAPTER 41

I didn't drive to Dave's. Instead, I headed straight to Lenny's Place, a local bar owned and operated by Valerie. Val bought the bar a few years ago from the retired owner but never bothered to change the name. I pulled open the heavy door and entered the dimly lit room. A couple sitting at the bar laughed and snacked from a bowl of peanuts as Val served their drinks. She acknowledged my entrance with a big wave.

"Hey, Rick, where've you been? I haven't seen you for a while. I thought maybe you moved away or something."

I nodded and walked on in. Jack was in his usual spot, curled up next to the end of the bar. His full name is Jack Daniel's—a proper name for a bar owner's dog. Jack is a lazy long-eared hound dog. He got his name due to his brown coat resembling the color of the golden, amber whiskey. I walked over to Jack, scratched his head, and spoke to him as though he understood my circumstances, "At least you can sleep in your own bed tonight."

Val overheard my comment. "Aww, what's the matter, Rick? You in the doghouse?"

"You could say that." I took a seat at the bar.

"Look, Val, I'm not much in the mood for talking, so just hit me up with a couple of beers."

"Will do," she answered, along with an affirming nod. She pulled out a pint glass and tipped it under the tap of my favorite lager. I watched as the golden liquid crawled up the glass, crested the rim, then spilled its frothy foam down the outside. She set the beer in front of me.

"Here you go. Just give me a wave when you're ready for that second beer."

THE WAR WITHIN

I stared into the foamy head and slid my fingers up and down the sweaty glass…thinking. I hadn't had a drink for an entire month. All I wanted to do when I got out of jail was to get back on track: meet up with my parole officer, pay off the fine, attend AA meetings, and work on getting my driver's license reinstated. If that wasn't enough, now there's one more thing added to my to-do list—Anna. If she knew I was sitting in this bar with a beer in my hand…I can hear her now:

You lied to me. You broke your promise. I can't believe anything you say. Practice what you preach. This is your last chance… My last chance! I'm getting really tired of people telling me what I can and can't do. I've had a rough day, and I'm going to have a beer…maybe two. After all, I deserve it. I lifted the glass to my lips.

Just as I was about to take a drink, I caught a glimpse of myself in the mirror behind the bar. I would swear my reflection spoke to me… *What are you doing here?*

Val watched as I set the glass back down onto the bar then she walked over to me.

"What's wrong? You find a fly in your beer?"

I was not in the mood for jokes, so I disregarded her attempt at humor.

"No, it's just that…well, there's something I have to do."

I paid my tab then went outside to use the pay phone. First, I called Alcoholics Anonymous. I noted the meeting place and time and assured them I would be there. Next, I dialed Dave's number to let him know I was on my way. But before I heard the first ring, I quickly hung up. I walked over to my truck, got in, and slammed the door shut. I closed my eyes and leaned my head against the window. *The last thing I want to do is go to Dave's.*

I started the engine and headed out of town. I drove through the small towns of Cornelius and Forrest Grove. Then a dozen miles later, I arrived at the lake. *Maybe here, I can think.*

I parked my truck, got out, and began walking along the lakeshore until I came upon a fallen log near the water's edge. I picked up a handful of pebbles then leaned back against the rough trunk.

One by one, I tossed rocks into the lake. The ripple effect from each stone was mesmerizing and my mind drifted back to a happier time.

"*Come on, Anna, just jump in! The water is warm!*"

She knew I was teasing. The water in this lake was never warm. She would tiptoe along the shore, wade in inch by inch until she was thigh-deep in the frigid water.

"*Ricky, I don't know how you can jump in all at once. It's soooo cold.*"

"*It's easy,*" *I said. Then I began wading toward her. She knew what I was about to do. I think she liked this game because she never tried to escape my grasp. I would pick her up, toss her into the lake, then splash in after her. I laughed as she squealed with delight.*

"*See, Anna, I told you it was easy.*"

After swimming, we would wrap ourselves in beach towels, cover the table with a cloth, and unload the ice chest. A simple picnic of sandwiches, chips, cookies, and sodas was our favorite meal to have at our favorite lake.

Lost in thought, Rick spoke as though Anna was leaning against the log next to him.

"When did we stop coming here?"

I pondered my own question. In reality, the true question was not *when* but *why*. The death of a relationship doesn't happen overnight. Like the ground fog back in the Valley, it goes undetected at first. Then its silent footsteps slowly tiptoe in little by little until its consuming power obscures everything around you. Before you realize it, you are blinded by the thick blanket of mist.

I wasn't blinded by the mist. I was blinded by my own selfishness. Now it's too late. Again, I asked myself, "Why?" There was no real answer, life just got in the way. *No, the real problem is me… I got in the way.* I'm such a screwup: prison, jail, alcohol, drugs, probation, fines, DUI, suspended driver's license, felony record, dishonorable discharge, failed marriage, AA. I'm only fooling myself if I think Anna will want me back. Maybe I should just go back to Lenny's Place and have that beer.

CHAPTER 42

I got into my truck and was driving back to Lenny's Place when the thought occurred to me—*I'm driving around without a proper driver's license*! I'm not supposed to be driving at all, but I need to drive to get to work. How am I supposed to get to meetings with my parole officer or AA? Hitchhike? If I get stopped, I'll get another fine. Oh, the irony of a vicious circle.

I slowed to turn into the parking lot when that inner voice nudged me to keep driving. A few minutes later, I parked in front of Dave's house, grabbed my duffel bag, and rang the bell.

"Hey, Rick. Come on in. You had me worried. I expected you a couple of hours ago."

"I should have called, but I went for a drive. You know, to clear my head."

"No problem. I made chili. Want some?"

Just then, I realized I had gone the entire day without eating. A sickening feeling had settled in the pit of my stomach, and it was not likely I could keep down a bowl of chili.

"Thanks, Dave, but I'm not hungry. I would like something to drink, though."

"Help yourself. Drinks are in the fridge."

I opened the refrigerator and momentarily stared at the six-pack of Miller High Life chilling on the top shelf. I was tempted, but instead of reaching for a beer, I grabbed a Coke and pulled the tab. Dave dished himself a bowl of chili, and we sat down at the table.

I was about to thank Dave for letting me stay at his place when he bowed his head.

"God is great, and God is good, let us thank Him for our food. By his blessings, we are fed. Give us, Lord, our daily bread."

"You pray over your meals?" I asked Dave. "I didn't know you were a religious man."

"Habit, I guess. I've recited this prayer at the dinner table ever since I was a kid. You know, Rick, you don't have to be religious to be thankful for a bowl of chili."

"Speaking of thanks…thank you for letting me crash at your place. And for keeping up with the business while I was gone. By the way, how's it going?"

"It's been busy. I've tried to stay on top of it, but I'm a little behind. Are you ready to get back into the swing of things?"

"Of course. But first, I have to meet up with my parole officer. I've already called AA, and I'll be attending my first meeting tomorrow evening."

*****

I pulled into the parking lot of the Hillsboro Presbyterian Church, turned off the engine, and sat for a few minutes before going in. I noticed a small group of people gathered at the side entrance of the building that led to our meeting place in the basement. They were laughing and carrying on as though they were going to a party instead of a meeting for alcoholics and drug abusers. I walked past them and made my way to the door where I was greeted by a man that looked to be at least a decade older than me. His long beard and mustache covered most of his face, so it was hard to know for sure.

"Welcome," he said as he offered his hand. We shook hands, and he continued, "Come on in. We're a friendly bunch here. Help yourself to some coffee and doughnuts. Take a seat and make yourself at home."

I wondered how I could possibly make myself at home in a strange place, around a bunch of strangers confessing their addiction, and talking about their *feelings*. If it weren't for my court order, I wouldn't be here. Just because I got a DUI and drink a few beers once in a while doesn't mean I'm an alcoholic. After all, I haven't had a drink, or any other addictive substance, for an entire month—thanks to my thirty days of incarceration.

I grabbed a bear claw and filled a Styrofoam cup with something similar to motor oil. I took a seat in one of the folding chairs that had been carefully arranged in a circle—not in the rows I had envisioned where I could sit in the back undetected. This arrangement forced everyone to face each other. The chairs slowly filled with a dozen or so people, all munching on doughnuts and slurping the black sludge they called coffee. A man sat in the empty chair next to me and we introduced ourselves.

"My name is Patrick Smith," he said. "But everyone calls me Smitty."

We shook hands, and I noticed a tattoo on his arm, a set of dog tags with the name Matthew Boyd and date of birth and death. The words inked below said it all: *Never Forgotten*.

Referring to the tattoo, I simply remarked, "Nam?"

"Yup. 1967. Me 'n my high school buddy, Matt, were drafted into the Army at the exact same time. By a funny twist of fate, we were in boot camp together, went to Vietnam together, then were assigned to the same outfit. We did everything together…except for the time he stepped on a land mine. I would have been right there beside him, but I had stopped to tie the laces on my boot. 'Go on,' I said. 'I'll catch up.' A minute later, I heard the deafening explosion that claimed my friend's life. That's when I began abusing alcohol and drugs to numb the pain. When I got out of the Army, I continued that lifestyle, if you could call it that. Then one day, I realized Matt would not want me to go through life without living. So that's why I've been coming to these meetings. I've been clean and sober going on five years now. How about you?"

Before I had a chance to answer, the leader of the group joined us in the circle of chairs, introduced himself as Gary, and welcomed the new attendees—there were three of us. I felt a bit uncomfortable while everyone clapped as though we had just won an award.

"Okay, everyone," began Gary, "let's start with the Serenity Prayer."

I know this one, I thought. When I got out of Leavenworth, Katie gave me a pocket stone engraved with these words. I kept it in my pocket for a while, then one day, I tossed it into the junk drawer in the kitchen. I suppose it's still there. I joined the group in reciting the words:

> God, grant me the Serenity
> to accept the things I cannot change;
> Courage to change the things I can;
> and Wisdom to know the difference.

I looked around as each person recited the prayer in his own way. Some bowed their heads while others sat with their eyes closed and hands clasped together in their lap. Smitty stood. He fixed his gaze toward the ceiling and placed his right hand over his heart as though he was reciting the Pledge of Allegiance. I noticed a tear roll down his cheek. Announcements were next, then Gary read the 12 steps and 12 traditions of AA. One alcoholic in the circle stood and shared his story of hope, strength, and recovery. Gary gave some words of encouragement, then it was over. My first AA meeting was finished. I grabbed another doughnut to-go and ate it as I drove.

Dave had already gone to bed when I arrived, so I just headed to the spare bedroom. I kicked off my shoes but didn't bother changing clothes. I lay down on top of the blanketed bed and closed my eyes. My thoughts replayed the day's events. Images flickered across my mind like an old newsreel. This day had exhausted every part of my being, and my emotions were running on empty. I tried to go to sleep, but I couldn't stop thinking about Smitty, his friend, Matt, my friend, Danny, and the scars Vietnam left on the soldiers lucky enough to make it home.

The pounding in my chest kept time with the whomp-whomp-whomp of the Huey's blades as they sliced through the air. One after another, they came. The storm of helicopters was a direct result of the Viet Cong's onslaught of surprise attacks. The Dustoff team had flown into harm's way, plucked our wounded soldiers from battle, then transported them to the hospital. Just as the war outside was bent on destroying life, we were trying everything in our power to save it.

THE WAR WITHIN

The emergency room looked like a postapocalyptic wasteland. Soldiers were practically stacked on top of each other, many with head wounds, missing limbs, and gaping holes where no hole should be. The chaotic din of soldiers crying out for help and doctors yelling orders had the nurses and medics running from one soldier to another. We were all trying our best to keep up. Blood was everywhere. The sickening odor permeated my nostrils, and I wanted to vomit. Suddenly, the room grew silent and still. I came to the harsh realization I could no longer help any of them.

I startle awake. I'm curled up on my side with my knees tucked tight to my chest. My hands are pressed hard against my ears in an effort to squelch the ferocious throbbing in my head. My heart is beating with such force I'm afraid it will tear through my chest. My stomach churns like a volcano only moments from erupting. I run to the bathroom and spend the next half hour heaving into the toilet. I fill my hands with water from the sink faucet, suck in a mouthful, swish it around, and spit it out. Then I wash my face and head back to bed. I peer at the clock on the nightstand and realized I had only been asleep a couple of hours.

I haven't had the hellish nightmare for quite some time. But tonight, from the dark recesses of my memory, it resurfaced. The year 1968 was a long time ago, but tonight, I was back in Vietnam… I had just relived the worst night of my life. I lay back down on the bed, but the last thing I want to do is fall asleep. I stare up at the ceiling for over an hour then get up and head to the kitchen. I open the fridge, grab a beer, and pull the tab. This time, I don't hesitate to take a drink.

CHAPTER 43

I downed the third beer when guilt washed over me. I tossed the cans into the trash and went back to my room. This time, I got out of my clothes and crawled into bed. As I lay there in the dark, I thought about my failure to leave the beer in the fridge, and the horrifying nightmare that triggered this latest binge—another broken promise to add to the long list of disappointments. Then I thought of Dave's dinner prayer... *God is great. God is good.* I once believed God was great and God was good, but I haven't experienced the greatness or goodness of God in a very long time...if it even exists. Then I thought of tonight's meeting and the Serenity Prayer: *God, grant me the serenity to accept the things I cannot change...*

Serenity—Calmness, peace of mind... How can my mind be at peace when all I feel is this war within?

Courage to change the things I can...

Courage—Audacity, bravery, guts... Do I have what it takes to change the things I can? I wish I could change the past, change the future, change everything about me.

And wisdom to know the difference.

Wisdom—Understanding, insight. Am I smart enough to know the difference?

Thoughts were bombarding my mind like a barrage of arrows sailing through the air in an archaic battle, each piercing my brain. I let out an exasperated breath in an effort to relax. I recalled Gary's words of encouragement at the end of tonight's meeting:

"*Remember, be gentle with yourself. Don't get burdened down thinking about next month, next week, or even tomorrow. In Matthew 6:34, the Bible gives us these words to live by 'Therefore do not worry about tomorrow, for tomorrow will worry about itself. Each day has enough trouble of its own.' Just remember—easy does it."*

Easy does it, I whispered. I closed my eyes and softly repeated… *easy does it.*

I woke with a pounding headache. I was in desperate need of coffee, so I got out of bed, dressed, and shuffled my way to the kitchen. Dave was standing at the stove, cooking bacon and eggs. He turned to me as I entered the room. His comment was less than comforting, "You look terrible. I take it you had a rough night."

"You could say that."

"How about some coffee? I made it like I like it, hot and strong. But if you want to ruin it, I have milk and sugar."

"Thanks. I'll take it straight." I opened the cupboard, pulled out the largest mug on the shelf, and filled it with the hot brew. I took a few sips then asked Dave, "What's on the agenda for today?"

"Leaves. Raking leaves. Fall has hit hard, and I think all the trees shed their leaves at the same time. Are you ready to get back to work?"

"Of course, I am. At least it will keep me busy. Mama used to say, 'Idle hands are the devil's workshop.' She said it was in the Bible. Whether it is, or isn't, there's a lot of truth to it. I just have to be done in time for the AA meeting tonight."

"No problem. Every day, the sun sets a little earlier than the day before. We'll be done in plenty of time for you to get to your meeting."

Each day, Rick and Dave raked leaves until winter had claimed the grass, trees, and bushes, leaving the lawn care business in a state of hibernation. Rick paid off his fine, tucked away a little cash, and regularly attended AA meetings. He was headed in the right direction—until he wasn't…

CHAPTER 44

Winter had left Rick with too much time on his hands. It didn't take long before he found himself back at Lenny's Place. In a few short months, he had blown through his savings and was unable to help Dave with food and rent. Dave finally had enough.

"Rick, after you got out of jail, Anna asked if you could stay with me for a few weeks. I agreed. I was more than happy to help you get back on your feet. Well, those weeks turned into months, and you stopped helping out with the groceries. I hate to say it, but I can't afford you. You're eating me out of house and home. I'll give you one more week, then you'll have to find another place to stay."

"You mean you're kicking me out?" *First Anna, now Dave. It's like déjà vu slapping me in the face.*

"Sorry, Rick. I have no choice."

The week went by quickly. I was packing my belongings into my duffel bag when I heard the phone ring. I thought about just letting it ring but then decided I'd better answer it. Katie said my name and then paused. I knew by her tone that something was wrong.

"Rick…I have bad news. Mama had a heart attack."

"Is she okay? Is she in the hospital? Is she—"

"You need to get here as soon as you can. The doctor said she needs surgery. Rick, Mama needs to know you are here."

It seemed strange to Katie that suddenly she was telling her big brother what to do and was also prepared for his excuses.

"Katie, how am I supposed to get there? I don't have a truck. I ran it into a ditch a couple of weeks ago. I didn't have the money to fix it, so I just let the tow truck take it away."

Katie had no doubt about how Rick's "accident" had happened. She was sure alcohol had been involved.

THE WAR WITHIN

"Don't worry about that. It's all taken care of. I've already purchased a bus ticket in your name, and it's waiting for you at the station. The bus is scheduled to leave at 2:00 p.m. Be sure to get there early to get your ticket. When you arrive in Fresno, I will be there to pick you up. Rick, *do not* miss this bus. I'm counting on you. Mama's surgery is scheduled for tomorrow afternoon, and we *need* you here!"

Katie hung up, leaving a stunned Rick to wonder why his sister would speak to him so sternly.

Today is moving day—now this! At least Anna would be sympathetic. I dialed the familiar number, our number, and gave her the news.

"Oh, Ricky, I'm so sorry. I love your mama as much as if she were my own. I will pray for her. I will also be praying for you and Katie."

"Thanks, Anna. Mama needs all the prayer she can get. Katie bought me a bus ticket, and my bus leaves this afternoon."

"If you need a ride, I'll be happy to take you to the bus station."

"Dave's not here to take me, so I will take you up on your offer."

I finished packing my bag and waited at the window, watching for Anna. Less than half an hour after our phone conversation, she pulled in front of Dave's house. I ran across the lawn, tossed my duffel bag into the trunk, and climbed in on the passenger side.

"Anna, thanks for taking me to the bus station. If I had to walk, I probably wouldn't have made it there on time."

"You're welcome, Ricky. I'm so sorry about your mama. Just go and be there for her and Katie."

We arrived at the bus station two hours early. I retrieved my duffel bag from the trunk of the car and waved as Anna drove out of the parking lot. I secretly hoped she would ask to stay with me while I waited for the bus, but there had been no offer, no hug, no sadness at our parting. Just one old friend who had done a favor for another—so much for sympathy.

I went inside and approached the ticket counter. The woman behind the desk slid open the plexiglass window and asked, "How can I help you?" I said I had a ticket waiting for me and handed her the ID she had asked for. She made a couple of notations then returned it with my ticket. I walked over to the waiting area and took a seat. I noticed the chairs were all connected to one another and bolted to the floor. Next to the wall were two vending machines— one with snacks and one with drinks. I managed to gather enough change from my pocket to buy myself a Mountain Dew. I returned to my seat and pulled out a book of crossword puzzles from my bag. I bought the book several months ago but had only completed a few of the puzzles.

The minutes ticked by as though they were traveling through molasses. I had already completed several of the puzzles, and my eyes were starting to blur. Finally, an overhead speaker blared the announcement that it was time to head to the bus loading area. I took a quick trip to the restroom then headed to the door.

CHAPTER 45

I climbed the steps, entered the bus, and settled down in a seat next to the window. A petite elderly woman walked down the aisle and stopped at the row where I was sitting. She wore an old-fashioned dress printed with small, pink rosebuds, and her hair had been colored a pale shade of blue. A small red purse hung from her bent elbow.

Gesturing to the empty seat next to me, she spoke softly, "If this seat isn't taken, I would like to sit here. I mean, if it's okay with you."

"Of course, it's okay with me."

She quickly sat down, smoothed out her dress, and placed her purse on her lap. Her small frame barely took up any space on the seat, which I'm happy about because it gives me ample room to stretch out. The fresh aroma of Ivory Soap quickly filled my nostrils.

After the last passenger had boarded the bus, we pulled away from the station and entered the on-ramp to I-5. As we made our way south, I recalled the last time I drove this interstate. Daddy was dying of cancer, and Mama needed my help with his care. I slept in my old bedroom, cared for my father, and helped myself to his pain pills.

Breaking the silence and my train of thought, the woman introduced herself, "Thank you for allowing me to sit next to you. My name is Ruby."

"Hi, Ruby, glad to meet you. I'm Rick."

We sat in silence for over an hour, then she spoke again, "I just want to let you know that I'm sorry."

I waited for her to continue, but she just sat there with her hands folded on top of her purse.

Finally, I asked, "What are you sorry for?"

"You."

"Me? You don't even know me. Why are you saying you're sorry?"

"I'm sorry you are worried and sad. It's your mother, isn't it?"

"Uh, how did you know?"

"The look on your face when I sat down. I know that look. You are worried about someone you love."

"Yes, my mother is in the hospital and is having heart surgery tomorrow. When I get to Fresno, my sister will be at the bus station waiting for me. It's important I be there for both of them."

"I see. This is not the first time you've been down this road. Am I right?"

"You're right. The last time I went back home, I drove this very highway."

"That's not the road I'm talking about. I'm referring to the road that leads to worry, doubt, and fear."

She opened her purse and pulled out a small New Testament. She patted the leather cover and said, "Did you know, right here, in God's Word, he tells you to cast all your care on him? Why does he say that? Because he cares for you."

"Well, Ruby, you can believe what you want. As for me, I don't see any evidence that God cares for me."

"Oh, Richard, if you only knew."

"What do you mean, 'If I only knew?' And by the way, how did you know my name is Richard?"

"Let's just say, a little birdie told me."

"Oh yeah? What else is that little birdie telling you?"

She didn't answer my question, but after a few minutes, she reached over and placed her hand on mine.

"I pray that God, the source of hope, will fill you completely with joy and peace. But, Richard, you must first trust him and believe. She pulled her hand away and held up the little Bible. You can find that verse right here in this book."

I just closed my eyes and leaned my head against the window. I was enjoying the quiet until Ruby began humming the old hymn "Amazing Grace." As much as I tried to ignore it, I couldn't. The song's tender melody, like a gentle breeze, swept over me with a sense of calmness and soothing familiarity. Although I haven't gone to church in several years, the words to this song came to me as though I had just heard them yesterday. As she hummed, in my mind, I sang along:

> Amazing grace, how sweet the sound,
> That saved a wretch like me.
> I once was lost, but now I'm found,
> Was blind, but now I see.
> 'Twas grace that taught my heart to fear,
> And grace my fears relieved.
> How precious did that grace appear,
> The hour I first believed.

I woke to people stirring about. Finally, I thought. We're here. We must have stopped in every little Podunk town along the way. I looked over to wish Ruby a good day, but she was already gone. Lying in her seat was the New Testament. I grabbed it and stood, hoping to catch her and return her forgotten book. But she was nowhere in sight. I asked the nearby passengers if they had seen the lady sitting next to me. They all shook their heads.

"You must be dreaming," said a gentleman sitting across the aisle. "There's been no one in that seat since we left Oregon."

"But the Bible…"

He just shrugged his shoulders.

"I guess you're right, I must have been dreaming." *But then where did this Bible come from?*

I tucked the book into my pocket, made my way to the exit, and waited while the driver unloaded the luggage from the storage space beneath the bus. When he tossed out my duffel bag, I grabbed it and walked into the bus station. Katie was standing at the door waiting for me. I gave my sister a hug and told her how much I missed her.

"Rick, you're really here? I expected to wait for you in anticipation of you walking through that door only to realize you never got on that bus, just like all the other times I bought you a bus ticket."

"Katie, I know. I know. This time, it's different. It's for Mama." *I didn't want to admit to her that all those other times, drugs were more important to me than seeing my family.*

"You know, Rick, I always look forward to our phone conversations, but they can never take the place of a face-to-face, warm embrace, big hug from my big brother."

CHAPTER 46

Katie drove straight to the hospital. We entered Mama's room, and when she saw me, she began to cry. I leaned over her bed and gave her a hug.

"Richard, I didn't know you were coming."

I looked over at Katie. "You didn't tell her?"

"No, I wanted it to be a surprise." *And I had to make sure you showed up.*

"In her condition? I don't think a surprise was a very good idea?"

"Never mind with that," interrupted Mama. "I'm so glad you both are here. It's been a long time since the three of us have been together. Richard, when I get back home, I would like you to stay with me while I recover from this surgery. Do you think you can do that?"

"Of course. I'll stay as long as you want me to. Katie and I will help out in any way we can."

"Thank you, Richard. Are you sure Anna won't mind if you stay?"

"Mama, Anna loves you. She wants you to get well. I am 100 percent positive she will have no problem with me staying with you for as long as you need."

I have yet to tell Mama and Katie that Anna and I are separated. I'll just keep it to myself until the time is right. Now my priority is my mother.

We visited with Mama in her room until they were ready to take her to pre-op. Katie assured Mama there was nothing to worry about.

"You'll come through the surgery with flying colors. I know you will. You'll be fine."

Mama reached for Katie's hand. "Tell me, Katie, just who is it you're trying to convince? I have every expectation of coming out of this surgery. I'll either wake up here, or I'll wake up in heaven. Either way, it's a win-win situation."

I quickly scolded my mother. "Mama! Don't talk like that!"

"Richard, you don't understand. It's not in my hands. Someone bigger is in control."

The nurse came into the room and informed us we had to leave. "Your mother will be heading to surgery very soon. Go on over to the surgical waiting room and we'll keep you posted on her status."

The waiting room was vacant, except for an elderly couple sitting in front of the TV watching a game show. Katie and I chose seats in the back of the room, as far away from the noise as possible.

"Rick, I'm worried. This surgery has a lot of risks. What if she doesn't pull through?"

"I know how you feel. I'm worried too."

Katie reached into her purse, pulled out a small Bible, and showed it to me. "Maybe we need to take a look at a couple of passages highlighted in this book."

"Where did you get that?"

"I arrived at the bus station a couple of hours early just in case your bus was ahead of schedule. I was sitting in the waiting area thumbing through a magazine. I wasn't really reading it, just flipping pages to pass the time. It was the strangest thing…

"A little old lady walked up and asked if she could sit in the empty seat next to me. She was kind of cute. She was neatly dressed, carried a small red purse, and I don't know if it was just bad lighting, but her hair was blue. And she smelled really good.

"'Sure,' I said although I was a little confused why she wanted to sit next to me when there were empty seats all around us. She asked if I was waiting for a family member.

"'Yes,' I answered and told her you were coming from Oregon because our mother is in the hospital, and it's important you be here for her surgery.

"'I can tell something is wrong,' she said. 'The look on your face tells me you are worried.'

"'I try not to worry,' I admitted, 'but I just can't help it.'

"She opened her purse, pulled out a New Testament, and handed it to me as she spoke, 'You know, Katherine, right there in that little book, God tells us to give all our worries to Him.'

"'I'm familiar with that verse,' I said. 'I just have to remind myself to believe it. By the way, how did you know my name? We didn't even introduce ourselves.'

"She just winked at me, stood, and walked away."

By this time, I was on the edge of my seat. I hurriedly told Katie about the woman named Ruby that sat next to me on the bus. How she knew about Mama and called me Richard when I had only introduced myself as Rick.

"Katie, you know what else? You just described her to a T."

I pulled the New Testament from my pocket and showed it to her. "She left this in her seat."

"Rick! You have the exact, same Bible!"

We each noticed pages bookmarked with ribbons. Both Bibles were marked on the same pages highlighted the same scriptures: 1 Peter 5:6–7 and Romans 15:13.

"Rick, I think we crossed paths with the same woman."

"It can't be. It's impossible to be in two places at the same time."

Katie raised her eyebrows and gave me a quizzical look.

"What are you saying? This Ruby person is actually an…?"

"I couldn't say for sure, but there's one thing I do know, God gives us what we need when we need it. Maybe we both need to take a look at this little book."

After Katie read the scriptures aloud, we tucked the Bibles away and headed to the cafeteria. We got sandwiches and took them back to the waiting room. Several hours passed without a word from the hospital staff. I think I had read every magazine in the waiting room, but nothing had calmed my growing anxiety. I had to stretch my legs.

"Katie, I'm going for a walk."

"Don't be long. I'm sure Mama's surgery will be over soon."

I walked up and down several hallways, trying to shake off my nervousness. I turned the corner to yet another hall when I noticed a sign over one of the doors: *chapel*.

I slowly opened the door and peered inside. The small room was empty, except for a dozen or so pews, a podium, and a cross hanging on the wall behind the platform. I stepped inside and took a seat on the back pew. For a few minutes, I just stared at the cross. I had mixed emotions. It seemed as though I felt the comfort of sitting in a familiar place; then, on the other hand, I felt as though I didn't belong. I stuffed my hands in my jacket pocket, and once again, I was reminded of the New Testament. I pulled it out and opened it. I reread the highlighted verse: *cast your care on him, for he cares for you.* I bent over, rested my elbows on my knees, and buried my face in my hands. I asked God to bring Mama through the surgery. I don't know if he heard me, but I asked anyway. Suddenly, a calmness swept over me, and somehow, I knew God would take care of Mama—if not for me, for her.

I walked back to the waiting room. Katie was visibly upset.

"Rick, where have you been?"

"I told you, I was going for a walk."

"While you were gone, the doctor came in and gave me an update on Mama. The surgery went well, and she is in recovery. We can go and see her after she's moved to a room in the intensive care unit."

After an hour of watching the clock, pacing, and rereading the magazines, we were finally allowed to visit Mama. We entered her room, and the nurse gave us strict orders. "You get fifteen minutes, then you'll have to leave. She needs her rest. You can come back tomorrow."

Mama was in no condition to hold a conversation, so Katie and I just sat there, watching her breathe. It seemed like we were only there a couple of minutes when the nurse came back into the room. She tapped her watch and said, "Time's up." We both kissed Mama goodbye and left the hospital.

Katie and I chatted while she drove to Mama's house. I even told her about the chapel and how I had said a prayer for Mama. "I'm not much on prayer, but somehow, I know she's going to be all right."

"Well, she's not out of the woods yet. She'll need time to recover."

"I know. That's why I'm going to hang around to make sure she gets well soon."

"Rick, thank you for being here."

I retrieved my duffel bag from Katie's car, entered the house, and went into my old bedroom. An eerie sense of déjà vu washed over me. The last time I stayed in my room was to take care of Daddy. Now Mama's the one who needs my help.

Katie was emotionally exhausted. She dropped Rick off and headed home. After a hot shower, she went to bed and quickly fell into a deep sleep.

The phone rang, and Katie woke with a jolt. *A call in the middle of the night is never good news.* With trepidation, she reached over to the phone sitting on the nightstand and lifted the receiver. Fearing bad news, she was barely able to speak the customary answer, "Hello?"

The doctor on the other end spoke softly, "I'm sorry to wake you, but I have some bad news. Your mother's heart was very weak. We gave her the best care possible, but her body just couldn't handle the stress of the surgery. I'm so sorry."

"What do you mean you're sorry? She came through the surgery. We saw her!"

"She suffered a postsurgery heart attack. We did everything we could, but she didn't make it. I'm sorry."

The phone slipped from her hands and fell to the floor. Katie's husband picked up the receiver, placed it back in the phone's cradle, and wrapped his arms around her. She buried her face in his chest and wept.

"Katie, you mean she's gone? But she was doing so well after her surgery. I even prayed…"

"I know, Rick. I prayed too. But God had a different plan."

"Yeah, his plan was to ignore my prayer. Maybe he never heard me in the first place."

Mama had made her funeral arrangements the same time she paid for Daddy's. All Katie and I had to do were put her directive in action. Anna flew to Fresno to attend the funeral. Mama and Daddy only rented the house they lived in, so there was no property to deal with.

The three of us were going through Mama's things when I came across her Bible. I handed it to Katie. "You should keep this. You'll make better use of it than me."

Katie took hold of it and hugged it close to her chest.

"You know, Rick, I'm sure Mama would love for you to keep her Bible."

"How about you keep it, and if I feel the need to read it, I'll let you know."

Katie agreed.

We spent the following week separating Mama's things into two piles: one labeled "Keep" and the other labeled "Donate." Katie offered her garage to store all the items we were keeping. After an emotional week of clearing out Mama's house, it was time to go home.

Anna used the other half of her round-trip plane ticket to return to Oregon, and I borrowed money from Katie for the bus fare home.

Home.

What am I thinking? I don't have a home.

CHAPTER 47

Mama's death and his divorce from Anna sent Rick in a downward spiral. He spent the following ten years in and out of jail due to his criminal activity in an effort to support his alcohol and drug addiction. He had no place to call home but never considered himself homeless. Friends were always willing to let him sleep on their couch. When he tired of one situation, he moved on to the next available place to crash.

Rick kept in close contact with Katie, calling her each week… unless he was in jail. He went through rehab several times, and each time, Katie thought she could help and would offer him another bus ticket to California.

"Rick, come and stay with me for a while. Change your surroundings. Every time you go through rehab, you go right back to your so-called friends. If they really cared about you, they would support your efforts to stay clean."

"Katie, you're right. I do need a change. I'll come and visit you. Maybe I can get a job while I'm there and stay awhile."

"Rick, I would love that. I'll get you a bus ticket and let you know the schedule."

Rick's bus was right on time, but Katie wasn't. An accident on the freeway had caused her to be nearly an hour late. She rushed inside and searched for her brother but had no luck finding him. She approached the ticket counter to verify his bus had arrived. With trepidation, she then asked if his ticket had been used. The attendant pulled up the bus schedule and gave Katie the news she already knew: "I'm sorry, ma'am, but the person holding that ticket never boarded the bus."

The attendant was startled when Katie shouted, "I knew it! Why would I ever believe he would follow through?"

Katie stormed out of the bus station and drove home. Her husband was waiting.

"Where's Rick?" asked Mark. "Never mind. You don't need to answer. He didn't show up, did he?"

Katie just hung her head.

"Katie, I love it that you want to help your brother, but when are you going to learn? How many bus tickets have you bought for him over the years? Four? Five? Ten? I've lost count. All with the same results. He didn't show up. You can't help him if he doesn't want to be helped."

"I know. I know! What do you want me to do? Give up on him?"

"That's not what I'm saying. It's just that some people have to hit rock bottom before they look up. Just be there for him and keep praying."

Katie picked up the phone and dialed the last number Rick had called her from. After several rings, he answered the phone.

"Rick! Why are you answering this phone in Oregon when you are supposed to be at the bus station in California?"

After a long pause, Rick questioned, "Bus? California?"

"Are you kidding me? You don't remember? When you got out of rehab, you said you would come and visit me. I bought you a bus ticket and…"

"Oh yeah. About that…well, I forgot."

"Really? You forgot? It didn't take long before you fell right back into your old ways, did it? Rick, I love you, but right now, I don't like you very much."

Katie slammed the phone down.

Three months passed without a word from Rick. Every effort to contact him proved unsuccessful. Even Anna didn't know of his whereabouts.

THE WAR WITHIN

I tell myself I've lived my life with no regrets.
But the truth is, I've regretted it all.

CHAPTER 48

Where am I? Katie is sitting by my bedside, her eyes red and swollen. Anna is here too. I don't recognize my surroundings at first, but after scanning the room, I realize I'm in the hospital.

Katie noticed I was looking around the room. She jumped out of her chair and took hold of my hand, "Thank God you're awake!"

Anna ran to the door and announced to the nurse at the desk, "His eyes are open. He's awake!"

What do you mean 'awake'? Why am I in the hospital?

Rick was unable to speak, but his furrowed brow expressed his confusion.

He closed his eyes and squeezed Katie's hand. Anna had returned and now stood at the other side of the bed. She took his other hand as she spoke:

"Ricky, you overdosed on heroin. We were afraid you weren't going to make it."

The nurse rushed into the room and checked the machine monitoring my vitals. "Welcome back, Mr. Clark. I'll let the doctor know you're awake."

The doctor walked into the room, examined Rick's chart, and listened to his heart.

"Mr. Clark, you're a lucky man. This is not the first time I've seen you in here. Your lifestyle, along with this last episode, has caused some damage to your heart. You'll be okay for now, but you'd better think about making some serious changes. If you continue doing what you've been doing, I *will* see you again. Only next time, if there is a next time, could prove fatal."

He then asked Anna and Katie to step out of the room while he removed Rick's breathing tube. In a few minutes, he came into the hallway and informed the two they could come back in and visit for a short time.

"We'll continue to monitor Mr. Clark throughout the night. It's late. Go home, get some sleep, and come back in the morning."

It was nearly midnight when Anna and I left the hospital. As she drove us back to her place, I closed my eyes and recalled the stressful events of the day. Had it really been almost twenty-four hours since she had phoned and awakened me from a sound sleep? I can still hear her words: *"Katie, your brother is in the hospital, and it doesn't look good. You'd better come!"*

I immediately called the airline and booked the first available flight to Portland. I quickly packed my bags, and Mark drove me to the airport. After landing in Portland, I was able to get a cab and headed straight to the hospital. The hours crawled by as Anna and I sat at Rick's bedside, hoping, praying, he would pull through.

It seemed I had just lain down on Anna's couch and closed my eyes when the aroma of brewed coffee roused my senses. I peered at the clock and was surprised to see it was nearly ten o'clock. I threw off the covers and headed to the kitchen. "Anna, shouldn't we be at the hospital? The doctor said to come back in the morning."

"Everything is okay. I've already called the hospital, and the nurse said Ricky is doing well. He ate most of his breakfast and they've already removed his IV. He's been moved to a regular room for observation, and he should be able to go home soon. You were tired, so I let you sleep. Let's have some coffee then we can go visit Ricky."

Anna and I walked into Rick's room. He was sitting up in bed with his hands folded on his lap. No TV noise, no music—only silence.

"Rick, what's wrong? Why the somber face? You've just dodged a death bullet. Aren't you happy?"

"Katie, I've been thinking. I never before gave much thought about dying, but what if I hadn't pulled through this time? Sure, I don't want to die, but the truth is…"

He paused and swallowed hard.

"I'm afraid to die"

"Why are you afraid?"

He didn't answer.

"Rick, let me ask you this, do you believe Mama and Daddy are in heaven?"

"Of course, I do."

"Why?"

"Because they were such good, hardworking people. They went to church, prayed, and believed in God."

"When you die, what do you think will happen to you?"

"Let's just say I won't be invited into heaven."

"Why?"

"What do you mean *why*? Katie, you know why. I'm not like Mama and Daddy. I'm not good. I don't understand it. Deep down inside, I want to do good, but I don't do it. And the bad things I don't want to do, that's what I do. I think evil lives inside me."

"Rick, do you realize you just quoted scripture? Even in Bible times, followers of Christ struggled with good versus evil."

"Don't you think it's time to stop this vicious cycle? This isn't the first time you've wound up in the hospital because of drugs. Each time Anna calls me, I think, *this is it. He's not going to make it.* At least when you're in jail, I can sleep at night knowing you aren't out on the streets using drugs. Several times now, you've gone to the hospital. You've gone to jail, gone to AA, and gone to rehab. The one place you haven't gone is to God."

"Remember this?" I held up Mama's Bible. "The answers to your problems are in here."

"Katie, I tried God once, and it didn't work out. Maybe you forgot that I was going to college to study for the ministry. I thought I was doing what God wanted me to do, but I guess I got it all wrong. Instead, I was drafted and sent to Vietnam, and God definitely did not go with me. That's when I started using drugs. Why not? Most of the soldiers were doing it. It was a way to escape the reality of being in the middle of a horrific war a million miles from home.

"The drugs got me kicked out of the Army, and I went to prison. When I got out, I went right back to using drugs. I would do all kinds of stupid stuff to feed my addiction. Each time I went to jail, I thought, *this time I'm getting clean. I'm starting over.* It didn't take long to forget about the promise I had made to myself and slip back into my old habits. The truth is, I don't know how to change. I've done so many things I'm ashamed of. Things you don't even know about. If I prayed, I'm sure God wouldn't hear me anyway. I've come to the realization that the only thing between me and God…is space. I don't think God would forgive me even if I asked."

"You're right about one thing. You don't deserve to go to heaven. None of us do. But the great thing about God is he doesn't give us what we deserve. Instead, he gives us what we don't deserve. It's called, *Grace.*"

Rick just sat there, staring down at his lap.

"Rick aren't you tired?"

He lifted his head. With a quizzical look on his face, he asked: "What do you mean?"

"What I mean is, aren't you tired of blaming God, running from God, trying anything, and everything to fill that void in your heart? My earnest prayer is that you will get your life in order and find the happiness you so desperately seek. I want to read you something."

I opened Mama's Bible and removed a sheet of paper.

> My dearest Richard and sweet Katherine,
>
> I thought the happiest day of my life was when I married your father. Nearly ten years went by, and we thought we would never be blessed with children. Then along came Richard. I never knew I could love someone so deeply. I was afraid of having another child because I couldn't possibly understand how I could share that love with another. Nearly nine years passed, and my little Katherine came along. I was mistaken. I didn't have to share that love. Somehow, although I thought it impossible, my love doubled.
>
> There are no words to express the deep, tender love I have in my heart for the two of you.

But I want you to know that as much as I love you, God loves you more.

Katie, keep your eyes on Jesus. Keep your heart happy—for the joy of the Lord is your strength.

Richard, one day you will realize that inner peace can only come from God. I pray your troubled soul will someday find that peace.

Love,
Mama

"Rick! Look at the date! She wrote this letter just a few days before she died. I was flipping through her Bible the other day, reading all her notations, when I found this letter. I think she had strategically placed it here in the book of 2 Timothy where she had highlighted this verse *I have fought a good fight, I have finished my course, I have kept the faith*."

"Katie, what are you saying? You think she knew she was going to die?"

"I don't know. It sure seems like a coincidence."

Rick closed his eyes, took in a big breath, and exhaled. A few minutes passed before he spoke, "Katie, you're right. I've let drugs control my life. And because of it, I've lost my marriage, my business, my home, and my health. So to answer your question, yes, I'm tired."

"Rick, why don't you just talk to God? Tell him how you feel. I think he's been waiting a long time to hear your voice."

I noticed a tear spill from Rick's eye.

"Katie, is it okay with you if I have a turn with Mama's Bible?"

I smiled and handed it to him.

He held it tightly against his chest, bowed his head, and began to pray.

CHAPTER 49

Anna picked me up, and I left the hospital with a renewed sense of direction. We had already talked about the immediate future before I was discharged. In truth, our conversation was more a matter of Anna talking and me listening: *"Ricky, over the years, you have broken promise after promise, but this time, I have a deep sense of assurance that you are serious. I'm a little hesitant to make this offer, but when you get out of the hospital, you can come to my place and sleep on my couch for a few weeks. That is, as long as you look for work and attend your AA meetings."*

I agreed.

We reached her place, she unlocked the door, and we walked inside. She set her purse on the counter and said, "Make yourself at home."

I reminded myself that this was *her* home—not *our*s. Although we were no longer married, I cherished the fact we had always remained friends.

She immediately made it clear that there would be no intimacy between us. I was just a roommate sleeping on the couch, and my job was to find a job.

The following morning, Anna had made a simple breakfast of scrambled eggs and toast. We sat down at the table and she said, "Let's pray over the meal."

"Anna, if you don't mind, I'd like to say the blessing."

"I don't mind at all. In fact, I would love it."

I took her hands in mine. As we bowed our heads, I thanked God for bringing me through one more hospital stay. I thanked him for Anna, a place to sleep, and food to eat. But mostly I thanked him for his grace.

"Thank you, Lord, for giving me another chance."

Anna echoed my amen.

I quickly piled my fork with eggs, but instead of taking a bite, I placed them back down on my plate.

"Ricky, what's the matter? Are you feeling okay?"

"I'm fine. Actually, I'm better than fine. I just have something I'd like to say…"

"Go on."

"Anna, I know you don't trust my promises, but I'm making one more, one I'm determined to keep. I'm going to stop all this nonsense, stay clean, go to church, get back to AA, and get a job. I just want to live a normal life."

"Ricky, this is an answer to prayer. I have every confidence in you, and in God, that everything will work out like it's supposed to."

After breakfast, Anna left for work, and I set to tidying up the kitchen. It's the least I could do. She works hard at her job, and now, I have to work hard at getting one. I know I don't qualify for just any job, but I need to find something I'm good at. Suddenly, I had a brilliant idea…so I headed to Walmart.

I walked into the store and purchased a seventy-nine-cent bandana. I walked out, turned around, and reentered the store. I grabbed a cart and headed straight to the electronics department. I scanned the aisle in search of the perfect item, a *big* item. I spotted a TV and hefted the large box into my cart then went to the office supply area of the store and located a roll of tape. I tore off a piece and carefully attached the bandana receipt to the TV box where it could easily be seen. I didn't really want the TV, this was merely a test, kind of like a job interview. I headed toward the exit and walked out of the store. Nothing happened. No alarms, no one stopped me. I turned and reentered the store. I walked over to the customer service desk and was greeted by a friendly associate. "How can I help you?" she politely asked.

"I'd like to speak to the manager."

She picked up the phone, punched a few numbers, and quietly spoke into the receiver, "There's someone here to see you."

The manager must have asked her what I wanted because she whispered into the phone, "He didn't say."

She hung up and instructed me to step to the side of the line and wait. "He'll be with you shortly."

I waited several minutes before a man emerged from a hallway. He approached me and introduced himself, "My name is Scott. I'm the store manager. What can I do for you?"

"Hi, Scott, I'm Richard Clark. The question is not what you can do for me, but what I can do for you." I immediately realized that line sounded like a cheesy cliché, but I continued, "I'm looking for a job."

"What kind of a job?"

"Security."

"You want to be my security officer? What are your qualifications?"

"Actually, I may be overqualified."

I held up the bandana and proceeded to explain what I had just done.

"See this?" I didn't wait for his answer.

"I bought it a half hour ago. I exited the store, turned around, and came right back in. I grabbed a cart and headed straight to the electronics department and loaded this TV into the cart. I taped the bandana receipt to the box and walked out of the store."

"You mean you *stole* the TV?"

"No, I didn't steal the TV. It only appears that I stole it. You see, when I walked out of the store, no one suspected that I had not paid for this large item."

"And your point is?"

"My point is...you need me."

"Once again, Mr. Clark, please explain to me how you are qualified to be a security officer in my store."

"Consider this an object lesson, a show-and-tell. I wanted you to see how easy it is to take an item out of the store without paying for it. I came back inside to explain how I can help you and get paid doing it."

"Mr. Clark, you said you may be overqualified for this job. Are you telling me you have a history of stealing?"

"Well, I wouldn't exactly put it that way. I'd rather look at it as my qualifications."

"Qualifications?"

"Look, I know all the tricks. I will be able to spot shoplifters and save the store from loss. I know I have a tarnished past, but that's just it. It's the past. I'm ready for a real, respectable job."

Scott slapped me on the shoulder and chuckled. "Did Brad put you up to this? My brother is always trying to pull one over on me. He thinks he's the master prankster, but I'll get him back. And when I do…"

I watched as Scott's eyes darted from side to side. He spun around in a complete circle while he scanned the store, no doubt trying to locate his trickster brother. Then he stood on his tiptoes to peer beyond the nearby display of tortilla chips and salsa. He gritted his teeth and questioned under his breath, "Where are you? I know you're hiding somewhere, watching all this go down."

I tapped Scott on the shoulder, interrupting his search.

"I don't know your brother, and I'm not joking around with you. Do I get the job?"

Scott's smile suddenly vanished as he turned to face me. "Don't tell me you are actually serious. You pulled off this charade just to apply for a job?"

"I don't see it as a charade. I really need a job, and I thought—"

He cut me off in midsentence, "I don't have a security job opening. Thanks for stopping by."

Scott took the cart with the TV and started to walk away. He stopped, turned to me, and commented, "By the way, thanks for the heads-up. I'll have my official security officer keep an eye out for you."

CHAPTER 50

I didn't let Scott's rejection deter me from continuing to look for work. I remained determined to get a job. When Anna came home from work that evening, I described my unique job interview at Walmart.

"Seriously? After all that, did you really think he would offer you a job?"

"I just thought I could show him how my experience…"

"Ricky, next time you have a job interview, you should use a different tactic. By the way, I have a surprise for you."

"Oh, Anna, you shouldn't have," I teased. "What is it? A new car?"

She handed me a plain run-of-the-mill white envelope.

I quickly tore it open and pulled out a small card.

"A bus pass?"

"Yes, a bus pass. See, it's better than a car. You don't have to buy gas or pay for insurance. Think of it this way, now you have your very own personal chauffeur to take you to your meetings and job interviews."

"Thank you, Anna. I will put it to good use."

I searched the newspaper ads and called several businesses in town to see if they were hiring. I filled out a few applications, but they all ended with the usual results—rejection. I wasn't in the mood to attend tonight's AA meeting, but I knew if I didn't go, it would be easier to miss the next one…and the next.

I entered the church, grabbed a doughnut and coffee, and sat down in the circle of chairs, which was quickly filling up with unfamiliar faces. I didn't see anyone from my old group. I guess it had been too long to hope things would still be the same. Norm, the group's leader opened with the routine announcements, upcoming meetings, then a job opening. *Did I hear him right? A job opening?* I sat a little straighter and listened to the details.

"The custodian of this church has given his resignation. When the church first allowed us to have our meetings in this building, they agreed to employ a member of our group to fill that position. If any of you are looking for a job, I have an application right here."

After the meeting, I approached Norm and asked for the application.

"Since you're the only one showing any interest in this job, I'm sure you'll get a call. Complete the paperwork and return it to the church office tomorrow."

Giddy with excitement, I went back to Anna's and filled out the paper.

"Ricky, you don't have the job yet. You haven't even turned in your application."

"I know. But I have a good feeling about this one."

"I hope you're right."

I woke up early, showered, and dressed in my best clothes. I rode the bus to the church and walked into the office. The nameplate on the secretary's desk read Dawn. I was in such a good mood when I handed her my application that I considered telling a joke about how the rising sun dawned on me. On second thought, I'm sure she has already heard them all. I held my tongue and kept my antics to myself.

Dawn took my application and said, "I'll pass it along."

"When can I expect to hear something?" I asked.

"I couldn't say. Pastor Evans is a busy man. He'll look over the application and call you if he's interested in an interview."

If she had meant to be cold, she had succeeded. I left the church with my excitement deflated. I'm not sure what I was expecting, but Dawn didn't seem to share my enthusiasm.

An entire week passed. I hadn't heard anything from Pastor Evans—not even a rejection. I had answered the questions on the application honestly. I didn't want to lie and jeopardize any chance I had in getting this job. *Had my honesty kept me from getting an interview? Just like I thought, no one wants to hire an ex-con.*

Tonight's AA meeting didn't deviate from the regular routine. When the hour was up, I tossed my coffee cup into the trash and walked toward the exit. A nicely dressed man was standing by the door. I had never seen him before and was sure he was not a member of this group.

When I reached the door, he greeted me, took me by the arm, and pulled me aside. Suddenly, I felt like I was back in school and the principal was taking me to his office. *Had I done something wrong?*

"I sat in on tonight's meeting," he said. "And I want to introduce myself."

He extended his hand. "I'm Pastor Evans."

"You're the pastor of this church?"

"Yes. I've read over your application, and I see that you have prior janitorial experience."

"I worked in the custodial department when I was in Leavenworth. Honestly, I thought my incarcerations would crush any hope of ever getting a job."

"You know, Rick, just because you've spent time in jail doesn't mean you don't deserve another chance. Are you still interested in the custodial position?"

"Of course, I am. When I didn't hear anything, I assumed I wasn't being considered for the job."

"Do you have time to chat right now?"

"Is this a job interview?"

"You could call it that."

I could hardly wait for the bus to get to my stop. I ran the few blocks to Anna's house and burst through the door.

"I got the job! Not only that, but it comes with a studio apartment. Pastor Evens said I could start the job and move in next week!"

CHAPTER 51

Two years had passed. Rick worked at the church, never missed an AA meeting, and regularly attended Sunday services with Anna at her church. He was given a generous raise early on and was able to save a portion of his earnings from each paycheck. He still didn't have a car, but the bike he bought from the thrift store was working out well. He rode it everywhere. When the weather was less than desirable, he took the bus. He and Anna spent more and more time together, eating, laughing, and going on long walks. It felt like old times.

Anna's birthday was coming up, so Rick planned a special evening.

"Anna, I want to take you out to celebrate your birthday. Would that be okay?"

"Ricky, are you sure? Can you afford it?"

"It doesn't cost much to live in that small apartment. Plus, I've been putting a little away."

"Well, if you're sure. But it can't be anywhere expensive."

"I have just the right place in mind. Can you pick me up after you get off work? Or should I give you a ride on my bike?"

"No thanks, I'll pick you up."

Anna parked in front of Rick's apartment, waited a few minutes, then honked the horn.

Rick came out, opened the car door, and climbed in.

"Is that any way to call on your date? Honking the horn? Where are your manners?"

"Oh, this is a date?"

"Well, we made plans...so yes, it's a date."

"Okay then, where are we going?"

"Just head to the mall!"

THE WAR WITHIN

"The mall? Are you serious?"

"Yes, I'm serious. We're going to the ice-cream shop inside the mall. You know the one where you choose a bowl and fill it up with as much ice cream and toppings as you can fit. Remember when we were in college and we used to go to that cute ice cream shop in Santa Cruz?"

"Of course, I remember. It was my favorite."

"I know. That's why I thought you would like ice cream for this birthday."

"Well, Ricky. You'd better be prepared to get me the largest bowl they have because I plan to celebrate!"

We were enjoying our gigantic bowls of ice cream when Anna pointed to a nearby photo booth.

"Look, Ricky. After we finish our ice cream, let's go over there and take some silly pictures. It will be fun."

"I don't know, Anna, that seems a little childish."

"Come on, it's my birthday."

"Well, since it's your birthday…"

Anna proceeded to give Rick details as to just how each photo would capture the two of them.

"The first picture is somber. We have no expression. Smile in the second. We put on our happy faces in number three, even show some teeth. Then we'll make the last picture silly."

I deposited the money, and we stepped inside the booth.

We followed her instructions, and by the last photo, we were laughing so hard that making a silly face required no effort.

We waited outside the booth for our photos. When they dropped from the processing slot and fell into the tray, I quickly grabbed them and turned away from Anna. "I get the first look!"

"Ricky! I want to see!" She grabbed my arm and spun me around. I handed her the photos, and she giggled at the sight of our happiness.

"Wait! There are two photo strips here."

What Anna didn't know is that I came to the mall earlier in the day and took photos of myself. In each photo, I held up a sign:

The first one read *Will*

The second *You*
The third *Marry*
The fourth *Me?*

While she looked at the photos, I knelt on one knee and offered up a simple promise ring, like the one I gave her with my first proposal. Then I began the speech I had practiced all day.

"Anna... I..."

Before I could speak another word, she knelt in front of me and covered my face with kisses.

"Ricky, I have never stopped loving you. I prayed this day would come. Yes! I will marry you...again!"

I placed the ring on her finger. She jumped to her feet and announced to everyone in the food court, "We're getting *married!*"

Everyone applauded. I even heard a few loud whistles.

Anna and I held hands as we walked through the mall. I stopped in front of a jewelry store and stared into the display case.

"Anna, which ring do you want?"

"Ricky, I don't want any of them. I still have the ring from our first wedding. It has been in my jewelry box all these years. I've been waiting for the day I could put it back on my finger. Also, I don't want a big celebration. We can just have the pastor of our church officiate. How do you feel about a Christmas wedding?"

"Christmas? That's months away. Why wait that long?"

"It will be here before we know it. Besides, there are things to do. We need to get the marriage license and save money for a honeymoon... And of course, I'll need a new dress."

"Anna, whatever you want. Christmas sounds good to me."

CHAPTER 52

"Katie! Your brother is in the hospital."

"What's wrong? Is he okay?" I was firing off questions faster than Anna could answer. She interrupted, "Katie! It's his heart. You should come."

"I'll be there as soon as I can." I hung up the phone and immediately called the airline. I had hoped by calling in the wee hours of the morning, I would be able to get a flight. I had no luck. All flights to Portland were booked until the following day. I knew traveling by car would mean a hard day of driving. December was not the best time of year for a road trip, but I couldn't wait. I had to get to Rick as fast as I could.

I quickly tossed my clothes into a suitcase, breathed a quick prayer for safe travels, and kissed my husband goodbye.

California's Central Valley is usually socked in with tule fog this time of year, but today, instead of it settling at ground level, it hovers overhead, allowing a clear view of the road. After several hours of driving, I pass snowcapped Mt. Shasta and soon peak the summit of the Siskiyou Mountain. Here, the snow has accumulated on the road and I have to slow down to a crawl. Visibility is poor, but I'm able to see a snowplow up ahead, clearing the way.

Thankfully, it wasn't long until I was over the mountain, and the road conditions were much improved. I knew I should stop and take a break, so after crossing the border from California, I followed the first exit, indicating gas and food. The outskirts of Ashland, Oregon, had a gas station and a nearby fast-food restaurant. After the car's fuel tank was full, I drove across the street to the restaurant. I went inside, ordered, and after using the restroom and splashing water on my face, I forced myself to sit down and eat my sandwich. I was back on the road a half hour later.

After a long day of driving, I pulled into the parking lot of Tuality Community Hospital in Hillsboro. I rushed to the information desk and asked where I could find my brother. The man behind the counter tapped on the keyboard and informed me that Rick was in CICU, the cardiac intensive care unit. He gave me directions, and I ran to the elevator. I stepped inside, repeatedly pushed the number two button, and waited while the doors slowly slid shut. I anxiously tapped my foot as the elevator seemed to crawl, inch by inch, to the second floor. "COME ON!" I yelled. "Can't you move any faster?" *I knew I should have taken the stairs.* Just as the doors parted, I saw Anna standing in the hallway speaking with a doctor. I quickly rushed over to them.

The doctor looked at me and asked, "Are you Katherine? Richard's sister?"

I nodded and answered, "Yes."

"Richard has suffered a myocardial infarction, more commonly known as a heart attack. We don't know how long he was unconscious before the EMTs arrived. When they got there, he had no pulse, but they managed to resuscitate his heart. We've placed him on a ventilator to keep oxygen flowing through his body. We are monitoring his brain waves, and...well, I'm not going to sugarcoat the seriousness of his situation. I've reviewed his records, and your brother's history of drug abuse has caused his once healthy heart to deteriorate over time. This damage has interfered with the heart's basic ability to carry out normal functions. I'm sorry, but it's unlikely he will wake up."

My knees weakened, and I leaned against the wall for support. My stomach churned, and I wanted to vomit. I thought of other times I had rushed to Rick's side. He had always pulled through. *This time is different.*

I looked into the doctor's eyes, searching for the slightest sign of hope. I found none.

My shoulders sank, and I could barely speak. "So this is it?"

"I'm afraid so. You are listed as his medical power of attorney, so we can't make any decisions without your permission. Go on in, be with him, and let us know what you decide."

Let us know what you decide... That angered me. *I'm not buying a pair of shoes. This is my brother. My family. My flesh and blood. How can I possibly make this decision?*

My mind continued to drift back to a conversation Rick and I had a few years earlier.

"Katie, I have something I want you to do for me."

"Let me guess. You want to borrow some money."

"No, I would like you to be my medical power of attorney."

I immediately began to choke up. "Are you sick? Are you dying?"

"No, I'm not dying, at least not today. But if the time comes and I'm incapacitated and can't make my own decisions, I want you to carry out my wishes."

"Rick, I don't want that responsibility. What about Anna? You could ask her."

"Katie, here's the thing…a few years ago, Anna's brother went to work for a company on the east coast. Her parents missed the grandkids so much that they moved across the country as well. I love Anna, but now that her family is so far away, I'm afraid she will keep hanging on to me with a false hope that I would someday recover. In reality, all she'll be doing is postponing the inevitable."

"And you don't think I'll do the same?"

"Katie, I trust you. I have confidence you will make the right decision, even if it's difficult. I don't want to be hooked up to machines for a long period of time. If I'm not going to pull through, just let me go."

"But, Rick, I don't want to have to make that decision."

"Katie, look at it this way, it's not your decision. It's mine. I just want you to speak for me. You know, be my voice."

I had reluctantly agreed.

Anna took my hand, and we entered Rick's room. I was not prepared for what I saw. My brother, whom I once believed to be strong and unshakable, lay in bed, eyes closed and motionless. He was attached to all sorts of wires, tubes, IVs, and monitors. His chest rose and fell in sync with the whooshing sound of the ventilator. *The only sign that he is still alive.*

Anna and I had been quietly sitting in Rick's room for several hours, both of us lost in our own thoughts. Finally, she spoke, "Katie, it's late, and I have to go to work in the morning. How about we go home and get some rest? When I get off work, I'll meet you here at the hospital."

I didn't want to leave, but I agreed. Then we each kissed Rick good night.

Day after day, I sat by Rick's bedside, hoping, praying he would wake up. I watched over him, read to him, and held his hand. I whispered in his ear and pleaded for him to open his eyes. Each minute was like sand draining through an hourglass, measuring time in a countdown to life's deadline. I sensed such an urgency. I needed for him to understand that his time was running out. I wept until I thought I would surely run out of tears. *So why am I still crying?* The feeling of an elephant sitting on my chest threatened to crush me. I wondered if I, too, were experiencing a heart attack.

Each evening after Anna got off work, she joined me at the hospital and took over my vigil. I had an opportunity to stretch my legs, get some coffee, and visit the chapel. When I returned to Rick's room, Anna and I would talk.

"Katie, I have to tell you something. Ricky and I had plans to get married on Christmas Day."

"Anna! Why didn't either of you tell me?"

"It's my fault. I wanted it to be a surprise, so I swore Ricky to secrecy. We were going to have a small ceremony with our pastor, then Ricky was going to call and introduce you to his wife, me. She opened her purse, pulled out the photo booth pictures, and handed them to me. This is how he proposed. He got down on one knee, right there in the mall, at the food court, and gave me this." She extended her hand showing me her ring.

"But now instead of wearing my new dress to our wedding, I'll be wearing it to his funeral."

"Oh, Anna, I'm so sorry. I was so focused on my broken heart that I didn't acknowledge yours. I have always considered you my sister, even when you two were divorced. That will never change. We are family."

Each day, the doctors asked me for permission to remove Rick's life support. Each time, my answer was the same: "Not today. Maybe he'll be better tomorrow."

I stayed by Rick's side for an entire week. Then I realized it was only three days until Christmas. I harbored an incredible amount of guilt for even entertaining the thought of driving back home to spend Christmas with my husband. I shared my thoughts with the medical staff, and they were quick to advise me that that is exactly what I should do—go home. "You need to take care of yourself, mentally and physically," they said.

I don't want to leave Rick...but they're right.

Early the following morning, I stopped by the hospital and told Rick I was going home for Christmas and I would be back in a few days. He didn't show any signs of acknowledgment. Still, I hoped he had heard me. The entire drive home, I wrestled with guilt. Going home for a couple of days felt like I was abandoning my brother. In my head, I knew that wasn't the truth, but my head and my heart didn't seem to agree.

I tried to enjoy Christmas at home, but I couldn't stop thinking about Rick. Although my sadness never left me, I felt a slight hint of comfort knowing he wasn't alone—Anna was with him. Then came the call from the hospital.

"There's been no change," they said. "We need your permission to take him off the ventilator."

"Stop calling me!" I yelled. "I *know* what I have to do! But I will *not* give my brother permission to die on Christmas!" I angrily hung up the phone.

It's true. I knew what I had to do. With my permission, Rick's life support would cease its work. The breathing tube would be removed and the whooshing sound that had kept him alive would be silenced. Then the last frail thread to my immediate family would be broken, leaving me all alone.

I fell into my husband's arms and sobbed my heartfelt words, "I just couldn't do it. Not on Christmas."

Mark took a few days off work, and the following morning, we drove back to Portland. Anna met us at the hospital. We entered Rick's room, and he was just as I had left him. The ventilator continued to mimic the sound of life. I watched as he inhaled then exhaled. But I knew it wasn't him doing the breathing. *It's the machine.*

My husband took my hand, "Katie, I know this is the most difficult decision you've ever had to make, but maybe Rick is just waiting for you to tell him it's okay to go."

Just then, the doctor entered the room.

"He is still unresponsive," he said. "We've done additional testing, and there's been no change. He's not showing any signs of improvement."

I knew what he wanted from me. But I just wanted to repeat what I'd told them before: *Just one more day.* But I knew Rick's time was up. The hourglass was drained, and I had no way of turning it back over.

I turned to Anna and Mark. "If it's okay with you, I'd like to be with Rick for a few minutes. Just me and him."

They nodded and stepped out of the room.

I sat down by Rick's bed, took his hand, and gazed at his motionless face. I recalled how his hazel-green eyes twinkled with mischief every time he teased me. I remembered his laugh when he would mercilessly beat me at board games and I would cry. I remembered his self-satisfied giggle when he brought a trunk load of snow to the hot Valley so I could build a snowman. I remembered his gentle touch when he held two baby jackrabbits and gave them to me to raise. I remembered how mad I got at him for locking me in the old outhouse. But most of all, I remembered that he loved me. And I loved him.

I leaned in and whispered in his ear, "Rick, I've been selfish, and I'm sorry. I've held you back far too long. This is not what you wanted. I made you a promise, and I'm sticking to it. I now know it's okay. It's okay for you to go, and it's okay for me to let you go." I kissed him on the forehead and walked out of the room.

Anna went in and spent some time with Rick. When she came out of the room, I called for the doctor.

I choked back the tears as I gave the order to remove Rick's life support. With the tube removed, he exhaled one final breath.

This day, the day after Christmas, is one I will never forget. Rick is free—free from the machines, free from the wires and tubes, and free from monitors that have kept him captive in a broken body.

EPILOGUE

Anna, Mark, and I, along with the hospital chaplain, sat in the quiet room in the hospital's lower level. We were waiting for Rick's body to be brought into the room so we could say our final goodbyes. As we waited, the chaplain made small talk and offered words of comfort. Each time I opened my mouth to speak, the viselike grip on my throat squeezed a little tighter, and my voice was reduced to a whisper. When the door slowly opened, Rick was brought in on a gurney. He was lying there, stripped of the hospital gown he previously wore, and was now covered with a blanket. *I know this is my brother, but somehow, he looks different.* I stared at his face and recalled that it had only been a few days since I whispered in his ear and begged him to open his eyes.

It's a strange thing. When life leaves the body, it takes with it the spirit and personality of the loved one we once knew. All that's left is a shell where that spirit once lived.

I reached out and placed my hand on Rick's shoulder. His skin, once warm and supple, was now cold and hard. I knew this was the very last time I would ever see him or touch him.

Two weeks later, Mark and I drove to Portland to attend Rick's memorial service. When we entered the church, Anna was standing in the entranceway, waiting for us to join her before entering the main part of the church where the service would be held. We made our way toward the front and found the seats that had been designated for Rick's family. My eyes were immediately drawn to the table situated at the front of the room. It was draped with an intricate lace tablecloth and held three items: a glass vase with a floral arrangement of red and white roses, an eight-by-ten photo of Rick, and a small box that was wrapped in blue velvet and secured with a golden ribbon. That small box held my brother's remains.

I barely heard a word the minister said. I just kept staring at the box. *I've been shortchanged. Cheated. He was too young to die. I should have had more time with him.* Although my heart was aching, I allowed my mind to focus on my cherished childhood memories with Rick, and how in the end, he had once again placed his trust in the only One who could carry him from this life to the next. I will always miss him, but I'm comforted by the fact that he is now with Mama and Daddy.

After the service, I walked up to the small table and gently placed my hand on the velvet-wrapped box. Choking back tears, I had to speak to him one final time:

"I love you brother."

"I'll see you on the other side."

AUTHOR'S NOTE

This story is a work of fiction based on my childhood memories with my brother, Gary. Although it weaves together facts of true-life experiences, it does not represent the entire facts of my brother's life: his giving heart, thoughtfulness, love for his family, his jokes, his ridiculous antics, and the debilitating addiction that controlled most of his adult life. Furthermore, it contains a mix of characters: some inspired by real-life figures of family, and others completely imagined.

In this writing, I have tried to paint a picture of the kind of person my brother was and how an unforeseen event changed his life and how his day-to-day choices led to a life of drugs, prison, and regret. I've seen firsthand how war can change someone in ways I could have never imagined possible.

I hold my brother's memory dear to my heart, and I grieve the loss of a life that could have been. It took a lifetime for him to accept God's peace and realize that redemption, available to all who ask, was only a prayer away.

Gary fought an invisible battle. Like so many of our veterans, the struggle is never over. They just keep fighting the *war within*.

THE PROMISE

Like a train racing down the track
Starting off slow, gaining speed,
Never looking back.
Because returning to back
Is not part of the plan;
Look ahead, keep moving forward,
Trust in his plan.
This train that I speak of is not really a train,
But time, precious time.
Starting off slow, gaining speed, it seems
Good times, hard times, dreams.
When life feels as though it's racing past
I must always remember to say,
"Thank you, Lord, for your many blessings,
Yesterday, tomorrow, and today."
From the start of life's journey to the very end,
The end is not really the end.
So you could say, the end is just the start
Yes, impossible to comprehend.
Although we miss those who have before us gone
We have a hope made possible through the Son,
That when *our* journey's end is just the start,
We'll meet again at that eternal reunion!

The Bible reminds us in James 4:14, that our lives are just a vapor, it appears for a little time, then vanishes away. No matter how long we live on this earth, compared to eternity—life is short.

If we confess our sins, He is faithful and just to forgive us our sins and to cleanse us from all unrighteousness. (1 John 1:9 New King James Version)

ACKNOWLEDGMENTS

To my brother, Gary, your unique personality, silly antics, and life experiences have given me the inspiration to build this story.

To Loyce Edwards, my sister-in-law, thank you for providing memories and filling in the gaps.

To my husband, Lloyd, I thank you for your encouragement and understanding of the countless hours I secluded myself to write this story.

Thanks to Bill Braun, Larry Mathis, and Victor Ulloa, all Vietnam veterans who were stationed at the Eighty-Fifth Evacuation Hospital in Qui Nhon, Vietnam. Your information about the Eighty-Fifth proved to be invaluable.

Thanks to Ken LaMaster, retired correctional officer at Leavenworth Prison, author, and Leavenworth Historian. Our conversations and your in-depth insight of prison life is truly eye-opening.

To Terry Pederson and the members of the Silver Valley Writer's Group, thank you for listening to my writings, offering suggestions, and extending words of encouragement.

To Diane Dames, my dear friend and beta reader, I would like to extend a special thanks for joining me on this writing journey. With your support, encouragement, and editing help, this book went from dream to reality. I could not have done this without you.

Last, but certainly not least, I thank my Lord and Savior for giving me the courage to write this story.

Gary, Vietnam, 1968

Gary was stationed in Qui Nhon on the
coast of the South China Sea, 1968

ABOUT THE AUTHOR

Sharlene was born in Fresno, California. Her entire childhood was spent in the San Joaquin Valley in the small town of Tranquillity.

She is a retired radiologic technologist and now begins a new career with this, her debut novel, *The War Within*.

Sharlene loves spending time with her two grown children and her grandchildren. She has traveled extensively throughout the US, camping, sightseeing, and has lived in six states.

In her spare time, Sharlene enjoys writing, sewing, and quilting. She now resides in the Idaho panhandle with her husband, Lloyd, and their rescue dog, Jasmine.

rmation can be obtained
testing.com
e USA
0240921

9 781638 147961

CPSIA info
at www.IC
Printed in th
FSHW0115